CORNERED BY THE WOLF

SHADOW SHIFTERS SERIES

MILA YOUNG

FREE BOOK!

Get a special Gods and Monsters story, Apollo's Desire, (only for the amazing Wicked fans on Mila's email list)

Click here to get started.

CORNERED BY THE WOLF

Their forbidden love will bring war to their doorsteps.

Daciana never expected to fall in love with a human. Hell, she never imagined that she'd abandon her pack and break the worst rule possible. But she did.

But a rogue werewolf is killing Daciana's friends, and she'll do whatever it takes to stop the beast. The police and her boyfriend, Inspector Connell Lonescu, are starting to question her involvement in the murders and when the pack alpha kidnaps Connell. Daciana must choose between saving the man she loves and saving her pack family from certain deat

CHAPTER 1

The door to the underground bunker rattled, sending twitches down my spine. I threw the books back onto the shelf, blew out the candle, and froze in the darkness. It might be Radu, coming to help with the research. Or it might be Sandulf, who'd be less than impressed with my presence here.

The door clattered again. My hands fisted as I silently prayed it wasn't Sandulf. If the alpha found me here, I'd never be able to explain it away. He'd see right through any excuse I made for being in the pack's library. I was the outdoors kind of girl, not the studious type. If he guessed I was researching the lupul elixir, I was dead. Or as good as dead.

For the third time, the door shook on its hinges. The smell of rain teased my nostrils, along with the earthy fragrance of trees, but no Sandulf.

After a long pause of nothing happening, I released a long breath. It was just a damn storm coming, and the gale continued to pummel the entrance. *Stop freaking out.*

I hurried up the stairs and slipped outside into the cold morning. With the trapdoor locked, I brushed foliage over the entrance with my foot. Lofty trees crowded the forest around me with minimal sunlight breaking through the canopy above. I inhaled the crisp, pine scents and bolted through the woods. The wind tore through the area, tugging my shirt and pants, tossing brown hair over my face. Another night spent alone where I'd lost track of time searching for secrets of the potion. Later that night I'd be back doing more research, though Radu's help would make it a lot easier. He'd missed our catch-ups three days running. That wasn't like him. He was never late. Maybe he'd given up on helping me?

I pushed the trepidation down, knowing it wouldn't do me any good to think about it, and Connell came to mind: his strong arms wrapped around me, loving whispers in my ears, and kisses that melted my insides. If I didn't find the potion before the next full moon, everything with Connell was over.

A loud footfall on the forest floor iced me over.

I held my breath. Darkness filled the gaps between trees where the sun didn't reach. A shadow flitted behind the broad trunks. I sniffed the downwind: timber, car fumes from the city of Brașov, and a barnyard scent.

The woods fell silent. Too silent.

Stop freaking out.

I rubbed the chill out of my arms and kept moving. The crunch of foliage beneath my boots echoed.

A fleeting prickling sensation slithered down my back.

I wasn't alone.

The moment I whipped around, something massive and dark struck, hitting me in the chest. I screamed.

I fell to the ground and threw my arms up in defense. My heart thumped against my ribcage, breaths raced. The foul stench of wet sheep and dung smothered my senses.

A black wolf the size of a small hatchback crouched several feet from me—ears flat, lips peeled back over pointy fangs. Rumblings rolled from its chest. Hot air steamed twirling upward from a snarling mouth, and it eyed me as if I were a free meal.

I couldn't breathe. A man-eating dracwulf, the same unstoppable animal said to eat entire villages, was in the Carpathian woods. I'd only seen drawings of this thing... what the hell as it doing here? The urge to transform into a moonwulf wriggled over my skin. But it wasn't a full moon, yet I swore I sensed my inner wolf rising inside me.

In slow motion, I climbed to my feet. "I'm not going to hurt you."

The beast lunged.

My blood ran cold.

I threw myself sideways into a roll, leapt to my feet and ran. The dracwulf was on my heels, swift and heavy, crashing through the underbrush. Each tree offered an obstacle to dodge around and stop the creature from jumping me. Low-hanging branches snagged on my clothes and hair.

We were too far from the pack house.

Too close to the city.

The forest floor flew under me.

The pack's bunker, perhaps? If I wanted to trap myself. Terrible idea. A hint of panic

crawled forward. What if I couldn't shake it? What if it caught me? What if... No more stupid fear.

Around the next tree, I swiped a hefty branch off the ground and spun to face the dracwulf, ready to finish it my way.

The animal collided with me, headfirst into my hip. I was thrown backward and crumpled to the ground like a broken tree, muscles and bones in shock from the impact. A horrid suffocating sound gushed from my lips. The beast came at me in a blur of speed, giving me just enough time to swing the branch out in front of my face. It was on me. Teeth latched onto the weapon and ripped it out of my grip.

I threw my fist into the side of its head as a shrill whistle sounded from a distance.

The huge wolf jerked up, muzzle creased. Unfazed by my punch, the animal bounded over me and dashed into the woods like it had caught sight of better prey.

That was my chance to escape.

I pushed myself up, but my body seemed to weigh a ton. My hip flared in pain each time I put weight on that side of my body. Where had the dracwulf come from, and where had it gone? Dracwulves were not meant to exist and this one damn sure wasn't scared of me.

With clenched teeth and stumbling steps, I hurried toward my Jeep.

I took deep breaths and shoved my fists into the pockets of my pants, touching the coolness of the key to the bunker. I glanced over my shoulder, the hairs on my arms lifting.

Where the hell did you come from?

Connell came to mind.

Five days until the Lunar Eutine, the next full moon—the pivotal moment when a moonwulf like myself would transform into a full-blown wulfkin forever. No longer controlled by the moon. Except I had other plans: to become human with a little help from the elixir potion I still hadn't found.

My palms stung. I glanced at the red, crescent shapes indented into the flesh from my nails. The chill had returned to my bones by the time I reached the vehicle. I was surprised my body didn't ache worse. Instead, it just felt bruised.

The pack needed to know a monster lived in our woods, so I'd pay them a visit. I climbed into the Jeep and drove along the curving track toward the pack house.

My cell phone rang.

I snatched it from the passenger seat. Connell flashed on the screen. Something tightened in my chest. I wanted to answer and hear his voice, listen to the way he said my name, but not right then or he'd hear my frazzled voice and ask a million questions. I'd call him back after I visited the pack house. I let it go to voice mail. The phone revealed he'd already called six times.

The cell rang in my hand. Connell again. I answered this time. "Hi there."

"Daci, are you okay?" Fear threaded his words, and it scared me.

"I'm fine. What's going on?"

"I called you all morning and no response. You're not at home or work. Where are

you? I've been so worried."

I swallowed the dryness in my throat. "Out in the woods tracking deer for work." I

hated lying. "Sorry, I missed your calls. Did something happen?"

He let out a loud sigh, and my stomach clenched. "This morning, a jogger found a dead girl in an alley behind your apartment. And the investigation team has been waiting for you before they clean up the scene. That's why I was trying to get hold of you."

My insides turned to mush. "That's awful. But why do you need me?"

"Your boss said you'd help us with identifying the animal, since we may need to issue a hunting permit to track and kill it. Please hurry back. I'll meet you in front of your apartment, okay? Drive carefully." He hung up.

The day was growing worse by the second, and my stomach dropped.

I'd assisted police in the past on multiple animal attacks, since I specialized in animal behaviors—but on domestic livestock, never humans... unless... The dracwulf attack poured through my mind. My next breath caught in my throat.

I slammed on the brakes and did a quick five-point turn

on the dirt track. Soon, I left the woods behind and sped into the city. Renaissance-style houses lined the thoroughfare, showcasing fashionable clothing boutiques, cafes, and restaurants. People wandered along the footpaths, oblivious of the monster stalking the Carpathian woods.

I arrived on my street in no time and slid out of the Jeep, rubbing my sore hip. Potted plants adorned the balconies of the concrete apartments along the road. Despite the bright flowers twirling around the metal railings, the rusted drains running down the cold white walls reminded me of the stories about families losing farms and livestock to the government in Communist times, then being forced to live in tiny apartments. I took hasty strides up the footpath and grimaced at the pain lacing through my side.

At front of my place, Connell leaned against the wall, staring at his cell. Despite the circumstances, the excitement of seeing him made me giddy. Dark blond hair framed his sun- bronzed face. Those broad shoulders filled out a tailored pinstriped suit, and his well- muscled physique would make anyone think twice before taking him on. Me... I just thought about pushing my hands all over those muscles, and already heat collected in the pit of my stomach, igniting the itch between my thighs. Damn he was gorgeous.

Connell glanced up with those chocolate eyes that made me forget what I was thinking. All angled cheekbones, strong, rugged jaw. He pushed off the wall.

What was I here for again?

I threw my arms around his neck. My body molded into his perfectly, my nipples pebbled against his chest. He always had this effect on me. This was what I had never experienced whilst hidden in the woods with the pack for all the years I grew up in the forest—such tenderness with a man.

"I missed you so much." Connell's arms swept along my back and pulled me tight. "I was worried something had happened to you." There it was again, the terror in his tone.

I took a sharp breath and pulled back, unable to stop my defenses from rising. "I'm fine."

He scanned me head to toe, his gaze like a soft caress. "Your shirt. It's ripped."

Peering down, I found gashes in the white fabric over my shoulders and arms. I poked a finger through one of the holes. Another favorite shirt destroyed. Great. "I fell over in the woods, but it's all good." In that moment, a flare of sharp pain throbbed down my leg, and I smiled through the ache.

Connell raked fingers through his hair and tucked his cell into the inside pocket of his jacket, revealing the gun holster at the side of his belt. "Are you sure?" His hand caressed the length of my arm before stroking my cheek.

I nodded, leaning into his touch, and wanted nothing more than to fall into his arms. No more talking.

"I love you so much." He plucked a twig from my hair. "But I don't want secrets between us."

Something hitched in my throat. I'd told Connell so many lies to conceal my identity as a moonwulf, I had lost track of them. "What do you mean?"

Only the wind swept past. Connell's gaze flickered around the place—everywhere but on me. "For over a week I've been calling you, and you never bothered to call back. Not even a text message to say you're busy. Nothing." He searched my face for an answer. "Then today I needed you for work, and you weren't anywhere. This whole time I thought I was giving you space because you were going to be busy at work for a while, but what if something had happened to you? I'd never forgive myself."

A shudder ran through me and heat crawled through my chest. Had I really let days pass by without calling Connell? I was certain we'd spoken just yesterday. Or was it the day before? 'I'm so sorry I didn't call you right away. Time got away from me."

He dug his hands into the pockets of his tailored pants. It

was obvious they were fisted into knots. "All I ask is that you let me know you're okay, where you are sometimes, and that you're still alive."

My response came pouring out. "I don't need to tell you where I am all the time."

"That's not what I mean." He pinched the bridge of his nose. "Shit, Daci. I thought you wanted to be with me forever. I don't get what's been going on with you lately."

I shook my head in disbelief. Everything I did was for Connell. For us. I'd never felt this way about anyone, and I was ready to leave my pack for him. Even if it was unheard of. That was why I needed the elixir. "Of course I want us to be together."

"Are you sure?" His voice shook.

"I can't believe you just asked me that."

The front door of the building creaked open, and an elderly woman with a bag on wheels shuffled outside. With pursed lips, she shook her head before hurrying down the street. Great, my whole neighborhood probably knew about my love life.

Connell glanced up to my apartment and back before loosening his tie from around his neck. "I know you haven't been spending the nights at home."

My breath quickened. "And you know this because . . . "

"I've driven past your place the last few nights, hoping to catch up with you. To see you. But you're never home. Where do you go every night?" His incredulous stare pinned me on the spot, and right then I was certain my legs would give out.

"Are you stalking my place?"

I couldn't tell him that I spent my time in an underground bunker searching for a potion that could turn me into a human for good. Or that if I turned into a wulfkin, I'd be forced to live with the pack, mate with one of them, and lose him forever. It would make me sound like a crazy person because, in his world, moonwulf and wulfkin didn't exist.

He drew in a quick breath of air. "Of course not. We haven't caught up for weeks, and I missed you. Daci, tell me what you want from me, or am I an idiot for believing something serious was happening with us?"

I reached out for him and took his hand in mine. "It's only you I want. Nothing else is going on. I've been working extra hours for a huge project at work. That's all."

His hand slipped out of my grasp. "Part of the problem with being an inspector is that it lets me know when someone is lying." His voice held a ragged edge. "After my ex-wife, I never thought I'd be able to love again. Then I met you. But now I'm getting that same feeling I got when I realized she wasn't telling me the truth." His gaze held onto me. "I don't want to go through that again."

He might as well have pulled the ring from a hand grenade because my heart stopped beating. "I'm nothing like—"

"Why can't you—"

"Let me finish," I said through gritted teeth. "I'm not like your ex-wife. I would never cheat on you, so don't compare me to her, ever. How could you even suggest it?" Pain squeezed my throat. "What do you want me to tell you? Something that isn't true so you can say all females are liars?" I struggled to hold my composure and hugged myself. "That's not going to happen."

Connell shut his eyes, his lips pressed tight together.

"All I ask is for one week to finish a project at work. Then you won't be able to get rid of me." I couldn't think of anything else around my trembling limbs and numb brain.

He opened his eyes slightly, and a shade of brown flashed, reminding me of his sexy look just before he had his way with me. My body tingled. I'd never wanted a man as much as I did Connell.

He pushed his shoulders back, and a hard expression slid over his face. "I don't want to talk about this now. We have to go to the crime scene." An edge of bossiness crept into his voice. He turned his back to me. "Ready?"

I couldn't speak.

A dracwulf had attacked me.

Connell hinted at breaking up.

Somehow my day had managed to suck even worse.

CHAPTER 2

*A*n icy breeze brushed past Connell and I as we started walking.

My boss, Vasile, ran Romania's Animal Research Institute, and unfortunately when

the police asked him for a favor, he rarely said no. So I was not happy with him for nominating me on this case.

"Why do I need to attend the crime scene anyway?"

Connell's tie hung crookedly around his neck, and frustration masked his handsome face when he looked over at me. "Our victim has severe lacerations to her jugular, carotid and trachea, which points to either a wolf or bear attack. We're hoping you can help us figure out which one it is and why it ate the victim in an open street. Apparently no one in the neighborhood heard a sound."

"That's horrible." I dropped my gaze and remembered the rabbits and deer I'd hunted, along with how the chase pumped the adrenaline in my veins. The greater the fight they put up, the more determined I was to capture them. In comparison, a human was easy prey. It would make sense if there was no food in the woods, but winter was weeks away.

"Daci, you're limping?"

I glanced up at the man whose eyes softened the more he stared my way.

"It's nothing, just a bump." My voice broke.

"Can I see?" He stopped and placed his hands on my waist, plucking my blouse

upward.

"Knock it off." I pushed away his arm and tried to sidestep him. "It's nothing."

He took my hand. "Stop being so stubborn. You'd say you were fine if you lost a leg."

He lifted my top slightly at my side and took in a quick breath. "You've got a purple bruise the size of a soccer ball." He ran careful fingers across my skin, and I bit my lower lip, holding back the moan in my chest. I craved his touch more than I wanted to admit.

Staring into his soft eyes, and at the way his lips parted, I considered leaning over and stealing a kiss.

"What did you fall onto? A huge boulder?"

I tugged my top down. "Just the ground. Don't worry about it."

He straightened. "You probably fall over all the time when you're tracking animals for work. And I'll always worry about you getting hurt."

Sadness wove through his words, and my chest tightened with anguish. "I love that

you care so much."

Connell rubbed the stubble on his jaw, and the crease at the bridge of his nose returned. "I'm confused. You keep pushing me away, yet you say you love me." His head shook. "I adore your strength and independence, Daci, but that doesn't mean you can't accept help or let anyone into your life." His voice grew sharp. He tucked his hands into his pockets and took a step back.

I reached for him and laid a hand on his arm, uncertain what words might cheer him up. I had spent no time with him over the past weeks, but time was a precious commodity I couldn't waste if I wanted a future with him.

"You know what, forget it." He gave a slight shake of his head. "I said I didn't want to talk about this now." He flicked hair off his face, nudging my hand away in the process.

We pushed into a stride, and as much as I wanted to make things better, I couldn't think of a single word to say, not when I worried so much about everything.

Unable to concentrate on anything but the hollow pit growing inside me, I mulled over the victim's unfortunate end, wondering why the animal struck. I prayed we weren't dealing with the dracwulf. Why would a wulfkin knowingly mate with a wild wolf and allow such a monster to be born, considering the punishment was death?

"Have there been other similar attacks?" I asked.

Connell kept silent and avoided eye contact.

"How many? When did—"

"You don't need those details."

"I do if you want me to work out what sort of animal did this. You're the one that wants my help, remember?"

I could tell by the way he rolled up his sleeves and held his chin high that my words annoyed him.

"The police assumed the first two were random, especially since they were months apart and outside Brașov, but then we found the third one this morning. We knew it was the same animal by the claw and teeth marks. Wolf DNA showed up in the tests, but it was soiled with bear and other animal DNA, along with something the lab's never seen before, and we dismissed it as contaminated evidence. The chief insists it's just a bear and scavenger dogs or other animals picking at the remains afterwards, which is why we need an outsider's expert advice."

Connell stole a glance my way, his expression pained. I did that to him, and I hated myself for it. The first time I met him was in the police station. I'd been assisting with a case when I sensed his gaze on me from an office in the far corner of the building. His smoldering eyes, and the sexy grin that pulled at the sides of his mouth, had imprinted themselves in my mind, along with the way he kept glancing at me over the folder in his hands. I wished he still looked untroubled and content like he had then, rather than having worry lines scoring his forehead.

Around the next bend, nosy locals clustered near the police tape blocking off an alleyway, which curved out of sight. Police cars and an ambulance littered the footpaths to make way for passing vehicles. A television news van sat in the adjacent lane. I couldn't believe a murder happened practically outside my front door.

"Follow me, and don't speak to anyone."

I ducked under the police strip, slipped past the crowd, and ignored their calls. I was only a few steps onto the cobblestone street when the scent of blood battered my nose. I tasted it on the back of my throat—something I'd never been able to do before outside a full moon. My senses usually matched a human's, so I didn't understand why my body kept reacting as if it were a full moon.

Farther into the street, I spotted a group of men. Ambulance workers wheeled a gurney toward a black cloth spread over something or someone on the ground. A man with a belly like a barrel snapped photographs nearby, while another in business attire gave the officers orders. Each one sported a badge around his neck. Too busy to notice our arrival, the officers continued scribbling in their notepads, chatting into phones, and collecting samples. Beyond the crime scene was a backdrop of cozy terrace houses, and the impressive Carpathian Mountains loomed behind them. Picturesque.

Except on this street, where the neighbors might never feel safe again.

An officer with a long moustache drew near. "Who's this?"

"She's with me." Connell gave a sharp nod to the man, sending him off. Then he retrieved surgical gloves from his pocket. "Put these on."

I took them out of his hand fast.

Connell did that thing with his eyebrow, lifting it in an arch.

"What?" I said. Two could play the grumpy game.

He took off to talk to the criminal division chief, a.k.a. his boss—an intense man whom I'd had the pleasure of meeting before. The chief always spoke in a carefully controlled tone, but the reddening of his cheeks gave away his usual annoyance. The smallest things set him off, and a murder case would certainly rate high on his irritation scale. A cool wind swished through the alleyway, bathing me in the same, faint odor I sensed in the woods earlier that day. It was the dracwulf, but I didn't want to believe it. Wulfkin carried timber flavors, and moonwulf like me reeked of humans. No bear—or other animal for that matter—wore the dracwulf's putrid scents.

Connell had said this was the third similar attack. That meant the dracwulf had been living in the nearby woods for a while. Surely my alpha, Sandulf had picked up the scent and tracks of the new resident in the woods.

I reached the victim.

The two paramedics lifted the covered body onto the gurney. Blood stained the cobblestone road beneath the body, collecting in the crevices. I approached one of the medics. "Can I take a quick look at the body, please?"

"Sure, but be quick."

I lifted the fabric with two hands and held my breath, scanning the victim's body— there were bite marks, scratches, and tears in the flesh. It was horrid. When my gaze rose to her face, I gasped at the familiar, open eyes.

Catalina.

I almost fell over.

My only friend in the city.

Killed.

A sudden coldness spread through me. I'd seen her the day before at my work picking up samples for testing. My mouth was parched. The fabric dropped from my hands.

The medic adjusted it over Catalina and pushed the gurney away.

Shivers crawled over my skin, and my stomach threatened to throw up what little I ate that day. I struggled to take air into my lungs. Suffocating on my own nausea, I spun on my heels, searching for Connell. Disoriented, I felt alone and lost—the same feelings Catalina must have had when she sucked in her last breath. My insides crumbled and my knees wobbled.

The dracwulf was responsible.

Sandulf had to know the animal was in the woods. Why hadn't he done something before it killed Catalina? The street ahead blurred behind my tears, and I wiped my nose with the sleeve of my blouse, terrified of what was happening around me.

In my next breath, I smelled the weak ammonium of urine. Not Catalina's. Not human. Dizziness challenged my balance, but I followed the scent deeper into the lane, houses away from the police, where the smell strengthened. Heat surged through me. A deep guttural sound rumbled in my chest. Was that my wolf? Couldn't be.

On the wooden fence framing a small cottage-style house, I found scratch marks. Something in the dried earth below the pickets caught my attention. Deep brown droplets dotted the ground like water drops. I pinched the soil and smudged it between my fingers. Red smeared the tips of my gloves. Blood, not water. The air was ripe with it, and heat poured through me once again. I ignored it. Hunched over, I followed the rough line of sprinkled evidence along two other lawns, heading toward the far end of the street where the woods lay.

The dracwulf attacked me on the same day it killed my friend. But why drag her here from the woods? Couldn't be due to hunger. Perhaps it was marking its territory?

Connell touched my shoulder.

I jerked upright to face him. "I found something." I showed him my fingers. "Catalina was attacked somewhere else, and then the animal carried her here in its mouth to finish eating her."

"Catalina?"

"Catalina Barascu. My friend. You don't know who the victim is?"

He glanced upward momentarily. "I remember you mentioning her before. She jogged with you sometimes. Right?"

I nodded, biting my lower lip, and the memory of her musical laugh wavered in my thoughts.

"I'm sorry you had to see this, Daci. If I had known who she was, I wouldn't have

called you." He offered a deep sigh, his eyebrows pulled down in concentration.

"When was the last time you saw her?"

"Yesterday afternoon." My gaze swept to the ambulance men rounding the curve of the street. She didn't deserve such a death. "I drove past her in the woods as I headed into the office." I ripped the gloves off, bunching them into my fist, as I decided I had to pay the alpha a visit.

Connell took the scrunched gloves out of my fist, tugging his off, too. "Does she live nearby?"

"Several blocks away." I turned away, my eyes beginning to sting.

He pulled me against his shoulder and wiped my tears with his thumb. I melted into him, needing the warmth of his touch. In the same moment, fire engulfed my insides, and I caught a whiff of Connell's arousing fragrance: sharp and musky. I inhaled, holding utterly still, one hand against his chest, the other sliding down his firm stomach. The undeniable hunger for sex with Connell right in that moment drove my pulse into frenzy. I pressed myself closer to him, my hand sliding lower, liquid heat pooling between my thighs.

What was I doing?

Alarmed, I shoved myself off him, and left Connell with a quizzical look. Perhaps the craziness of the day had finally got to me. One second I had been crying over Catalina and the next I wanted to jump Connell's bones. What was wrong with me?

"Are you okay?" He reached out for me.

His touch threw my heartbeat into overdrive, so I jerked back.

"I'm a horrible person."

"You're not horrible, Daci. You're busy at work, you have no time for me, and it's probably that time of the month for you."

I stiffened. "What!" I pressed hands to my hips. "Why would you even say that?"

He rubbed his face, and his cheeks blushed. "I . . . I really don't know. You're being affectionate, and then you're ready to fight me. For weeks you avoided me. You've got to see why I'm confused what's going on between us."

I crossed my arms and let out a long breath. "You really want to do this here." My voice rose with each word, and several heads turned in our direction.

His eyes squinted, and he lowered his voice. "I don't know who you are today." He marched off toward a couple of plainclothesmen and the chief.

I didn't know who I was, either, but something felt wrong, like a boxing match was taking place inside me, with every single emotion fighting inside the arena at the same time.

Burning heat flushed through my body, and despite the autumn chill, sweat collected at the back of my neck. I wiped my brow and focused on taking slow breaths.

The chief was coming my way. His hands tucked into pockets, and the badge on his chest gleamed beneath the sun. "Were you and Catalina good friends?"

His direct question puzzled me. "I guess so. Though we didn't spend a lot of time together. Just when we both had free time."

"Is there any reason you—or anyone—might want to harm Catalina?"

My shoulders flinched back. "What sort of question is that? Of course not."

Connell's approach diverted my attention. The desire to punch him pulsed through my veins. He brought me here, and then abandoned me to the chief's interrogation.

The chief didn't notice his arrival. "I want to simply understand your relationship with the victim, since you saw her yesterday, and today she's dead near your apartment."

A frown captured Connell's expression. "Chief, we all agree, an animal was responsible. So how can Daci be involved?"

I butted in. "I see hundreds of people every day. And if one dies, will you suspect me as well?"

"Calm down." The chief's voice was strained. "Until this case is resolved, please don't make plans to leave town. We may have more questions. And Inspector Lonescu," he turned to Connell, "don't ever challenge me in front of others again." He called to the officer with the handlebar moustache and asked him to write down my short statement of when I saw Catalina last, along with my contact details.

I reviewed it and signed it.

Connell ran a hand through his hair and folded his arms. He mouthed the word 'sorry' when he looked my way.

The chief's gaze gestured to the crime scene and back. He studied me, his thick eyebrows lowering, and licked his lips. "So what animal do you think is capable of this?"

I shrugged. "A wolf."

He tilted his head to one side. "You mean a pack of wolves or dogs?"

"No. The tears on the body are suggestive of a single wolf struggling to rip flesh, as

opposed to two or more wolves tearing the carcass in a tug-of-war manner. Plus, the animal who did this was really strong, so it wasn't a dog."

The chief exhaled a long breath. "Why a wolf and not a bear?" He gave me a glare that could scare off a cast of vultures. "Plenty of bears wander down from the woods, rummaging in people's garbage. We've got a dedicated team of park rangers trapping bears every night so people don't fear going outside. What if this girl was in the wrong place at the wrong time, and she crossed paths with a hungry bear? That seems like a more logical reason to me. Sometimes the obvious reason is the right one."

"Bears mark their territory by clawing trees as high as they can reach to show other bears how big they are. They don't scratch low fences or spray their mark like wolves do." I pointed to the fence, not holding back the annoyance in my voice. "Can't you smell it? You don't need me here to tell you what any moron could see." A swirl of anger spread through me, and I laced my fingers behind my back to stop them curling into fists.

Connell coughed and raised an eyebrow.

I had to calm down before I exploded.

The chief's nose made a whistling noise as he breathed. "That could be any local dog."

My jaw set tight. "The wounds on Ca . . . the victim aren't

common and unlikely to be a dog. Anyway, the wolf didn't attack the girl here. She was dragged from elsewhere. There are blood drops leading in from the woods if you check."

"Yes, Inspector Lonescu told me."

"Perhaps we should let her see the other files?" Connell suggested.

After a loud smacking of his lips, the chief responded, "Not yet. Until we find out that

she wasn't the last person to see Catalina, I'd prefer you work with her today on the case. Decipher the animal's behaviour and where the girl was dragged from."

The balding man turned his attention to me for a moment, drilling me with his gaze as if to intimidate me, then called to the forensic team with a wave and turned to Connell. "I want whatever is responsible caught before the end of the week. There's bound to be a witness, someone who saw or heard something." The chief inspected the fence and surrounding ground, prodding his chin with a finger.

I strode angrily away, despite the stabbing pain in my hip. What was I doing anyway? Helping the police catch a demonic wolf that no human should know exists after they accused me of being involved, and in the process I kept pushing away the one person I adored beyond anything? On top of everything, something was happening to me. I was changing, and the idea of my inner wolf freeing itself early mortified me.

Connell grabbed my arm. "What's going on with you?"

I tugged myself free. "I'm sorry for what I said. I just need some fresh air."

His rigid posture softened. "I feel terrible that you had to see your friend like that." He seemed genuinely concerned.

"I'll be fine." My throat was dry again.

"The chief doesn't think you're a suspect, if that's what's worrying you. It's standard procedure. It would apply to me too, if I saw a murder victim the day before she died." An expression of regret creased his brow.

"I don't want to fight anymore. Please. My place tonight. Eight?"

"Lonescu," the chief called out.

Connell's gaze lingered over me like he might answer me, and I yearned for him to

nod or do something. But I had to get away from the smells of blood, and Connell's sex musk, before something bad happened.

He spun away, as if I were nothing but his colleague, rather than the woman he loved. I rushed toward the back end of the street. A crawly sensation pinched my skin like a thousand ant bites. *God. No. Not here.* The full moon hadn't arrived yet. My muscles twitched, and I ran.

At the end of the lane, I caught a glimpse of the Braşov Hollywood-style sign adorning the mountain. I dashed into the woods, behind the first few lines of trees, and knelt onto a bed of dried pine needles.

Breathe.

Inhale.

Exhale.

Too many unruly things were happening at once, and I had to keep my head straight. A thunderous gasp rolled from my mouth. My hands clutched the grass. Inside, I felt her, my wolf, stirring. My transformation urges had ignited too early. Days before they should.

Without any reservation, my own change pushed forward. My limbs quivered uncontrollably.

Images of Connell finding me flashed in my mind.

An inferno seized my body, and a half-howl, half-shriek, tore past my lips. On all fours, my wolf poured out of me like a broken dam, spilling free and uncontrollable, ripping my clothes to shreds. A bronze pelt cloaked me. The injury on my hip flared with pins and needles.

I shook off the human remnants, trotting in a circle. Colors blended and shadows glowed with a gray hue. I was a moonwulf outside the full moon. I'd always been able to control my wolf when I turned, which apparently was unusual for a moonwulf, but this was new.

Footsteps closed in from the lane, and Connell appeared at the wood's shore. "Daci? Where are you?"

Crouching low, I watched through the foliage and gaps between pine trunks. I contemplated transforming back into human form, but how would I explain being naked and my clothes shredded. I wasn't even sure I could control a safe change back.

A wrinkle claimed Connell's brow as he swept the area with his gaze. "Daci?" He inched closer.

Only a few trees stood between us.

My pulse hammered.

He shook his head, then threw his hands into the air. "Can't believe she took off."

There was a crooked frown on his face, and something else—despair. He rubbed his arms. His posture slumped slightly.

My heart bled. It sickened me to not respond when I lay right there. Maybe that was my chance to reveal who I was. He'd just as likely shoot me.

He gave a heavy sigh, and then walked off.

I glanced down at my house and car keys cradled in a nest of dried leaves and branches. A quick nudge of foliage covered them. I crept deeper into the woods and bolted away from the city.

CHAPTER 3

Confused and broken, I sprinted through the woods farther from the city and deeper into the forest. I'd given Connell my heart and planned to walk away from the pack, yet he doubted me. Sure, he wasn't aware of my sacrifices, but wasn't love about trust and forgiveness? I wanted to throw it all in his face and tell him he could keep his stupid love. But I couldn't do it when I'd give my life for his.

If I found the elixir recipe to stop my transformations, then I could live like a normal person, and Connell and I could be together. But that wasn't my only concern anymore, now I seemed to turn into a moonwulf days before the full moon, too. And how could I selfishly pursue the answer to my problems when a dracwulf was taking innocent lives? I had to do something and quick before the police started searching the forest and got themselves killed.

I decided to track down the dracwulf. If only I had visited the pack during the last twelve months, I might have sensed the dracwulf lurking deeper in the woods and stopped it before it killed Catalina. A guttural snarl burst past my throat, and dread crawled through my chest like a snake's venom poisoning my insides. Too many *if onlys,* and I hated looking back.

Every so often I spotted prints in the soil too small for the animal on my radar. A splashing sound reached my ears, and I trailed the source to a narrow stream twisting down the mountain. The water tasted sharp and icy. With a quick splash to my face, I continued my trek through thigh-high undergrowth.

Night crept over the skies, and I still hadn't located the dracwulf. I had to speak to Sandulf about the beast and to Radu about the potion. I broke into a stride. The woods whizzed past until I spied lights peeking through the trees ahead. Overgrown foliage spread over a timber-framed house where vaporous tendrils of smoke floated from the chimney, dissipating into the pitch-black night. Five wulfkin in the pack, not including me, lived in that house.

A fluttery feeling rolled through me. Returning to the pack home felt surreal and somehow comforting. Everything seemed older and smaller, or maybe I'd forgotten the simple life of a wulfkin.

I hurried across the path toward the pack house, but the fresh scent of kindling and musk stopped me.

"It's good to see you, Daciana." Enre's voice carried on the breeze.

I'd recognize his deep tone anywhere—he was my ex. "How are you in wolf form outside the full moon?" Behind me, Enre leaned his shoulder against Sandulf's Land Cruiser. Black strands of hair stuck to the sides of his face with rainwater. His hands disappeared into the pockets of his faded jeans and he wore no shirt or shoes. The muscular swell of his torso and carved arms made him a prime target for all females. I'd been there already, and while he was gorgeous, I didn't feel a connection. Not like Connell.

I willed myself to transform, and like slithering into a coat, warmth slinked over my skin, the fur vanishing, and I morphed into my human form, brown hair tumbling over my shoulders. A light sprinkle of rain licked my skin, and the ache in my hip from the dracwulf's attack no longer hurt. Nothing like a good transformation to speed up healing.

Enre strolled forward, eying me up and down, his hand caressing his chin. "I missed your *al naturale* form."

"Get a grip." Nakedness amongst wulfkin was as normal as breathing air.

He drew closer, his blue eyes tracing the length of my body. "Do I still have a place in your life, or did you forget me while living in the city this past year?" He shook his head, spraying me with water in his damp hair. "I remember my rohang time," he said. "It was fun, but I never forgot my wulfkin roots when I returned home."

Enre's heart was in the right place, but most of the time he let his wolf control him, which meant he acted before he thought. That included the words that came tumbling from his lips. Sure, I'd spent the last twelve months amongst humans—a rite of passage before becoming a full-blown wulfkin. And he was curious whether I'd forgotten about him. I hadn't. Though I had no intention of returning to pack life. "What are you talking about?"

The rain drizzled around us. Surrounding trees swayed, branches rubbed against one another, and the wind picked up.

"The years we dated. How do you remember me? As the wulfkin who loved you unconditionally, a mistake, a fling, or the hottest lover you've had?" He ran his fingers down my cheek and my lips.

I threw back his arm. "Yep, you're still the same Enre I remember."

"As the hot lover. I knew it."

I couldn't help but laugh, despite the narrowing of his eyes.

He inhaled deeply and gritted his teeth.

I had forgiven dozens of stupid things he did when we dated, and it got to the point where I realized no matter what I tried, he was never going to change. In comparison to Connell, I doubted I really loved Enre. It was a lust thing. Though I didn't hate him—far from it—Enre was part of me, and always would be.

"Anyway, who let the forest take over the house?" I asked. Knee-high grass covered the property, a dead tree lay halfway across the driveway, vines spread over the roof gutters.

"Things have changed since you left. We're too busy running errands to do anything else."

"What errands?"

"You'll see." He shrugged and made his way toward the entrance. Thumping the door open, he vanished inside. A delicious aroma of raw meat teased my senses.

I trailed after him, greeted by a wall of warmth and fur scents: powdery, milky, and musty. The stone fireplace blazed, throwing amber light into the darkest corners.

Fawn-colored skins masked the gashes in the wooden floorboards, with scratches stretching out from beneath them like tentacles. These were reminders from when the pack wrestled Enre's wolf into submission, and with that thought, the incident resurfaced. Enre and I were in a brawl over a young child loose in the woods. I blinked away the memory, resisting the urge to rub the wound that refused to completely heal on my leg.

Enre emerged from the hallway and threw me a T-shirt. "Put something on before you freeze."

I smiled and dragged on a black top that fell to my thighs. It smelled of his wolf, earthy and musky. "Where is everyone?"

"Some are setting bear traps near the city. Others are out back." He gave me a long stare as if he was waiting for me to say something, then brushed past me and out the front door.

He was acting strange, like he couldn't wait to get out of the house. He said the pack had been running errands, and members were away that night. Gatherings were compulsory, no matter what, except for those on rohang, of course. Had the rules changed? A year ago, no one would have dared break them: don't kill humans, don't let humans know we exist, never abandon your pack, attend gatherings, and don't create a dracwulf. Well, someone had already broken the last two.

Heavy footsteps approached from behind, and unlike Enre's light stride, I sensed Radu before he spoke. "Is it really you at home?" His arms coiled around my waist and he lifted me off the floor. "You're here to stay now." His chuckle filled the room, and he carried me into the kitchen, while I pretended to struggle. Yeah, it was an act. No one knew we spent nearly every night for the past few weeks together, pouring over books, drinking too much coffee and snacking on rabbit jerky.

The exposed ceiling beams continued through the kitchen. Aside from a counter along the enormous window and several knives attached to the wall, the kitchen remained bare, lit only by the moonlight streaming through the window. Years ago I'd convinced Sandulf to buy an oven for my meals outside the full moon, and after months of nagging, he purchased an old-fashioned wood stove. Once it was installed, I cooked my own dinners and the waft of bacon and eggs had the wulfkin salivating. My meals soon turned into enormous feasts for everyone in the house. Those were great times. Now the place no longer felt cozy. It was bare of voices and laughter, replaced with the cold of an abandoned house.

My eyes settled on plates of raw meat on the counter.

Radu dropped me on my feet. "Look what I caught." His voice carried a natural, low tone, and each time he smiled, the tiniest creases formed at the edges of his eyes, reminding me of our childhood games in the woods.

Botolf pressed his hip against the counter in the darkest corner of the room and stepped into the moonlight. He wore the widest smile, along with a cherry-colored shirt covered in white palm leaves. I rushed over and embraced him. My arms wrapped all the way around his chest, something I couldn't do twelve months ago. Firewood and soap cologne emanated from this wulfkin who had nurtured me, alongside Sandulf. Though he was reaching 150 years of age, he looked no older than seventy. I'd forgotten how much I missed him.

"There's something different about you tonight." His voice was heavy. "You smell earthy."

Maybe he inhaled the recent resurrection of my inner wolf or traces of the victim. Hesitant to panic the wulfkin with news on the dracwulf's killing binge, I bit my tongue. "Same old me."

"You're here to join us for the run, then?"

I pried myself out from his embrace, uncertain whether I could coax my wolf back out for the run, even if I wanted to. It seemed she had a mind of her own of late. "I'll never keep up in human form."

Radu approached us, and his silvery eyes met mine. His strawberry-blond hair, stubble and sideburns set him aside from the pack, not to mention the fact that he was a standout when in the company of humans. It was something he hated, and he avoided them at all cost. "Even if it was a full moon, you'd never catch me."

I shoved my shoulder into his. "Hey, don't dare me."

He nudged me back, his lips curling upward. "Oh, you're dared."

"Give me a couple of nights, and you're on. I'm faster than you in moonwulf form,
and you know it."

Radu moved toward the counter "This will be fun." He chortled, imitating an

exaggerated malevolent laugh.

Botolf stared at Radu, who pawed the meat. "I sure hope you're not planning to eat

before Sandulf does?"

"No." Radu's cheeks reddened. He glanced my way.

Botolf patted Radu's shoulder. "Coming out to help set up the table?"

"Be there soon."

Botolf headed out back. The second the door slammed shut, I dragged Radu to the

farthest corner of the kitchen. "Where have you been the past few days? What's going on? Did you find anything?"

Radu's words dropped to a hushed whisper. "Sandulf's got everyone running around for the council while he does who-knows-what. For the past few days, I've done nothing but chase bears away from the city. The damn things keep going through people's garbage. I didn't know how to get in contact with you to tell you I wouldn't be there, since Sandulf's been watching all of us." He shook his head. "I don't know what's going on with him." Radu leaned against the wall. "He's been out in the backyard most of the afternoon, just staring into the woods. He hasn't spoken to anyone today. Everyone's on edge, but no one knows why."

Looking at Radu's gaze flit around the room, a burst of guilt hit me. He smoothed and re-smoothed his gray T-shirt.

The dracwulf was the problem, and Sandulf's behavior meant he had to know about it. But why not tell anyone else? As tempted as I was to spill everything to Radu, I decided to wait until after speaking with the alpha. "I'll talk to him and see what he says, but first, have you found anything on the you-know-what?"

His chin dipped to his chest. "I've gone through all my books, including the ones I took from Sandulf. No mention of the recipe or ingredients. One entry said something about salt, but nothing else," he murmured.

My stomach dropped. I wouldn't give up on Connell. Ever. "There has to be something else. Otherwise, why did they mention it the books?"

He rubbed the back of his neck and stared with concern in his eyes. "Are you sure this is what you want?"

I nodded. "Please don't tell the others."

"Give me some credit. Do you think I want to face Sandulf if he finds out? You've always stuck up for me, and I'll have your back. That was our pact."

I grabbed his hand and squeezed. "What are we going to do?"

"There's a couple more books under the broken board next to the fireplace." He leaned in closer. "Right at the back, but I haven't had enough time without someone in the house to grab them."

I bit my lip. "Okay. Once the pack's left for the run I'll get them. That'll work." I gave him a hug and we stayed like that a few moments, both shaken from the secret we held that could easily get us killed, and I was glad for his friendship.

When the back door scraped open, we both flinched and stepped apart. Botolf halted in the laundry room. "I'm not even going to ask." He crossed the dark kitchen. "Daciana, Sandulf wants to speak to you alone, outside."

A chill ran down my spine.

CHAPTER 4

$\mathcal{P}$ushing past the back door, I stepped into the night. An autumn breeze swept hair over my face, and I flicked it off.

Sandulf stood in the far corner of the yard, watching me.

I wet my lips and strolled closer, keeping my head high despite the tingling claiming my fingers and toes. Why should I be nervous? After all, I needed to tell him about the dracwulf's kills, but I also knew he wouldn't forget the small tidbit that my rohang was over, and I still hadn't returned home. I steadied my breathing, reminding myself if I found the potion in the books stashed in Sandulf's secret hiding spot, then none of it would matter.

Moonlight caught on the crest-shaped emblem on the breast pocket of Sandulf's uniform. As a member of the Romanian Rangers Association, Sandulf protected a large portion of the Carpathian Mountains with his team—basically, the pack. His job ensured a home for his wulfkin, and he had the authority to close the forest if needed.

Sandulf took me in his arms and squeezed. "Good to have you home, Daciana. The pack's missed you."

My muscles tightened, and I was tempted to ask if he

missed me too. My loyalty lies with the pack. Always would. But my heart belonged elsewhere. So I changed topics. "I heard the council's been keeping everyone busy lately." I broke free from his arms.

"Too many damn bears for my liking." His words flowed while his gaze swept the woods at my back. "The council has us setting traps for bears since they're scaring the locals." He gave me a bemused smile, and looked me up and down. "You home for good now?" Something twisted his expression. Holding the position of alpha meant Sandulf never stopped thinking and questioned everything, so I didn't fall for his phlegmatic look. Beneath it lay a ruthless leader.

"The police came and saw me today about an animal attack in the city. They're about to send out a hunting party."

One of Sandulf's eyebrows crept upward. "That explains your smell."

"They found a dead girl on the street this morning, mauled and eaten." I swallowed the tension in my throat, not wanting to admit the victim was a friend, a human—*Catalina, I'm so sorry.* "This morning I was also attacked in the woods by a dracwulf, whose scent was all over the crime scene. I think it killed the human." I started pacing, unable to keep still. "I thought the dracwulf were only legend. That thing tried to eat me."

Sandulf's eyes darkened beneath his frown with the kind of look you reserved for your enemy, not a family member. If it wasn't for the paleness crawling over his cheeks, I might have mistaken his lack of response for disbelief. His brows pinched together before he asked, "Are you certain?" His voice sounded weary.

I stopped. "Of course I am. I've seen illustrations and read enough descriptions to know what a dracwulf is. I have a bruise on my hip the size of my head to prove the attack." Though since my hip no longer ached, the mark had probably healed.

"I see." His words were almost a whisper as if they formed part of his thoughts and accidentally slipped out. The swelling scent of perspiration and wolf told me he knew something.

"I was at the crime scene this afternoon." I paused, thrusting back the memories of Catalina. Us jogging, laughing, and sharing stories about men. "It murdered the girl right behind my apartment. Plus, there were two other killings in the past few months. Sandulf, you must have detected something in the woods, or known a predator had moved into your territory."

He gave me a long stare, a warning to watch myself. "She's trying to claim territory, that's all."

I almost choked on my next breath. "What! That's all?" Three people had lost their lives, including my friend. "Did you know about the dracwulf and the other killings? And you did nothing about it?" My voice grew brasher and louder. "What is going on?"

His hands fisted to his chest, and he stormed past me, into the tide of dense evergreens leading into the forest. I assumed he wanted privacy from the other wulfkin, and I followed him, until we were a good distance away.

When Sandulf turned to me, his chest thrust out and his nostrils flared with each inhale. "The dracwulf is my child. I reared her, hoping . . . " His jaw set, and he rolled his sleeves up.

My mouth fell open. He raised a dracwulf and let it attack people. He'd pretty much signed our lives away. Whatever rules an alpha breaks, the whole pack bares the punishment. And in the case of a dracwulf, the punishment is instant death carried out by the reigning wulfkin clan, the Varlac.

"Don't you dare judge me," he said. "I know what I'm doing."

"You mated with a wolf and let the cub live."

"And?" He cracked his neck. "How different is that to what you and Enre do in the woods when in wulfkin form?"

"But that's not breaking any rules, or endangering us or humans."

Sandulf blew out a noisy breath. "I don't need a lecture from you." His voice hardened.

"Fine. But you've made a mess of this, and now we need to fix it."

"Watch your words around me. We will do this my way."

As tempted as I was to blurt out that his way hadn't gone well so far, I bit my lip.

"What's the plan then?"

"You stop the police from sending out a hunting party."

"Okay, I can do that." At least I thought I could.

"I'll stop the dracwulf."

I nodded. Something in my gut told me it wouldn't be that simple, but what could I

do? The resolve in his eyes was real.

A spasm twitched along his jaw line. "The other wulfkin are not to know of the attacks. Right now I don't need the rest of them panicked. Understood?"

I didn't know what to say. I stood there, numb, still trying to process what he'd told me. He broke the biggest pack rule and now asked me to help him cover it up.

"There's another reason you should return home. The pack matters right now. You will become a true wulfkin in a few days, and I need you ready."

I folded my arms. "Ready for what?"

A low rumble rolled off his chest. "A nearby wulfkin pack has been slowly claiming bits of our land close to the Bulgarian border. They think I don't know, but I do. And I want us ready for when the time comes to challenge them." He kept staring at me as if he could read my secrets. "Just remember, Daciana, if this neighboring pack takes us over, they will most likely kill all of us."

My head spun. Heat climbed up my legs and back. "What's the big deal? We've had packs encroach on our territory before. The issue here is the dracwulf."

He laughed. It was bitter and fake, and echoed in the woods around us. "I don't expect you to understand." His facial expression didn't waiver. For someone who barely controlled their emotions, he appeared surprisingly calm. "This isn't a small pack I'm talking about, but the largest in Eastern Europe. Our pack is in danger."

Shit! This was very bad news, and my arms trembled. How could our small wulfkin pack defeat the largest pack?

A loud commotion erupted from inside the house and distracted us. Wulfkin tumbled out the back door carrying plates of raw meat, which they placed on a wooden table near the house. The gathering had commenced.

Sandulf unbuttoned his shirt, exposing a solid, hairy chest and leaned into me. "Be careful, Daciana. No one is to know of the other pack or the dracwulf." He took off, disrobing while striding closer to the house.

Was Sandulf endangering or protecting the pack? The uncertainty set my insides on fire despite the frigid wind. Maybe it was just me having the longest, crappiest day in the world.

If I moved back into the pack house to help him, Connell would ask a trillion questions I couldn't explain. If I ignored the pack with a loose dracwulf and encroaching danger from another pack, I'd never forgive myself. That left me with two things to do: find the elixir and help Sandulf stop the dracwulf, all in five days before the full moon when I planned to join Connell forever. Sandulf could deal with the encroaching pack. My number one priority was Connell. Without him, I didn't want to exist. Hell, this was going to kill me.

Outside the house, the other pack members retreated in a semicircle around the alpha and mimicked him, discarding their clothes behind them. Sandulf insisted we ate before every run, following Enre's escapade of once munching on someone's pet pony a few years ago.

I joined them and slipped in beside Radu at the edge of the circle, eager for the run to commence, giving me full access to the house and the hidden books. Then I'd spend the rest of the night in Connell's arms.

The alpha ate first, as was the ages-old custom, the pack members got seconds and any leftovers were given to the moonwulf. Me.

Sandulf huffed into the wind several times, and soon twitches swarmed his body. His skin split down his back. The wulfkin around me imitated his huffs, louder and louder. Their heat poured over me, and sweat collected at the nape of my neck. Sandulf's limbs and bones lengthened, and a tail sprouted from the base of his spine. He collapsed on all fours, his elongated fingers and toes dug into the soil. He convulsed, and a mud-brown pelt coated his frame. Black fur covered his snout, ears and underbelly. The breeze carried his scent to the back of my throat—timber and fresh earth.

His howl pierced the night.

My limbs had a mind of their own, quivering nonstop. Watching transformations in the past never affected me. But right then I yearned to join Sandulf as he tore into the raw steaks, smacking his lips while the rest of the pack salivated and waited their turn.

Sandulf swung around. He snorted, shook his head and trotted into the woods.

Then the other wulfkin started to morph into their wolf forms. Their bodies shuddered, skins split and an overwhelming cloud of scents hit me.

I reeled back, needing fresh air. My legs gave out beneath me, and my knees hit the ground. A change pushed through me, like it had earlier in the woods. Not again. I concentrated hard and struggled to keep my inner wolf at bay.

Around me, bodies twisted into wulfkin form, grunts and snarls escalated. The fresh- turned soil, pine scents and the wolves' wet musk drove me wild. I crawled backward, desperate for distance between them and me, but a long breath gushed past my lips, and the floodgates burst open.

I screamed. My wolf spilled out. A fast and desperate half-growl, half-howl ripped free, and my paws touched earth.

Something swept against my back with the intensity of a gale storm, and Sandulf was there, right next to me. So close his meat-breath heated my face. His nose grazed the side of my head and body, sniffing, inhaling my scent into him. He growled, and his ears flattened. He snapped at my legs.

What was he doing? Warning me? I recoiled. My wolf wanted to stand up for herself, eager to snarl in response.

He barked in my face, and then sprinted into the woods.

The other wulfkin charged after him, all except Enre, who closed in on me. His silvery ears shone in the moonlight against his brindled gray pelt. He brushed his head along my ribs and moaned. Again he prodded me, and then he bolted into the evergreens until they engulfed him. I watched the tall grass thrash and sway where he passed.

A blaze coated my chest. An urgency to join the others. My adrenaline spiked. All I could think about was catching up to the pack. I pounced into the woods and raced after them.

CHAPTER 5

The phone's strident ringing woke me up, and I glanced over at the bedside clock blazing 5:13 A.M. Too damn early for anything.

Tempted to dive back under the covers, I checked the caller ID: Connell. *Crap.* The previous night's events came pouring back: me turning into a wulfkin outside the full moon, running with the pack all night, collecting my keys from the woods, and ditching Connell again. On top of that, I never retrieved the old books for the elixir. *Double crap.*

I pushed my legs over the edge of the bed, scrunched the sheet in my fist and answered the call. "Hi."

"Where are you?" The panic in his voice turned my stomach.

"At home."

"What happened to you last night?"

My throat dried up as my mind whirred with excuses. "I uncovered something in my research and got stuck into it, not realizing it was past midnight when I checked the clock. I didn't want to wake you and went straight home. I'm sorry."

"I suspected you wouldn't come. Looks like I was right."

"Come on, Connell, give me a break. I'm working on

something majorly important. When you're on a case and spend nights in the office, I don't give you shit about it."

"That's not what pisses me off. It's that you never tell me anything. Send me a message if you're going to be late or not turn up, anything to let me know what's going on. It feels like you're only staying with me on until something better comes along."

"That's not true. I only want you."

Silence.

I lowered my head and stared at the dirt beneath my toenails from the previous night's run.

"We found two more bodies this morning. The victims were located on the opposite sides of the city." He paused. "Why would a wolf bolt across the city after a kill? They attack in packs, don't they?"

A shiver rippled down my spine, the possibility of two more dracwulf kills made me furious. There was no convincing myself the attacks weren't related to the others; I felt the truth in my gut. Worse yet, I wondered whether the dracwulf was simply hungry or territorial, and Sandulf had to know. I flopped onto the bed and curled into a ball.

When I gave no response, Connell continued. "I need you to review the reports from the previous attacks today and visit the new scenes to see if you believe it's the same animal."

I cringed at the innocent wolves who could lose their lives over Sandulf's stupidity. "Your team can test the evidence and see if it's the same predator without me."

"We have limited testing resources in this country, so we need your expertise to move things along."

The way he said "your" sounded full of contempt, and it pained me to hear him talk like that.

"The chief wants a hunting party issued this weekend, preferably with Romania's Animal Research Institute's approval. He's already spoken with your boss, Vasile."

I climbed up and paced the room, shaking my head. Typical Vasile to agree to anything the cops asked.

"If I could leave you out of this, I would, but I can't. Trust me, I tried."

"I appreciate that. Where should we meet?"

"Piaţa Square. Half an hour?"

"I can do that."

He hung up.

A snarl ripped past my throat at the terrible start to the day. Who could blame Connell for being upset? I'd be livid if he kept avoiding me.

I threw on a pair of Levi's, boots, and a gray hooded top. The bathroom mirror reflected gray wolf eyes from my recent transformation, and already the silvery color was fading into a darker shade. I pulled every strand of my nest-style hair into a ponytail and rushed outside into the morning twilight.

In the heart of Braşov lay the Town Hall, which framed Piaţa Square and overlooked the courtyard like an angry gargoyle. In the southeast corner, a blackened Gothic cathedral peered from between two modern buildings with its medieval heritage and weather-beaten stonework.

I parked myself on the circular step enclosing the spring fountain and watched the carrot-colored sun start its climb. Stray dogs chased pigeons through the area, and the wind howled as it carried the mountain's chill into the city. The cold stone numbed my backside, and I pulled the hood over my head, thinking about how everything around me was starting to unravel. I could only blame the upcoming Lunar Eutine for my sudden transformation the previous night, and on some level that bugged me. If the impending change started showing signs already, I had to find the elixir without delay to ensure I remained a human and stayed that way forever. Then there was Sandulf creating a dracwulf. What was he thinking? I blew a long, exasperated breath and stared at the mist forming in front of my face.

Footsteps clapped the pavement ahead of me. Connell strode closer. His shoulders hunched forward and his hands dug into the pockets of his trench coat. Dark lines shadowed his eyes.

I climbed to my feet and tightened my arms across my chest. Even before he spoke, I sniffed alcohol on him; sweet rum mingled with perspiration. "You look as tired as I feel."

He combed a hand through his blond hair. "Didn't get much sleep last night."

I bit my lip and reached over to touch him. He walked past me, knocking my arm away.

"Did the rum help?"

He lifted an eyebrow. "No."

"Is there anything I can do to make you forgive me?"

"I'm not in the mood." He tucked blond strands behind his ears and his fingers scraped the growing stubble coating his jaw. "You ready?"

I blew hot air into my cupped hands, ready to scream at him, and force him to forgive me. Anything to stop the guilt crawling through my chest. I couldn't stand him being upset with me. "Okay."

We hurried to his Audi parked near Piaţa Square. Once inside the car, I strapped my seat buckle and coughed from the vanilla air freshener fumes tickling my throat. "Who are the victims?"

"The first was a young man who must have been outside when it happened." Connell started the engine and made a U-turn. "The second, an elderly man attacked in his own bed."

"Really?" I scratched my hip. "Wolves don't break into people's homes, unless they're in a fairy tale." I laughed at my own joke and didn't manage to break through Connell's hard exterior.

He shook his head. "That's the problem. If it wasn't a wolf, what animal was it? The initial tests on the dried urine from the last scene proved inconclusive—again. It was contaminated with human components this time. We're waiting on the blood samples, which will take longer, but I suspect they will match the initial ones and lead us nowhere."

Wolves spent their time searching for vulnerable prey, not breaking inside people's homes, and a dracwulf should be no different. Yes, the animal would try to claim territory, but why such elaborate attacks?

We veered right. The streetlights revealed identical red-roofed merchant houses and pasty-white walls threading the path. No one strolled outside at such an ungodly hour. If it were my choice, I'd be snuggled up in bed too.

At the end of the road, an ambulance and several cop cars clustered on the curb. Connell parked behind a silver hatch-back. Two uniformed officers caught my attention as they emerged from a nearby house. One clutched a black note-book, while the other kept his hand on his gun's butt. They exchanged frowning glances and hurried toward the next house.

I would hate to be those guys.

"If the scene is too much for you, you can leave anytime." Connell climbed out.

I took slow long breaths, reminding myself to inhale and exhale slowly, and followed him. A faint metallic smell danced on the wind. Hunger pains swirled in my gut, and there she was again, my wolf, squirming inside me. The last thing I needed was a repeat of the previous night. I tagged alongside Connell, going onto a narrow trail between two houses, skirted by fences.

Ahead of us, a tall policeman staggered out from behind a break in the high fence, crossing the lane before heaving his breakfast. Connell retrieved surgical gloves from his pocket and handed me a pair. "Will you be okay for a moment? I need to tell them you're here."

"Yep." My inner wolf pressed on my insides. Not a good sign.

Connell vanished behind the fence.

With my eyelids shut, I focused on the aromas. Fresh timber, metallic blood, and a sugary tang combined into a horrible concoction. Beyond the initial smells, I caught the same scent from the other crime scene. It was the dracwulf, all right.

Connell's gentle voice reached me. "Are you going to be sick?"

I opened my eyelids. His deep-blue shirt was a contrast against his pale cheeks, and I resisted the urge to reach over and touch him. "No, I'm fine."

"Ready to go in?"

"Let's get this over with." And for once, I was glad I hadn't eaten breakfast.

We walked into the backyard, and I came to an abrupt halt. Strips of green and white fabric were scattered around the concreted yard. My gaze drifted toward two skeletal trees at the rear of the area. Red pieces clung to the branches, like the devil's Christmas baubles. I skimmed the cement and found no body. Beneath a thick tree closer to the house, a number of bones were clumped into a mound, and flashes of flannel pyjamas poked out from them. The man's scalp lay near the heap, yet somehow his locks remained untainted by blood.

He had been eaten alive. I fought back my gagging reflex. The messy trail traveled up the tree to an oversized branch, sodden in red. The man's remains sickened me. My wolf retreated.

If I had to guess, I would say the beast dragged the victim into the tree and gorged on him, discarding the scraps. Wolves wasted little meat from a kill, but they never climbed trees. Several oversized bloody paw prints stained the cement surrounding the remains and trailed toward the back of the yard. A black crow landed on the leftovers and pecked at the morsels. The nearest cop shooed it away.

I inhaled and found the marking scent. Following my nose, I went to the far corner where dried rose stems lined the back fence.

Connell joined me. "I've never heard of wolves climbing trees." His voice teased on sarcasm. He looked over his shoulder. "And this is one mother of a wolf. Looks at its paw prints." Connell wasn't smiling, and his expression was tightening.

"They don't climb trees, but the same predator is responsible." I showed him the faded wet stain on the wooden fence. "Wolves are notorious for marking their territory."

Connell's raised eyebrow questioned my suggestion. "So you still believe it's a single wolf, and the same one?" He removed his gloves.

I peeled the latex off my hands. "Perhaps the last victim ran from the wolf, so it chased her. This guy was in his own backyard, most likely jumped on. The behaviour doesn't make sense, but yes, I do think it's a single wolf. The paw prints make that clear. And the probability of two rogue wolves attacking in a similar manner is unlikely."

He gazed at me for a long while. "How well did you know Danu Illie?"

I stiffened at his sudden interest in my work colleague. "As much as anyone at the institute. What's this about?"

"This is his house and his remains." He glanced over to the tree and back.

My hand flew to my chest. Was it a coincidence that I knew the last two victims? I couldn't take another look at what was left of the guy who always worked longer hours than me, wore a smile despite losing his wife years earlier, and made me feel welcome from my first day at the institute. God, he didn't deserve a death like that. I wiped my eyes.

Connell's voice brought me back from my thoughts. "When was the last time you saw him?"

"Last week. We went into the woods to collect a couple of dead deer." Perhaps the dracwulf watched me, sensed my wolf side and followed the guy. But what was the connection and why? I spent time with lots of people from work.

"Daci, look at me." I raised my head.

"What's going on?"

How could I tell him anything? A dracwulf attacked and killed two people I knew. I wanted to believe it was by accident, except there was no convincing myself. "I need to go home." My voice grew high-pitched.

"Daci, please, I know it's hard for you, but you have to see the next scene. I can't let you go until you do." He started to leave.

I didn't move at first and patted my pockets. No cell phone to call Sandulf. Did I really want to find out what Connell insinuated, and then have the cops believe I was involved? It was ridiculous of course, but drawing attention to myself was the last thing I needed. I tagged after Connell, throwing my gloves into the makeshift bin, deciding to rush over to the pack house after the next scene and demand Sandulf tell me what was really happening with the dracwulf.

All the way to the car, Connell remained quiet, and we drove in silence toward the second crime scene. I slumped in my seat, fire clawing my stomach. Was Sandulf involved in the killings? He had to know about them. So why had he not stopped the animal?

I was suffocating in the car, and the vanilla fragrance irritated my nose. I turned to watch the buildings and cobblestone streets pass us to distract myself. A world I might never be a part of again blurred past. A feeling of emptiness spread through me at the thought of not finding the elixir.

Connell touched my thigh. "Are you okay?"

I turned in my seat, bringing my knees up. "I'm not sure what to think. What are the chances of getting a few days to study the previous crime reports, and avoid trigger- happy shooters targeting anything that moves while I gather my thoughts?"

"Let's worry about that after the next scene." A quick glance over, and I saw that he hid something from me. A secret. And it hit me. My gut dropped.

"I'm not here to help you with the case, am I? I'm being investigated."

He said nothing for a long while. "With your connection to the victims, the chief questions your advice and refuses to accept it. He's already demanded another specialist from the institute to help with the case. He's informed your boss."

I swallowed the knot in my throat and couldn't believe my expertise was being questioned. "How could I possibly be involved with these killings?"

"I'm having enough trouble trying to work out where you spend your nights, but no, I don't suspect you, and you're not being investigated. I thought I'd bring you here in case you had some insight to share. A lead we missed."

"Why? If the chief doesn't believe me, why bother?" I folded my arms and shook my head.

His fingers pressed to his brow for a few seconds, and his gaze never left the road ahead when he spoke. "You picked up things at the first scene that helped, and I want to believe you're not involved."

The words hurt. On some level, he didn't believe me either. Things were getting worse, and the night of the trans- formation was days away. Unless I found the elixir, Connell was lost to me forever, along with my job and everything I'd built for myself in the past year.

He took a sharp swerve onto a road barren of shops or houses. I gripped the door handle to steady myself. The street we traveled presented a back way to the rural districts where the fields expanded and villages hadn't changed in two centuries.

We sped past empty lots and suburbia without a word. The flat street continued ahead, and no other cars traveled alongside us. I guessed the police had shut the road. We neared a small farmhouse, which was the color of dead leaves. Wooden shutters protected the windows, and gray blotches marked the black roof tiles while a picket fence enclosed the home. Police cars congregated on the front lawn and one vehicle had its lights flashing, with no sound. Connell parked behind them.

"We're here." He climbed out and slammed the door shut.

The frostiness nipped my skin once outside, and my pulse thrummed for so many reasons. I followed Connell into the front yard and onto the porch. Autumn had peeled the fruit trees bare of leaves from the snow season approaching. I tasted winter, like a melting icicle on my tongue. The cops at the other end of the terrace shifted their attention in our direction, and resembled football players huddled before a game.

Connell creaked open the front door, and a wall of smells hit me. Blood shoved forward first, then the reek of fermented cabbage. The main room easily accommodated five to six adults. With our arrival, the standing space became restricted. Hand-crocheted doilies decked the mustard-yellow couch, television, round dining table, and telephone.

I tore my gaze away from the photos of the victim or the family and stared at the tiny kitchen. A young woman in a white lab coat held a transparent bag storing see-through containers with red fragments inside. Similar bags sat on the counter. Connell headed down the hallway. I slipped past the police officers to reach him.

A female's voice called out, "Inspector Ionescu, do you have a moment?"

Connell and I turned to the officer collecting samples at the same time.

He leaned closer to me, shoving latex gloves and booties into my hands. "The room is to your right. I'll join you shortly." Connell hurried into the living room.

The flavors in the air teased my tongue, and my wolf stirred. My hands trembled as I pulled the latex gloves over my fingers and shoe covers over my boots. I stepped into the room, and my gaze fell on the atrocity. The bedroom carpet was plush beneath my shoes, though I couldn't ignore the dracwulf smells assaulting my nostrils.

I stooped over and couldn't remember moving closer to the mess, yet I stood inches from the chaos. I backed into a wardrobe and tensed. The whispers from the police faded into the background, along with every other sound. Only my heartbeat reverberated in my head, faster and louder. The scene imitated the previous two attacks, except the bloodbath was contained within one room and the butchery appeared worse. Blood and fleshy chunks smeared the walls. Still fresh, the lumps of meat slid down the wallpaper at their own pace, and every now and then, a tiny movement on the wall caught my attention.

Sandulf should be seeing this and lying to the police, instead of me, and maybe then he'd realize the danger the dracwulf posed to the pack.

Unnerved, I stared in disbelief at the mangled human remains. Pillow feathers and broken glass speckled the bed. The area could easily be mistaken for a chicken slaughterhouse. The shattered window above the double bed delivered no fresh air to the room.

Hard footsteps approached, and Connell's rum fragrance found me. I stepped into the hallway, ripped off the gloves and booties, bunched them into a fist, and stuffed them into my pocket.

Connell offered his hand, and I took it at once. He guided

me through the crowded house, into the freezing outdoors and around the side of the house, away from the police officers.

My inner wolf whined with hunger pains, and my insides craved for Connell's touch. I inhaled the clean air, forcing myself under control. It took several deeper breaths to clear my mind.

"Sorry I left you there. It's horrible." His hand held my shoulder, squeezing ever so lightly, and then traced the length of my arm.

My mouth opened. No words formed. We were thrown into a difficult situation that pulled us apart, and I didn't want to give up. He didn't either. It was obvious in the way he looked at me. If he continued to believe in us, then we would get through this. What other options did we have?

I turned and wandered farther down the path after picking up the scent of urine. The noise of Connell's footsteps treading the dusty earth fell close behind.

Dried grass coated the yard. A clothesline spun back and forth with the wind, and a chicken coop remained intact. Not a single bird chirped nearby. Everything fell silent. A red flag in the soft earth marked where an enormous paw print indented the muddy soil.

Connell shifted closer. "It's the large print again. This thing must be a monster wolf."

At first, I speculated whether he was being sarcastic, but the stern look on his face told me he wasn't joking. He leaned in, hovering his palm over the footprint. "It's bigger than my hand."

I faked a smile. If only he knew what prowled in the woods, he might never leave his house again.

A breeze brushed past us, and I traced the scent back to a dried stain on the steps of the rear door of the house.

"That stuff is toxic." Connell wiped his nose. "How do you

think the animal got across the city so fast? Could someone have driven it?"

"What sort of question is that?" I gave a slight shake of my head. "It ran." Such a dash wasn't impossible for wolves or a dracwulf. Hunger or territory propelled this creature, and the attacks seemed calculated. Was my involvement calculated, too?

Connell stared at the murky sky and rubbed his hands together for warmth. "Let's head off to the station so I can give you the reports."

"Wait. The chief doesn't want me involved, remember?"

"He doesn't need to know. I want the killings ended, and you might find something we've missed."

Every part of me screamed to walk away and let the chief suspect me. I'd then spend the next few days stopping the dracwulf and uncovering the elixir. Yet, the way Connell stared at me with those chocolate eyes made it impossible. Despite everything, he still believed in me. How could I turn him down?

We made our way to his car and took off.

"Did the house look familiar to you?" he asked. "No." My breath jammed in my chest.

"The victim was Ghiţă Tere."

A fluttery feeling swam through my stomach. I had worked with the guy, so it was official. The dracwulf had gone mad, killing only people I knew. Their lives stolen for no reason. The connection was me. But why? The numbness returned to my body.

"I did a bit of research," Connell said, "And found out Ghiţă supplies the institute with traps and snares."

"So? I could've told you that."

"Hear me out. Your boss told me you met up with Ghiţă earlier this week to set traps in the woods. I also learned that Danu helped you collect dead deer from the woods last week.

And you said you'd bumped into the first victim while driving to work in the forest."

"What are you saying?"

"You spent time with each of the victims in the past week in the woods. Could someone be watching you and targeting people you're with? But why only those with you in the woods? Maybe an animal . . ." He gave a loud *tsk*. "Doesn't make sense."

My breathing stopped. What if the dracwulf followed me and took out those people? But why? I didn't even know the creature existed before today.

"Who else have you spent time with in the woods over the last few weeks? Think."

I wracked my brain, going over everything, and no one else from work came to mind. "No one."

Connell paused while he took a sharp turn down a side street. "I rang up Vasile and he said he doesn't know if you were at work late during the last couple nights since he left early. He also confirmed he hadn't seen Ghiţă for months, since the guy only deals with you directly and gets updates from your reports. This is why the chief is on your case. I want to help you, Daci, but you have to tell me where you've been spending your nights."

If they investigated me, I'd have no alibi for where I've been without bringing Radu into this, and that meant drawing attention to pack members who preferred to remain hidden from the human world. Plus, I'd have to prove where I lived previously, leaving me with no option but to go into hiding, leaving behind the man I loved.

Connell's fingers drummed on the steering wheel. "You keep disappearing during the nights, and I only have your word to go on." He reached over and caressed my leg. "Tell me you weren't somehow involved."

"Of course I wasn't." I took a deep breath, and my stomach fluttered as I thought of Radu. Why hadn't the dracwulf attacked him if we'd spent the last few nights together?

Connell cleared his throat like something strangled him.

I glanced over.

He licked his lips. "I told the chief you were with me both nights to get you off the hook."

I was blown away by Connell's confession. He had lied to the police for me, risking his career and everything he'd worked for, based only on my word. And despite the overwhelming love I felt from his actions, my insides shattered like glass. I couldn't tell him the real truth, ever. I was the world's biggest hypocrite. "Are you sure that's what you want to do? I don't want to get you in trouble."

"It's done. Plus, I don't want you to be interrogated as a criminal where I can't protect you. This is why I need your honesty."

We drove in silence for a while. He soon pulled into the police station parking lot and leaned close. I guided his golden strands out of his mocha eyes. His sweet rum scent coated me as he kissed me in an urgent kind of way. Perhaps we both felt the uneasiness of our situation. After all, I'd dragged him into my mess. I melted against him, staying there until he pulled back.

"I won't be long." He climbed out and hurried around the side of the building.

The weight of guilt pressed down on me. I didn't need

another person to worry about as well as everything else. What if the dracwulf targeted Connell next? With the cops thinking I was involved, I couldn't vanish into the pack house, especially if the police started the wolf searches in the woods. Sure, I might get away with it if I hid deeper in the forest, but that was not my intention and neither was losing my love.

When Connell returned, he handed me a huge pile of manila folders. "Hope you like reading." He started the engine and reversed out. "I'll drop you off at work to do your research."

Of course I wouldn't find any similar cases at work, unless I resorted to mythology books. "Take me home, my car's there." I started flicking through the top folder. Interestingly, the early attacks were not related to me. So, that was something, I guess. The attacks mirrored each of the others in style and method. Only body parts remained, and I imagined the victim's family burying bits of their loved ones. My hands trembled at the idea that Sandulf let the dracwulf munch on five people and referred to it as the animal trying to claim territory, *that's all.* I smacked the folder shut.

"Everything will be okay, Daci." Connell pushed the sleeves up on his shirt "We'll find the killer soon. And you won't be a suspect." He reached over and ran the back of his fingers down my cheek. I leaned into his touch, desperate to feel his warmth against me. Something to forget the insanity that was my life.

In no time, we reached my street. "I'll call you later, okay?" I reached over and stole another urgent kiss.

"Please keep in touch. I can only protect you so much."

Once Connell took off, I retrieved the keys from my pocket and ran down the street to my Jeep. Once behind the wheel, I sped toward the pack house in the woods, with I the windows rolled down to let in the crisp mountain air.

I decided to force Sandulf into hunting the dracwulf with the entire pack and make him see why the animal had to die. Sure, not all the wulfkin were hunters like Enre and me, but with our combined strength we could stop the dracwulf, or at least capture it. The blame for the deaths lay squarely on Sandulf's shoulders. Why had he kept the secret from the pack for so long? Not like I would have judged him any worse than I already did.

I parked near the house, got out, and hurried across the gravel driveway.

Enre's panting voice labored behind me. "Aren't you a sight?" He walked close, and the way his cut-off jeans clung to his body would make most girls gush.

Enre's gaze slid down my body. "Is there something you're not telling me?" Thinking blood stained my clothes, I checked for marks. Nothing. "Huh?"

He pounced forward as if he were in wulfkin form. "Your frequent visits. They make me think your ulterior motive is me. You're eager to come back home, aren't you?" My words came out breathless. "Stop playing around."

A scent of gamey rabbit meat floated on his words. "Maybe I want to play."

"I don't."

The back of his fingers brushed my cheek. "Sure you do."

I shoved my hands into his chest, and a growl rumbled in my chest.

He stumbled backward.

"Back off." My wolf leapt awake.

His eyes were ravenous. "There it is again, your wolf outside the full moon."

I let out an exasperated huff. "I know."

"How are you doing it?"

"No idea." My chest fired up again. "I can feel her stretching inside me."

"It's probably the upcoming Lunar Eutine calling you early."

"I doubt it. Radu said he's never heard of this happening before."

Enre's chin dipped to his chest. "Radu reads every book in the world, but it doesn't make him an expert on all things." He shoved his hands into the pockets of his jeans and slouched on one leg.

His pose reminded me of the male models parading luxurious brands in magazines. Too bad it didn't do anything for me. I had fallen for him hard a few years earlier. Two years in a relationship ending with a scar that refused to mend despite my fast healing was not a solid foundation for a bright future.

"Sandulf told me you'll be returning any day now."

Oh really? The decision to return was mine, even if Sandulf would disagree. In truth, I was already exhausted talking about me. I needed the elixir and to get on with my new life.

"I know you think you want what's out there." Enre pointed behind him toward the city, never taking his gaze off me, and clearly not hiding his disgust. "But your call is in here. With us. With me."

My throat constricted. I had no plans on returning, or being with Enre, or following any call. But how could I say that? It meant rejecting the family I'd known most of my life, and I wasn't ready to break their hearts. Not yet, anyway.

He sniffed the air around me. "Why do you smell so human?" His nose scrunched up.

I had enough of talking, considering he might sense a specific scent on me. "Is Sandulf here?"

"Nah, he's at work, but Botolf's inside."

"What about Radu?"

"Sandulf's got him working on bear traps for the council, so he's out."

Just great. I left Enre standing there and entered the house through the front door. The main room was unusually bright with every window open, shutters pulled up, and a heavy scent of honeyed timber floating in the air.

Botolf lounged on an extra-long deer pelt in the center of the room, hidden behind a newspaper. Should have guessed. When Sandulf was out, Botolf opened every possible door and window in the house for fresh air and light.

He shuffled the paper in his hands. "Nice to see you again."

"Why aren't you at work?"

"Aside from the ongoing dramas with bears, the onset of winter quiets the forest, and not many trekkers are out in the bitter winds."

A breeze swirled into the house, and I rubbed my arms. "It's freezing in here."

Botolf lowered the paper and peered over the top of it, his white eyebrows lifted. "This is beautiful. I miss the chill that clings onto my skin, reminding me of when I lived in the woods with no house to protect me." He pushed himself to a sitting position, crossing his legs. "Lately, I've been reminiscing about the old days when I was a young pup and roamed the mountains freely." He spoke in hushed, excitable tones. "Home was anywhere I wanted it to be."

As an elder, Botolf was slowing down and Sandulf often gave him days off with different excuses to avoid admitting he needed rest.

He said, "There's a pile of your clothes I found in the cupboard when cleaning up. I assume since you haven't taken them with you to the city, you no longer want them. Let me know, and I'll get rid of them."

An urge to sit back and chat with Botolf tugged my heart. I wanted to tell him my intentions, my love for Connell, and even how I planned to track down my real human mom. And most of all, I yearned to talk about the crime scene I just came from, anything to get it out of my head. But how could I break his cheerfulness when I might soon leave the pack forever? At his age, I didn't want to burden him with such details. The gentleness of his gaze made me feel like the worst person in the world. I wanted to beg for forgiveness, cry in his arms, and have him tell me everything will be all right. Instead I nodded and smiled, relishing every happy second.

His mouth curled upward. "When you return, it'll be like the old days. Plus, we all miss your home cooking."

My throat choked up. I blinked and looked at the wood paneling at my feet. "Yeah, I miss those times too." God, I was going to start blubbering.

"What's wrong?"

I had no idea how to leave them. For years, I had dreamt of joining the wulfkin. Now, my emotions were torn between loyalty and devotion to family and my love for Connell, and my heart won. Still it hurt. I met his quizzical stare. "Just tired."

"I assumed since your wolf came early last night, you're starting to feel some changes and it's worrying you."

Botolf voiced my exact fears. If I stayed there any longer, I'd break down and tell him everything. "I'll go and check those clothes now."

I rushed into the hallway toward my bedroom. Sandulf had granted me a room of my own, a haven for privacy and growing up, he'd said. Though I was expected to join the pack's sleeping quarters in the larger room where everyone shared the floor, and despite my moonwulf status, the pack always huddled asleep around me, especially Enre.

In my tiny area, light spilled from the enormous window with curtains gathered at the sides. Two furry bearskin blankets covered the floor space. At the edge of the fur waited a pile of clothes. I knelt down and fumbled through the old jeans, tops, and sweatshirts from my younger years. Carefree days when hunting game in the woods and catching the eye of Enre were all I cared about.

Then I sensed him and looked up.

Enre leaned into the doorframe. "I've missed you." He strode into the room and seated himself on the blankets, his arms hugging bent legs. His hand crept along the fur, impersonating a caterpillar, and I laughed. He stared at me with his ocean eyes.

"Enre, has Sandulf told you he created a dracwulf?" I didn't care any longer for Sandulf's rules. He broke most of them, why shouldn't I?

"Yeah, he told us after the gathering, once you left."

"And did he tell you the dracwulf killed five humans?"

He said nothing, though his expression grew solemn. I guessed no. He poked his chin.

"Are you sure? He wouldn't allow his child to kill."

"He did. I attended three of the crime scenes with the police. The dracwulf's scent lingers at each one."

He turned away. "Why wouldn't he tell me? I'm the pack's lead hunter."

"You should hunt in the woods tonight, and I'll patrol the city."

He looked at me. "When did you speak to Sandulf of the killings?"

"Last night, before the gathering."

A loud exhale rolled off his lips. "He just hasn't got around to telling me perhaps.

That's all."

"So what do you say to patrolling tonight? Like we used to."

"It's not a full moon for you."

"Yeah, but my wolf is ready, and she came out last night. I'm ready to hunt."

"This isn't like other hunts. I don't want you hurt." Enre inspected his legs, flicking off a twig entangled in the frayed ends of his jeans. "Once I've spoken with Sandulf about this, I'll handle it." He leaned back onto his hands. "Do you know why I hunt?"

I shrugged. "Because you're a hunter, and it's your job."

"It's more than that—so much more. I love the chase. My adrenaline soars, and in those moments, I feel one with the earth, the air, and the trees. Nothing stands in my way, and there is only one thing on my mind, to rip into flesh and taste fresh meat." He leaned into my shoulder. "I've seen this desire in you as well." A smile curled on his mouth. "But don't push yourself yet."

An incident flooded my mind again. "But I want to control my wolf side." I leaned into my knees, lowering my gaze. "And not attack other wulfkin."

"It happened once. Can't you let go of the past?" He pushed off the fur blankets, stomped toward the doorway, and pressed his forehead into the wooden beam. "I'm sorry I attacked you." A grumble hugged his words. "When we run, we free our wolf, and the damn child was in the wrong place at the wrong time. Who allows their kid in the woods at night anyway?"

"Maybe you're losing control of your wolf?"

His cheeks flushed a pinkish hue when he faced me. "I don't think you're in a position to offer advice, considering you're still a moonwulf. Once you join us as a wulfkin, you can dish it out with the rest of them."

The hairs on my arms rose. "Don't speak to me like that."

His gaze fell. "You know I didn't mean it."

The lump in my throat grew.

"All the times I've taken you out hunting with me, were you never tempted to hunt down whatever you wanted? And feel liberated?"

"Of course." I resisted adding how much I fought the urge

with every bit of my strength, and that control was the one difference between us and wild animals such as the dracwulf.

"Then you know it's our true nature, and all we're doing is suppressing the part that will eventually burst free."

Exasperated and guilt-ridden for raising the topic, I changed tactics. "Have you thought of joining Sandulf and becoming a park ranger?"

Taking a seat near me again, he drew his knees into his chest. "One day, I will become the alpha of this pack. Until then, I will train to become the greatest hunter. That's my job for now."

I caressed his arm. There was no doubt he was unmatched when it came to hunting, but was he leader material? Maybe.

"My parents are Varlac members, and until I take my own pack, I don't exist to them." Heat radiated from his body in waves. He'd never before revealed his fear. "That's how it works in the Varlac clan. Once I had hit puberty and passed through the Lunar Eutine, I was kicked out of the pack to find my own way. To prove myself as a worthy son. And when the time comes, I will take down any opponent who stands in my way." Enre's expression softened. "You've always been there for me, ever since you joined us. That's why I know we were meant to be."

"Can't you let it go?" I climbed to my feet and strolled over to the window, staring out at the peaceful sway of branches in the wind before facing him.

He leapt up. His gaze darted in my direction with a pouty and suggestive expression.

"Please, don't look at me that way."

His lips tightened like he was about to say something. Instead he walked out.

A suffocating sensation gripped my chest and twisted. If only I had turned into a wulfkin when I was younger, everything would have been simpler. But then I would never have known true love or Connell.

I charged out of the room. "You can toss the clothes," I said to Botolf. "I'm off. Bye." I dashed outside, ready to rip off someone's head.

CHAPTER 7

By the time I reached my apartment, the anger
bubbling inside me was ready to pop. No Sandulf.
No Radu. No empty pack house to check for the hidden
books. Time was running out. I contemplated telling Botolf
or Enre, but I couldn't make them chose between me and
deceiving their pack leader. Dragging Radu into my deceit
was bad enough.

At home, I found a message on my phone from Connell
confirming he'd meet me at Florica's Kitchen, a small eatery
in the heart of the city. I knew the place well; I'd been there
more times than I could remember, and the owner even
knew me by name. He was a nice chap, even if he did stink of
homemade brew. Considering my need to eat, and the uncertainty of Sandulf's return home, , an hour with Connell
couldn't hurt.

Dressed in black leather pants with a long sleeve V-neck-
line top, I combed my messy brown hair and headed out.
Connell held my heart, but with the elixir recipe still out of
my reach and the Lunar Eutine approaching, my future was
still uncertain..

Soon, I arrived at the restaurant where Connell waited in a curved booth.

Rhythm-charged violin music played on several speakers attached to the walls. The tables nearby were crammed with couples, and a family huddled in another booth. Bronze chandeliers adorned the ceilings, casting silhouettes against the sandstone walls, and a scarlet rug sprawled across the room. A saccharine wine scent tickled my nostrils, as did Connell's spicy cologne.

Our legs bumped beneath the table. His black knit top hugged his chest; no matter how he dressed, he looked stunning. He pushed his sleeves to his elbows, exposing strong, tanned forearms. I placed my hand on his arm, reveling in the heat for a moment, and imagined our lives together always.

"I ordered you some mititei," he said. "Hope you don't mind, but I know how much you love them. We can change it if you want."

"No, that's perfect."

The waiter appeared and placed the food in front of us, then walked away.

"I hate things being so out of my control—especially lying. It's wrong," Connell said.

"And you've been distant lately. I can tell your mind's elsewhere, but you won't let me in. I keep trusting and believing you. I really hope you're telling me the truth about everything."

He didn't waste any time. I took a nibble of a meat roll, flavoured with spices and garlic, and broke off a piece of crusty bread, racking my brain for a response. After swallowing the food, I said, "I'm sorry you had to lie for me, and I'm not hiding anything."

Liar. I twisted in my seat, unable to get comfortable.

Connell gulped half the wine in his glass, and a tiny red drop stained his upper lip. "I guess coincidences can happen.

I checked the first two scenes from months ago, and there was no link to you that I could see."

He ate one of the mititei with one bite, and I tried to pretend his snooping didn't irritate the hell out of me. My toes kept tapping the inside of my boots. Radu had to find the elixir, or such dinners would become distant memories.

"This meat's a bit undercooked." He wiped his mouth and surveyed the rest of the food on his plate, pushing it around with his fork. "Anyway, I have something to tell you."

I swallowed the food and turned to face him. All kinds of ideas swarmed my mind— he discovered something about me, or he got caught lying, or the cops were going to arrest me, or he couldn't be with someone like me anymore. My head hurt.

"I've never told you this because I wanted to forget about it." "What is it?"

"Today I received a phone call I hadn't expected."

"A-ha."

"I don't want to hide things from you."

I fiddled with the tablecloth in my lap, too afraid to ask.

"Today is my two-year anniversary since I left my ex-wife."

I tried to hide the excitement inside me. Who cared about his ex? It wasn't a dumping conversation. I ate two more mititei.

"My divorce papers were finalized ages ago, but today she reminded me of memories I tried to forget."

I caressed his arm and nodded my head. At least I wasn't the only one with a past. Who doesn't have monsters in their closet? I shuffled closer to him while taking another bite of food.

Connell fell silent. Sadness captured his expression, and all I wanted to do was take him into my arms and love him until every last bit of sorrow vanished from his body.

"She called to complain about her misery."

"I hope you told her you're taken?"

He wrapped his arm around my waist and pulled me into him. "I don't know why she upsets me so much. She cheated on me with a guy from my work, right under my nose." His gaze locked on the couple in the opposite corner.

"Do you still love her?" I cringed while voicing this thought.

He gave me his full attention. "Don't ever think that." His hand stroked my back and drew me into his side. "I love only you, even if you drive me nuts sometimes." He kissed my forehead. "I don't want any surprises between us, and that's why I'm telling you this. That's why I get so upset when you disappear for nights."

I tensed as a hysterical laughter bubbled in my throat—I was the queen of secrets, and they had the ability to freak out Connell.

He finished off his wine. "I do feel better now."

I folded my arms around Connell and held him close. "Everyone has a past." A part of me was relieved by his confession, while another part fretted about holding so many truths from him. Anyway, we were talking about his problem, he wasn't upset with me, and it would be rude of me to trump him with my own secrets.

With that thought, the urgency to meet Sandulf and stop the dracwulf steamrolled over me, but it exhausted me at the same time. I needed a bit of time out, and dinner Connell was ideal.

Over dessert, he asked, "What about you?"

"What about me?"

"Do you have any exes I should know of?"

Enre was my first boyfriend, but I never loved him the way I did Connell. "Nothing to worry you." I sat up straight.

"Really? You have no past love interests?"

"Of course I do, but they're not comparable to what you and I have."

He shrugged.

I stood up to imply I was ready to leave.

Connell paid. We strolled outside into a feisty wind, which blew hair into my face and ruffled my top. Connell embraced me as we briskly walked along the cobblestone street. The city fell behind us, as did people. Buildings melded into the night, faded streetlights guided our path, and the hint of rain teased my senses.

Connell guided me toward a closed shop, blackness peering back from the glass. He placed his hand against the wall behind me, leaning in closer. He was stunning—and mine. "Sorry for ruining dinner."

"Well, it seems you now owe me two hundred kisses."

My hands crawled higher on his chest to the softness of his neck.

He nuzzled his lips against my ear and kissed it lightly. "Last time I counted, I owed you fifty. How did we jump to two hundred?"

"Accumulated interest."

His warm breath tingled on my lips, and I brushed my mouth against his. He ran his fingers down my back. "I'll have to check your calculations."

"You'll have to be extra thorough because—"

My words died. Enre's musky scent hit. I untangled myself from Connell's embrace and pulled free.

"What's wrong?"

I ignored Connell and scoured the area.

Enre rounded the far corner of a side street. *Crap.* Dressed in black, he meandered forward, his arms dangled by his sides, looking directly at me. My pulse accelerated. He seldom entered the city. Considering he wasn't running toward me with some earth- shattering news, I guessed he wasn't here for pack business. And that pissed me off.

"Enre."

Connell turned to the wulfkin.

I held my ground and faked a smile for Connell's sake. "What brings you here?" I kept my voice steady.

Enre flashed Connell a menacing grimace. "To see for myself what you're up to."

Connell gave Enre a steely look, uncertain whether he should intervene or wait.

"Don't be silly. What are you doing here?" I asked again, my voice lowered.

"You suggested we patrol tonight. I came to find you. But I see you've already got

company."

My laugh trembled, and I was certain Connell picked up on it, especially when he mouthed the word 'patrol,' because his brows lifted.

I gave a forced smile at Connell. "Just a saying."

Enre grabbed my arm, and I snatched it back.

Connell was at my side. He stood a few inches taller than Enre. "Hey, pal. The lady's

busy. Come back another time."

Enre's lips peeled back, and a snarl droned in his chest.

"Are you growling?"

Enre shoved his palm into Connell's chest, sending him back a few paces. "Watch yourself."

I elbowed Enre in the gut and placed myself between him and Connell, who'd already started sliding up his sleeves. *Joy.* Just what I needed.

Connell attempted to slide past me, but I stepped in his way. His gaze locked on Enre who looked ready to pounce, and said, "Who do you think you are?"

"Hey!" My voice snapped them out of their staring rivalry. "Way too much testosterone is being thrown around. Breathe. Both of you."

Connell spoke over me. "No one touches her like that. Apologize."

Enre's chest vibrated against my hand.

Connell glanced my way. "Move out of my way, Daci."

"Connell. I can handle this on my own. I know this guy."

"Shit, Daci. This guy comes here, shoving you around and you expect me to just sit back and do nothing? Forget it." He faced Enre, his fists curled into a ball.

Enre sidestepped me and raised his hands. "Look, I don't want to hurt you, so calm down."

Connell gave a snorted laugh.

I couldn't handle it any longer and dragged Enre to a darkened spot by the wall. "Connell, give me a moment."

My hushed words rolled with a snarl toward Enre. "What are you doing? Are you trying to expose us?"

Enre gave Connell a quelling glare. "Who's he?"

"A friend."

"Is he the reason you won't get back with me?"

"Don't be stupid." I peeked over my shoulder at Connell who looked ready to intervene. "You said I shouldn't patrol tonight. Plus, you never come into the city."

"I wanted to understand what you loved so much about this place." He inched closer, forcing me back. "But I never expected to find you with a man." His expression was pure loathing.

That ache returned to my stomach and anger hammered forward— the anger I wanted Enre to sense. His timing was out of place. "Is either Sandulf or Radu back home?"

"Nah." He shook his head. "I don't like this guy. He stares at you funny."

"Fine, you don't have to like him. Just go back into the woods."

Hurting Connell with more lies was the last thing I intended.

Something growled out of the lane from which Enre had emerged. We both froze, our gazes darted in that direction.

Connell's voice cracked. "What was that?"

I dashed to the street corner.

Connell tugged my arm. "No, stand back."

I shook him off and concentrated. Everything fell still for a second. Food wrappers scratched the concrete road. I inhaled the distinctive wet-sheep-and-dung stench. Peering around the corner, a lone black figure the size of a small car crouched low in the darkened lane. It was the dracwulf. Hot wisps floated from her muzzle, and her predatory eyes glowed out of the night. The huge animal didn't behave like any wild wolf I'd seen, though she stalked her prey in silence. We couldn't face the monstrous dracwulf while Connell was near. It would reveal too much and place him in peril.

Quickly, I pulled back and gave Enre two flicks of my hand, then pointed to the alley to signal the target was in sight. Enre moved to my side and slipped into the lane, crouched low to the ground.

Connell, whose cheeks paled, inched closer to me, his gaze locked on the intruder. I couldn't live with myself if the animal hurt him. I prepared to defend Connell, even if it meant exposing my real self. I caught his wrist. "Move away from the alley."

"Daci, what's he doing?"

I reached inside of me for my wolf, searching for the warm fur that caressed my insides, but sensed nothing. Zilch. Where was she?

Around the corner, I watched Enre slide along the wall, hidden by shadows, closing the distance between him and the animal. A pool of light sprayed the blackened creature as she inched through it. She lifted her enormous head and roared, fangs shining.

A tremor gripped me, and the tiny hairs on my neck stood up. I was a moonwulf and had no fear, but my survival instinct told me to back away.

Connell took hold of my arm. I brushed him off.

My gaze remained on the dracwulf. A breeze swept my back. She sniffed the air, her ears pointed and her fur bristled, then she leapt straight for us with jaws open, her claws grating against the ground. Enre charged the immense fur ball as his hands snapped into knife-sharp claws.

I stepped backward, colliding into Connell, causing him to lose his balance, and stumble out of view of the lane. High-pitched snarls, scraping sounds and guttural whimpers fused into an explosive cacophony.

The dracwulf's body flung out from the shadowy alley, smacking the asphalt beneath a lamppost. Light sprayed over her brown pelt, exposing a monstrous wolf with knife- sharp fangs. Just as fast, she pounced upright, and threw herself at us.

Connell stepped in front of me as Enre emerged from the darkness, his arms back in human form. Enre threw his shoulder into the great beast whose body hit the concrete hard, and a gush of air rushed from her flared nostrils.

Connell dashed forward, but I caught his arm. "Don't."

The dracwulf shot back to her feet, but this time she looped around and slashed a paw at Enre's neck, throwing the wulfkin onto his back. Blood flowed from his injury. It all happened too fast. The dracwulf hovered on top of Enre. She sniffed his face with bared teeth and growled a territorial, aggressive sound, then set her stare on Connell and me. She started turning toward us.

Enre punched the beast in the throat. She whimpered a bit before dashing down the dark lane she had come from.

Connell mumbled, "Dear God!" We ran to Enre, helping him to his feet.

Enre scrambled closer to the wall, letting the building take his weight as his chest heaved.

"Are you okay?" I asked.

Connell muttered something in the background, but I couldn't make them out. Enre clasped his neck.

"Take off your shirt." I helped him tug the top off and

folded it, before pressing it against the wound. "Hold this tight to stop the bleeding."

"I could have taken it, but..." his gaze shifted to Connell, "he's here."

Connell's shoulders bowed forward. "Christ! How did you do that? What was . . .?" His voice broke off. "Can't be."

Enre was hurt, but I couldn't risk the dracwulf hurting Connell. Was she after Connell or me? "Wait, where's your gun?"

Connell raised his palms. "I didn't bring it, figuring it wasn't needed for dinner." He marched up the footpath and back. "We need to take your friend to the hospital." With the phone at his ear, he started phoning in the sighting of a wild animal on the loose, demanding police start searching the streets.

Enre shrugged his good shoulder. "I'll be all right. You worry about yourself."

"What the hell was that thing?" Connell surveyed the street, his voice panicked. "We need to evacuate this area in case it attacks someone else." He stopped alongside me and murmured, "Why would he try to attack it?" Scratching his ear, Connell shot a questioning glance at Enre. "How did you do that?"

I grabbed Connell's arm, drew him closer, and held onto his hand. His pulse thudded in my ears. It drowned out all other sounds, as a raging river would do, unstoppable and magnificent. "I believe we just found our killer. An oversized wolf."

Connell shook his head. "It's a wolf all right. A goddamned monster-sized one."

"I'm pretty sure we scared it for now."

He dropped my hand and stepped to the curb, pressing his phone to his ear. He was
calling the chief, giving him a summary of the attack and

that the wolf was heading east, requesting backup to hunt it down.

Double shit.

Enre had protected the wulfkin's existence at the expense of letting the animal escape. I whispered in his ear, "Do you think the dracwulf followed you here from the woods?"

I was grasping at straws, not wanting to believe it watched us talking earlier that day outside the pack house. I touched Enre's arm, noticing the blood dribbling down his chest.

He shrugged. "Maybe she fancies me."

I raised an eyebrow. Great, he was already making jokes.

CHAPTER 8

The way Connell's brow creased signalled alarm bells. "Daci, I'm going after the wolf. Take your friend home and stay there."

Connell encountered a creature that should never exist in the human world, and to top that off, I would have to explain my connection to Enre and his behavior. If the cops caught the dracwulf, the Varlac would toast our heads on a spear. Our wulfkin pack might as well count their days, unless I caught the animal first with Enre's help. No use waiting for Sandulf, who I suspect wouldn't be a fan of hunting down his child. Otherwise he'd have done it by now. Like he said he would.

"At least wait until backup arrives," I said.

"I think I know where the wolf's headed," Enre said, as he leaned against the lamppost. "I saw it coming out of the woods on my way here."

I glared in his direction and stopped myself from shoving my fist into his face.

Connell's eyes were on Enre. "And you didn't think to say something before, or that's it's strange to see a giant wolf? But then again, you wrestled it with your bare hands." He joined Enre beneath the light, his arms folded tight. No other people or cars frequented the area; despite the recent fight, only a wind whistled through the shadowy streets.

Enre shrugged. "Didn't know it would attack us."

I never expected to see Connell in such close proximity with another wulfkin, especially Enre. The possibility of either of them saying the wrong thing, or revealing a bit too much information would make the rest of my life unbearable.

Enre gave me a quick glance, and the side of his mouth twitched ever so slightly. I knew the look. We'd used it in hunting. Distract the prey. In our case, get Connell and the cops out of the way.

"I saw it near the farming district," Enre said.

While I didn't know the exact location of the dracwulf's den, I did know Enre's directions were on the opposite side of the city where three of the attacks took place, not to mention far from the pack house. It would buy us some time.

Connell's nose scrunched up. "That's miles away. What were you doing out there?"

"I live there." He adjusted the bloody fabric against his neck, and his face had lost a lot of color. Red marks painted his hand and cheek.

I gave a slight nod in Enre's direction. Connell was too savvy to fall for too many more lies.

Connell looked at me. "He needs to go to the hospital and quick."

"Your place is closer," I said. "I'll clean him up first to stop the bleeding."

"Take a cab to the hospital." Connell placed hands on his hips.

"I'll be fine," Enre butted in.

Connell shook his head. "Okay, I'm going to get the car from home anyway, so come to my place if you prefer." He drew a hasty breath and stared at me for a hard second. Yeah, he wanted answers about Enre all right, but it wasn't the place for a drawn-out argument. And he was in a rush.

"Let's move." Connell nudged us into a brisk walk.

We hurried, and I slipped a few steps behind them to avoid any awkward moments.

The fear of Connell hugging or kissing me in front of Enre seemed less likely given the frown he wore and the dirty looks he kept throwing my way, but you never know. What a mess everything had become.

Connell stuck out his hand to the wulfkin. "I don't think we've been properly introduced. I'm Connell, an inspector at the local station."

Enre gave him a sideways glance. "Enre."

Connell dropped his hand. "How do you know Daci?"

Enre's cheeks lifted, and he cast me an amused smile. "Daci?" He hummed and nodded his head. "What has Daci told you about me?" His voice strained when he said my name, and joy, now he knew Connell's nickname for me.

"Actually, nothing. I've never been introduced to any of her friends or family. Sometimes I don't think I know her at all."

That hurt, and I intervened, despite wanting nothing more than to dig a hole and hide in it. "I've known Enre for a long time. He's a family friend." I forced a smile.

Enre's brow bunched. "Yeah, she's a hard one to figure out."

My stomach dropped. The conversation was derailing, and fast.

"We first met at the police station. She was helping us with a case involving slaughtered animals. But she is—"

I shoved both them off the pathway and stepped in between. "Geez, can we hurry up? Connell, you don't have time to waste." I smacked Enre's arm a few times and grasped his shoulder hard. "Your loss of blood must be making you light-headed. You're mumbling."

I felt Connell's hand on my back. "Daci, you're hurting him."

Enre's face pinched, and he squeezed his eyes shut for a moment. I let go and looked back at Connell. "Can we hurry up?"

"It's just left on this street. You know that."

I screamed in desperation and frustration, hoping Enre did not just hear what Connell said. "I want to get there already. Can't you see?" I nudged at Enre, who had a bemused gaze. "He's becoming delusional, and you need to catch the wolf."

"Daci, are you okay? You're acting really strange," Connell said.

I ushered them with my hands. "Less talk, more walk."

I was certain both men considered the idea I might have lost my mind, but better that than allow a conversation about my relationship with Connell to kick off. No doubt, Enre would accuse me of choosing a human man over him, and yes, while that was what I planned, I couldn't bear for him or my wulfkin family to discover the real reason for my leaving. I'd rather they believe my decision was based on something more heroic or that I emotionally connected with my human family—not that it was for a human lover. In my heart, I couldn't live without Connell, but I refused to argue this point with the pack every day until I found the elixir recipe.

We fell silent, and I let Connell take the lead. By the time we arrived at his townhouse, my throat was dry and panic had settled in. More blood rolled down Enre's arm, and the color in his face now resembled a sheet of paper.

The concrete townhouse mirrored others in the district. No plants or trees surrounded the house, only a metal railing for a fence. The inside of his place was minimalistic and neat with white walls and wooden floorboards. Everything from the trimmed potted plants in the corners, to the black leather couch, to the flat television on the wall, to an overflowing antique bookcase was spotless and seeped a bachelor-pad vibe.

Enre banged the front door shut behind him and stood there with arms folded, gritting his teeth.

Connell entered the darkened living room lit by moonlight streaming through the windows. He opened the cupboard beneath the bookshelf and retrieved a bottle. The bitter-honey aroma teased my appetite.

Enre sniffed the air. "What's that?"

"Rum, the cure for everything." His British accent strengthened. He stuck the bottle out toward Enre. 'It will help with the injury."

He snatched the neck and gulped several mouthfuls.

"Take it easy." Connell ripped the bottle out of his grasp. "Get him fixed up. I need to get my stuff." He strode out of the room.

I snatched the bottle and hauled Enre after me. We made our way through the dark kitchen and flicked the lights on in a bathroom large enough for a small party. Inside the cabinet, I found dressings and bandage tape, along with aftershave, razors and a pack of rubbers. My cheeks warmed as images of Connell and I in his bed flashed in my mind.

"Daci?"

"What?" I slammed the cabinet door shut.

Enre sat on the lid of the toilet. I grabbed a towel and drenched the corner of it in rum. "How did you know where the bathroom was?"

I fumbled with the bandages and didn't meet his eyes. "All bathrooms come off the kitchen. That's how houses in the city are built." I lied way too easily.

Blood caked the injury. I wiped the wound and not once did Enre wince. His hands gripped my hips and squeezed each time I touched his cut. The once white towel had turned red, and the bleeding continued to trickle from the three gashes. I prepared the bandages and taped short strips to the side of his neck. His shirt was stained, but at least, the wound was clean.

I said, "You're going to smell like a drunk now."

"Will it make you want to kiss me?" He squeezed my butt.

I recoiled. "Stop it." Enre's leg kicked out and slammed the bathroom door shut. A gleam traveled behind his eyes, and the muscles beneath his skin started to twitch. He cracked his neck. His musky scent poured over me.

"What are you doing?" I backed into the shower door.

"Don't push me away, Daciana. Or is it Daci? Not after I've waited for you so patiently." His smirk widened. "I can't remember the last time we did it in wulfkin form. Let's do it here. Now." His hands reached out for me.

"Come near me, and I'll rip your arm off."

A thudding at the door made me jump.

"What're you doing in there?" Connell asked. He entered the bathroom, and stood in the doorframe, all six foot three, broad shouldered, with smoky, jealous eyes that drove me wild.

I snatched the bottle off the basin and pushed past him into the kitchen. Connell followed. "Gotta go, Daci. Does he need a lift to the hospital?"

"No, it's just a small scratch. Nothing to worry about."

The way he looked at me, with his serious glare, parted lips and folded arms knocked the breath out of me. What if he'd had enough of my lies and decided it was over? Enre was just another piece of my life I forgot to mention to Connell, and after today's confession in the restaurant, would he forgive me so easily? Sometimes I wish I wasn't born a moonwulf.

His gaze fell to Enre. "Take care, buddy."

He walked away. The front door banged shut.

My feet refused to move. I had endangered him to the dracwulf.

"What are you, his lover? Why does he look at you that way?"

I shot Enre a snarl and stormed out of Connell's townhouse.

After a few minutes, Enre joined me outside. We didn't say a word, but broke into a sprint in the opposite direction Enre gave Connell. My clothes would most likely end up destroyed, yet while running up alongside Enre toward the forest, a new vigor leapt awake in my chest.

I might get the chance to rip something apart after all.

CHAPTER 9

*E*nre and I spent the rest of the night scouring the nearby forests and city with no sign of the dracwulf. The sun rose and we headed to my apartment. I had that sinking feeling in my stomach, the one which said, *We're wasting time*. No sign of the dracwulf. No elixir. Everything was crap. I slouched on the sofa and stared out the kitchen window at a white- chested hawk circling the sky. I wondered if hawks faced impossible problems, such as selecting the best tree for nesting, what critter to eat each day, finding a mate. The bird dived out of sight.

My foot rapped on the wooden flooring, and I speculated about Connell's reaction from the previous night. He looked pretty upset, though how much of that was sighting of the dracwulf or finally meeting a friend of mine I couldn't tell, but I bet my life the latter played a big part. With his encounter reported to the chief, police would comb the woods and probably shoot any wolf in sight. And if they managed to capture the dracwulf, how would they react? A ferocious, new wolf breed might tip them into panic mode. On the bright side, Connell could no longer suspect my involvement. I hoped.

Enre sat on the couch near me. He wore no shirt, insisting the newly applied antiseptic cream would stick. The blood had coagulated around his neck hours ago, and the flesh around the wound blushed pink.

He nudged my shoulder. "Did you hear me? Sandulf needs to know." He touched his neck and shifted, causing the cushion to bounce beneath me.

"He already knows the problem is out in the woods." I folded my arms. "So, why hasn't he done anything about it?"

Enre's nostrils flared. "I'm sure he's tried." His words tumbled free, filled with eagerness to satisfy the pack leader.

I slammed a hand into the cushion between us. "The animal attacked us last night, and we didn't sense Sandulf in the woods once. He wasn't home either. He's not going to kill his own kin."

"He was probably tracking the dracwulf deeper in the forest."

"You don't find it strange that Sandulf keeps heading into the woods on his own?" Glancing at the kitchen windows, I spotted the hawk again.

Enre jolted to his feet and marched across the cobalt rug toward the entertainment cabinet displaying my shoes. "Why do you doubt him?"

I leaned over my thighs and avoided staring at his chest. "I'm not doubting him. I'm anxious. Police will be all over the forest. How will the Varlac react to not only having a dracwulf on the loose, but humans finding the animal? And the last three attacks were people I knew. I think the dracwulf is targeting me, somehow."

He scoffed. "You're sounding pretty paranoid."

"I'm not paranoid. Sandulf broke two rules that can get the entire pack killed. Aren't *you* worried?"

He let out a long sigh, and then punched his fist into the wall, tearing a great hole through the plasterboard. "Of course I am, but I can't tell Sandulf what to do, that would be challenging him."

"Why'd you have to do that? This isn't the pack house. I've probably lost my damage deposit now."

"You tell this Connell guy to hold off the cops, and we'll get rid of the dracwulf."

I massaged my temples, certain I'd used up all my excuses, and after the incident on the previous night, Connell would not back down until he knew the truth.

"And what were you and the bloke doing last night anyway?"

My hand fidgeted with the zipper on my boot. "Walking."

"Really."

"I've helped the police with some cases, and we're friends." I lowered my voice, even if the words stung. Fatigued, I resisted the urge to close my eyes and never open them again. I missed Connell already. He felt too far away.

The wulfkin's pupils drifted upward, and he folded his arms.

I didn't want to argue. "We're both exhausted. Go home and sleep. I'll do the same." "Daciana." He inched closer. "Give me a chance. Let me take you to dinner and show you I have changed." He threw himself onto the couch beside me and searched my face for a response.

My lips pinched. "This isn't the time to talk about this. There are more important things going on."

He frowned and tilted his head forward, lost in thought, and when he finally looked at me, a cheery smile spread over his lips. "Once this is done and you've become a full wulfkin, we'll go on a date. Like the humans do." Satisfied, Enre nodded to himself. His eyes gleamed.

Glad someone was jolly, though I doubted the date thing would ever happen. I didn't want to burst his bubble, so I said nothing. I jumped up and headed to the front door. "The dracwulf seems to only hunt in the early morning hours before dawn, and I want to catch it. Also if you see Sandulf, tell him about the attack last night and that he has to stop the beast." I opened the door, and the new day's chilliness wrapped around me. "I'm tired now."

He snatched his shirt off the couch, strolled outside mouthing the word *bye*, and disappeared down the stairs.

I smacked the door shut and half-slumped against the wall. Too many people were involved: Connell, the police, my work, the pack, and I had no idea how to smooth it out and keep everyone happy. The simple fact that Sandulf didn't tell the pack to hunt down the dracwulf made him guilty. Maybe I should lead the police to the monster, tell them what I know and help them catch it, even if it got me killed. At least then, no one else would die. Though such a sacrifice would mean sending the whole wulfkin pack to their deaths, and I doubt I'd have that in me.

My life was spiraling out of control. I marched into the bathroom for a hot shower. Afterward, as I dried myself off, the phone rang. I leapt into the living room and snatched the receiver. "Hello."

"Daci?"

I recognized the stricken voice right away and had no idea how to approach the previous night's topic with Connell. No excuses came to mind, only trepidation, which inched along my skin. "Yeah, it's me."

"We need to talk. How did your friend survive the attack? I think it was a bear. No, the animal growled like a dog. Maybe a rabid wolf?"

"Maybe the cops should hold off hunting it until we know for certain what it is?" It sounded lame even to me, but I had to try.

His voice was breathless. "We can't afford for another person to be attacked. I spent all night in the woods, and found nothing. We were going in circles."

At least Enre's distraction worked, though the situation exhausted me. "What did you say to the chief?"

"That an overgrown wolf was in the city, but I didn't mention you or your friend." He paused and just the soft inhale and exhale of his breath filled the void.

He lied for me again, and I felt sick to my stomach.

"They already suspect you're somehow involved, Daci, so I had to cover you. Plus, the chief needs the institute to sign off the hunting release forms today. Apparently the council is involved now and hesitant to allow a wolf hunt. It's a mess."

The rapid movement of events scared me more than facing off the dracwulf. Once the police found the beast, all hell could break lose. The Varlac would find out through the media that a monster roamed in our woods and piece it together. Then our heads would roll. At least Sandulf did one good thing and encouraged the council to protest against the wolf hunt.

"I keep thinking about it, and I think the animal is following you, Daci. Have you seen it before, or been in contact with it?"

"No."

"And who exactly was that Enre guy? He seemed unhappy about my presence around you. And don't tell me I'm imagining things. How can we build a relationship if you keep things from me, and why haven't I met this guy before if he's your family friend?"

He spoke the truth. I could feed him more lies, but nothing came to mind. Emptiness.

"I don't want to talk about this over the phone."

The phone on his side fell silent.

"Connell, are you still there?"

"Yeah," he said.

"The truth is I love you above anything else, and would do anything to make this work between us. I don't want to lose you."

"I have to go. I'll call you later." The phone clicked.

My legs wobbled, and I leaned into the wall. Despite everything, he still lied for me.

The urge to confess the truth—unload my burden and come clean—was overwhelming. I planned to leave my family for Connell, break pack law, and yet I kept driving him away with secrets. By the time I'd become human, Connell might change his mind about me. Perhaps revealing a small truth might buy me time. I put the receiver down.

I needed to visit Radu, or rip apart the pack house until I found the book, regardless of who saw me. My head spun from a lack of sleep, so I stumbled into my room. Kneeling on the double bed, I drew the blinds shut, threw the towel on the floor and slipped underneath the covers for a quick nap. My mind drifted to Connell, and soon the dream world captured me.

My eyelids fluttered open to darkness as if a nightmare startled me awake. Climbing free from the tangle of bed sheets, I staggered into the shadowy kitchen and ate a large, cold steak. The oven clock read 7:52 P.M., and I almost choked. I'd slept the entire day. I washed my hands and checked the phone machine, which blinked the number six.

I hit the message button.

"Hi Daci, it's Connell."

The machine clicked onto the next one. "Daci, I'm trying to get hold of you."

I bit my lower lip. The next message started. "It's two P.M. Where are you? Your cell's going straight to voicemail. I came over and you weren't there."

I gasped. The following three messages grew more frantic and desperate. How heavy had I slept to not hear the front doorbell and phone ringing? The right thing to do was call Connell straight back. I dialed his number, my hand quivering. It went to voice mail.

"Hi Connell, it's Daci. Sorry I missed your call. I fell asleep at home. I'm heading out to work. Give me a call when you get a chance." A part of me was relieved he didn't answer. Perhaps a bit of distance would give me time to work on my excuses.

Taking a deep, pained breath, and closing my eyes for a few seconds, I redirected my guilt to the real problem. Finding the elixir to ensure I kept Connell, and stopping the dracwulf before I turned. Nothing else mattered.

Dressed in gray tartan pants, joggers, and a black sweater, I headed out.

I abandoned civilization and drove toward the forest, swerving into the trekkers' parking lot. Once in the woodland, I picked up a bear's scent, which reminded me of dried clover. Back-tracking, I inched around a few trees and shrubs to avoid the animal who might be with cubs. A few steps ahead of me a huge, brown bear rose on its hind legs, its wild eyes locked on mine for a few seconds. The animal looked around as if scared, then turned and ran. Strange.

Quick to find the majestic tree Botolf and I termed "old man" as kids, I scattered the blanket of dried pine needles with my foot to uncover a timber door and unlocked it. I dragged the panel open. A warm glow emanated within the shadowy burrow. I scrambled down the stairs, shutting the door behind me.

The underground post was Radu's research area, plus a confinement for moonwulf during the full moon. Sandulf preferred not to hold them at the pack house in case any unexpected visitors arrived. After all, he was the head park ranger.

A battery-operated lamp illuminated the space. Two prison booths, each the size of a horse's stall, sat against the cement wall. A wooden desk and crammed bookshelf lined the other side. Modern was not a word used to describe the den, nor was rustic or cozy. A rug, the color of a moonless night, extended the length of the room, and I suspected it provided Radu comfort more than décor.

The door to the makeshift kitchen opened and Radu emerged with his face tucked inside a book. He wore a sweatshirt and slacks. Strands of strawberry blond hair poked outward, and his stubble encroached on beard territory. He saw me and beamed a smile, dog-earing a page before closing the book. "I'm glad you came."

I embraced him and we both sat down at a small table..

Radu leaned back and rubbed his chin. "At the gathering when you transformed outside the full moon, how did you do it? There's no record in my books of a moonwulf ever changing outside the full moon. I've been searching."

"I didn't do anything—it just happened. I can feel her surfacing inside me, like she isn't quite settled."

"After the gathering, Sandulf was in a strange mood. He was broody and pacing through the house. Maybe he's worried for you."

I remembered his aggressive reaction when I first changed. It sure didn't feel like he was worried about me. "Let me know if you find out anything in your books."

He gave a slow nod.

"What about the lupul elixir?" I asked.

His gaze fell to the paperback on the table and tapped the cover. "I took a chance

while the others were in the yard and retrieved two books from Sandulf's stash. But there was another, older one I couldn't reach since I worried someone might catch me. I'll keep trying."

"You took the books? What if Sandulf finds out?"

"I'll return them before he knows it. They're useless anyway. The only thing I found out was something about a wild petunia, but it was out of context. I don't know how it relates to the recipe, if at all."

Now up on my feet, I walked over to the prison cell, gripping an icy cold bar. "I'll get the book tonight. We'll return to the pack house, you distract everyone outside, and I'll take it."

Radu was staring down at his hands.

I implored, "I need to know if I have an elixir recipe or not, because then everything changes. I can't keep pretending something might happen. I have to know."

"I don't want you to leave the pack."

"Radu, it's something I need to do for myself. Sandulf will never let me be free, or do what I want." I walked over and gave him a hug. "I'll still be around, and we'll see each other. Don't worry, you're not getting rid of me that quickly."

He smiled, and on the inside I cringed at the lies I kept dishing out to avoid dealing with the hard facts. If I turned human, I might never see anyone in the pack again.

"What about the dracwulf. Anything there?" I asked.

"No." His head jerked up. "Sandulf told us not to worry about her, he'll take care of

it."

Heat engulfed my chest. "She attacked Enre and me last night in the city." I threw my hands on the table, unable to control the buzz shooting through my limbs. "Plus, a human inspector was with us at the time."

He clutched his throat. "Did the human see the dracwulf?"

"Yes, along with Enre fighting it with his bare hands."

He expelled a long breath and stood up, pacing to the bookshelf and back. "Does

Sandulf know?"

"I asked Enre to update him. But what worries me is that Sandulf doesn't care that the dracwulf is running rampant in the city and apparently following me. The police are now organizing a hunting party for a huge wolf." I looked Radu in the eyes. "What if the humans uncover the pack or the dracwulf?"

A harried, wild look captured his expression. "The dracwulf has berserk tendencies and is almost unstoppable. When Sandulf told us not worry, I assumed he and Enre had found the lair and would finish her off."

"As of this morning, Sandulf hadn't spoken to Enre about hunting the animal." I slumped back into my chair. "Sandulf has no intention to take out one of his own."

One of Radu's eyebrows cocked up.

"He's been using the dracwulf to kill humans I know. For some reason, the animal is targeting anyone I've spent time with lately. So be careful."

Radu rose and strode to the cells. "Why would she do that?"

"Territory? I don't know." I rapped my fingernails on the old leather jacket of a book on the table.

"Maybe Sandulf is involved?" Radu scratched the side of his head, causing more hair to stick out. "If he already suspects you're not planning on returning, you're in deep shit because he has the right to kill you."

CHAPTER 10

*R*adu and I returned to the pack house, with barely a word exchanged between us during the drive. He feared for my safety, and I feared for everyone else's. The more I thought about what Radu said, the more sense it made. *God.* Had Sandulf found out about my plans?

Enre and Matias finished lighting the fireplace in the main room of the pack house. No one else was at home.

"Where's Sandulf?" I asked.

Matias, who was nothing more than disciplined muscle with an army-style haircut, shook his melon-shaped head and threw a log into the fire, causing it to spark up. "Him, Botolf, and Lutia are out at the Braşov council. Something about wolf hunts."

I approached the blaze and warmed my hands. My skin crawled, and I couldn't stand still. I needed a distraction, or I'd find myself running to Connell and blurting out the truth.

I glanced over at Radu and winked.

He stepped outside, and seconds later come running back in, his hands flying about. It was a bit over the top, but it got everyone's attention. "I think I just saw the dracwulf in the woods. Come quick!"

Enre's expression hardened, and he bolted after Radu, with Matias charging behind them. The second the door slammed shut, I threw myself to the right hand side of the fireplace and fiddled with the floorboards. I pressed down on each of them, until one creaked. With a bit of pressure in the center, a corner popped up, and I pried it open revealing a knife and wooden box.

I stuck my hand in and searched the sides, careful not to move things around too much. Bottles, pieces of paper, dried twigs, a tiny rib cage, and pieces of dried animal pelt. I stuck my arm farther: more bones. What had Sandulf been doing? Secretly eating squirrels?

From outside, Enre said, "There's nothing there, you're dreaming."

I dug my arm in, shoulder deep, and touched a book's spine.

"I'm sure I saw it." Radu's voice was right outside the front door.

Lying flat on my stomach, I pushed myself against the floorboards and clawed at it.

My fingers slipped off the edge of the book. *Come on.*

The door started to open.

My thumb snagged the corner. I snatched the book and heaved it out. In one quick

movement, I thumped the board back into place, jumped to my feet, and stuck the book into the back of my trousers.

The boys walked in.

"So what'd you find?" I asked, hands on hips, and my pulse thudding in my ears.

"I think Radu's getting paranoid with all this talk of a dracwulf," Enre said.

Matias approached the fireplace, and I slid away, inching toward the hallway.

"You ready to hunt then?" A smile curled on Enre's lips when he glanced my way.

I held my breath for a second and let the excited sensation fill me. Radu would spend the night studying the book. With Enre eager to kill the dracwulf, together we stood a better chance of doing just that. Connell was already pissed at me, and the hunt was for our future together. Eliminating the beast meant the police wouldn't find anything in their search, the Varlac no longer posed danger to the wulfkin, and the guilt of leaving my pack family, deep in trouble, lessened. "Let's do it."

Radu strolled over, and I half turned, allowing him to view the book at my back. Enre nudged Matias with his shoulder.

"Feel like hunting?"

Matias scowled. "Sandulf made it clear he'll take care of it. I'm not going against him."

Enre sauntered across the room, and Radu took the opportunity to snatch the book from me, hiding it behind his back.

"That's your choice. I'm not waiting any longer. He can thank me later." Enre swung the door open.

I looked at Radu. "You in?"

He shook his head. "I'm with Matias. I have no plans on going against Sandulf."

"Then can you tell Sandulf I'm moving back home, and he has nothing to worry about," I said.

Radu didn't smile. He knew I had no intention of following through with my promise.

But I didn't want any more people to die if Radu's suggestion had any truth to it. Enre and I hurried outside into the howling wind. We sprinted deep into the forest. Exhilaration swelled beneath my rib cage, and my pace quickened. The waning moon materialized from behind a cloud pocket. Wisps of fog teased the woodlands, like apparitions ready to take corporeal form. Each time we dashed through a patch of mist, I lost sight of the path. A wintry gale haunted the forest, and I rubbed the cold out of my arms.

Soon Enre slowed to a walking pace, and I tagged alongside him. "Sandulf never asked me to help him hunt the dracwulf, even after I told him what happened in the city." He clenched his fists. "As an alpha, he's not supposed to hunt on his own, that's why I was appointed." He smacked his palm into his fist. "I don't understand what's going through his head right now. He hasn't been himself for a while, but I just thought it was the loss of his female." He shook his head. "But I have no regrets in doing this. We should have gone out the first night he told us."

"Agreed." In truth, Enre's bold move surprised me as his loyalty to Sandulf outmatched anyone's. So who was I to question Enre? After all, once we stopped the dracwulf and Radu found an elixir recipe, my life should return to normal, all before the Lunar Eutine.

We hiked in silence against the thrashing wind.

Several hours of scouring the perimeter near the city revealed no dracwulf. Exhaustion replaced my enthusiasm, so we proceeded to the opposite end of the forest, combing the land near the city, hoping to catch the predator in action. The added complexity that the cops might also be searching the woods meant we remained in human form. Not the ideal situation, but since the previous hunts for the creature were time wasters, we figured our chances were slim at best anyway.

On a shrub in front of us, we saw brown fur tangled between several branches. Even before I sniffed the fuzz, I knew to whom it belonged. My shoulders tensed, and I shot a glance to Enre whose gaze fixed on the hair. I pointed to the woodland ahead. Oldest trick in the book; hunt downwind, and lucky for us, the wind played in our favor.

I breathed in the pungent wet dog fur-and-dung smell. It was the dracwulf, all right. Plants sported broken brushwood, making it obvious a large animal had traveled through the woods with haste. We soon found another patch of tuft tangled in a branch, which meant one thing—we were getting close.

The scent took us down the sloping mountain. Enre seized my arm, and I stopped. His gaze fixed on something over my shoulder. The tightness around his mouth revealed both dread and excitement, and I knew exactly what he'd found.

My senses awakened, as did my inner wolf, as the dracwulf's scent nipped my nostrils. I turned and found the beast between two trees, hunched low with her back to us.

The mutt's body was larger than any moonwulf I'd encountered. Through her thin hide, the solid muscles across her back tensed and bulged. Covered in brown fur and striped gray along her haunches, the dracwulf's solid stature epitomized strength and power. The formidable predator we observed in the city, with extended spiky ears, was homed in on the prey she was tracking. Unlike most crazed moonwulf who hunted anything that moved, this creature was intelligent enough to avoid detection, knowing the perfect striking time.

Not many things scared me, but the beast's proximity caused my hair to stand on end.

An owl hooted overhead. The creature, distracted by the bird, raised her head to the sky and spotted us. She sprung to her lanky legs. Rigid shoulder blades protruded from the fiend's sides, fur flared down her spine. She greeted us with teeth bared and ears flattened. Slobber leached from exposed fangs and a hostile growl thundered. These were very bad signs.

Enre let go of my arm. "I'll take the right. You go left."

My response came in throaty hums. There was no time to transform, but Enre had taught me how to draw on the wolf's strength while still in human form and achieve a partial change. I breathed deep, searching inside. My pulse intensified, and the desperate urge to release my inner wolf was stronger before, and that surprised me.

"Go!"

I dashed past trees and bolted for the great beast's hindquarters. Only one thought

raced in my mind: stop it or be killed. I snapped my arms into wulfkin form—my job was to immobilize the fiend while Enre tackled it straight on.

I reached the predator first. With my claws ready, I leapt onto the beast's back and tucked my feet in front of her hind legs, slashing at her back.

She whined and bucked. Blood surged everywhere and splashed hot across my cheek. My claws dug deeper, and I rode the wild wolf clutching handfuls of fur.

Enre punched the mutt's muzzle, and with a sudden snap, the dracwulf seized his arm. I released my hold and scuttled closer to the head, hooking my arm around her throat. She released Enre, and attempted to bite me. I continued to claw at the pelt, and fought against her struggle to break free. Her wails had no effect on me.

Blood seeped from her injuries and weakened my grip. She continued to buck and I lost my grasp, flying a few feet into a tree. Enre was less fortunate. His left arm dangled immobile by his side, yet he readied himself for another round of assault. I leapt to my feet.

Then the animal suddenly paused and moved away, bolting down the mountain into the dense woodland. Why had she fled so quickly?

Enre hurried to the side of the hill. "The trail falls sharply, then swings to the left." He cocked his good hand to imitate the path.

The thumping heartbeat in my head blocked the rest of Enre's words. My talons retracted. "I don't think she's there."

All of a sudden my balance gave out, and I fell to my

knees. My body ached. I no longer sensed my inner wolf lingering in my chest. I staggered to my feet and used a tree for support. As before, I dug deep within myself, but she was gone. Not a single strand remained. My strength from minutes ago withered. What was happening to me? This couldn't be happening at a worse time.

Uneasiness crawled along my skin as if something watched us. Then realization hit me faster than a speeding truck: the demonic beast now hunted us. *Shit!*

Enre's body contorted, appearing enlarged, his skin split and black fur burst free, shredding his clothes.

"She's back," I whispered.

Leaves crunched nearby. I listened for noises.

Enre snarled.

Twigs snapped on the other side of us.

"She's circling," I yelled. "And she's bleeding from the neck, so attack there."

I strained to peer into the woodland, the area speckled with mist between the trees, covering bushes at every turn. From a few feet away, Enre turned to me with wide wolf eyes.

A dark figure stood motionless beside a tree not far from where Enre stood. We saw the beast at the same time and darted forward. I prayed adrenaline would bring my wolf back. She lunged for Enre, head-butting his face. Enre crumbled onto the ground, his muzzle and chin dribbling with blood. He started to raise his quivering body, even as the dracwulf loomed over him, ready to strike again.

I rounded a massive tree and threw my weight into the monster's side, only to be flung backward. The damn thing didn't flinch, not against my human form —I may as well have thrown myself against a building. Yet I had no plans of leaving Enre alone, even for a second.

Then the horror happened all at once. Enre rose off the

ground. The beast latched onto his side, and his cry cracked the night's silence.

I screamed.

The beast twisted her body in my direction, Enre dangling from her teeth. Her lip was peeled upward with a snarl. Enre's body morphed back to a human form.

I rushed forward and attacked the dracwulf with my fists, head and legs, anything to halt her carnage. Enre dropped from her jaws onto the rocky forest floor.

The animal's teeth snapped menacingly at me.

I retreated, colliding into a tree trunk at my back. I shielded myself behind the trees, begging for my wolf to resurface. I refused to die like that. Enre crawled away on his belly. The predator raised her muzzle and released a screeching howl, loud enough for the entire population of Romania to hear.

She leapt to the side, rounded the trees and collided into me, the force knocking me off my feet. She ripped into my hip with her knife-like teeth. At first, there was no pain, just pure shock. I wailed, and the prickles rippled through my body. Her jaws released their clasp, and I flopped onto my back, certain half my waist remained in her mouth. I rolled my head back in time to spot Enre standing behind the creature, with a hefty branch in his hands.

She snaked around and seized his ankle in her mouth. Enre's body fell backward and smacked the ground hard. The beast hauled him into the forest.

"Daciana!" His hands scrambled on the forest floor searching for leverage.

On my feet, my legs quivered, and I collapsed. Quick to raise my gaze, I watched in horror as the creature lugged his body farther from me, his arms thrashing behind him.

Desperation and fear tightened in my muscles. I rose, despite my side stinging to high hell, and my skull convulsing. I hobbled in the direction the demon dragged Enre. Pure adrenaline carried me forward and I continued my pursuit even as my posture sagged sideways. Each step burned, but the thought of losing Enre thrust me forward.

Enre's weight slowed the dracwulf's rush, and I kept them in sight, but the distance between us lengthened. Then the fog and darkness snatched them away.

My foot jammed beneath a tree root, and I lurched. The forest floor came out of nowhere. I hit the ground, and my mind plunged into a darkened abyss, blacker than the night surrounding me.

In my vision, I floated mid-air with Braşov at my feet. I struggled to view the heavens, and the closer I looked at the stars, the more they resembled Enre's eyes. Hundreds of blue crystals blinked and stared in every direction. They swayed closer. I kicked and punched them away.

***

I jerked awake. Leaves lay tossed across the forest floor. Tree branches trembled and the blustery weather was merciless. I curled in a ball, guessing that several hours had passed since I fell. I pressed the wound at my side and uncontrollable quivers seized my body, pulsing through my torso like electric currents.

Enre was lost and perhaps eaten. I had made a fatal error: I assumed I held control of my wolf outside the full moon. God, his capture was my fault. Tears burned in my eyes, and my throat constricted. But I needed to believe there was a chance of Enre's survival and pushed off the ground, searching for city lights. I staggered for what seemed like hours and winced with every step. When I finally crashed past the front door of the pack house, I screamed for help.

Botolf emerged, wearing flowery pyjamas. Sandulf followed and flipped the lights on. They both looked shocked, taking in all the blood and leaves covering my body.

The pack leader's voice trembled. "Daciana, what happened?"

Botolf rushed over to me. "Lean against me." I let him take my weight and we limped over to the single chair in the house. Then he vanished into the hallway.

Sandulf asked again. "What happened?"

I opened my mouth to speak but only a squeak shrilled. I took a breath and hit upon my voice. "We found the dracwulf. Enre and I couldn't stop it."

My body convulsed. Botolf returned with a bucket of water and several towels. He started to clean the wound on my hip. My teeth gritted each time he touched the lesion.

Sandulf touched my cheek. "Where's Enre?"

A breath lodged in my throat. "The beast took him."

"What?"

My words dragged and slurred. "I have to find him."

"You're not going anywhere in this state," Botolf blurted.

"It's my fault. My wolf didn't come out." I lost control of my emotions, and tears fell free.

Botolf squeezed my shoulder, his expression showing his horror.

Images of Enre eaten alive numbed me. I swayed with nausea and clung to Botolf's arm to steady my body as I leaned out of the chair. For my own sanity, Enre had to be alive.

Otherwise I couldn't live with myself, knowing the role I played in his death.

Sandulf slipped his finger beneath my chin, lifting my head, until I caught a glimpse of fear in the pack leader's eyes.

"I couldn't stop her. I wanted to, but no matter what we did, she kept attacking." I cupped my face.

Sandulf groaned. "You'll be okay."

"She's headed west."

"Let your body rest."

"He might be alive." I thrust myself off the seat, nudging Botolf in the process. "I need to find him now, before it's too late!" My legs gave out, and I collapsed half on the chair, half in Botolf's arms.

Sandulf's growl pierced my ears. "I told you to return home and then no one would get hurt." He rubbed his mouth. "Not Enre," he murmured to himself. Then to me, "What did you do?"

I glanced at the alpha, his cheeks paler than snow.

"He's . . . bitten. We can . . . him . . . " My words broke off. Hyperventilation made it difficult to breathe and speak at the same time. The realization of what had happened slithered along my neck like a slick tongue. A swirl of black spots returned to my vision. The bigger they became, the farther I dropped into the pit of my darkened mind.

CHAPTER 11

I felt sunlight on my face. I stirred awake in the pack house bedroom. For a few seconds, I lay there fighting the fog from my sleep. Outside, the wind whistled and rattled the windows. Then like a train at full speed, the memories hit: Enre's body being dragged by the beast, his eyes harboring the horror of someone about to die, and my own devastation at being abandoned by my inner wolf when I needed her most.

My head felt as if a vice squeezed it, and I touched moist bandages at my side. A spasm traveled through my body. I tugged the bear-fur to my chin.

The previous night's events played on my mind, and I couldn't find the off button. I wondered whether Enre was still alive, lying in a pit somewhere on the forest floor, alone and hurt, or perhaps the dracwulf . . . *No.* I didn't even want to give thought to such a possibility. I scrunched my eyelids tight and shook my head. His capture had been my fault.

The wooden floorboards groaned. Someone stood outside the door. I wiped my cheeks and supported myself on my elbows. "Come in already."

The door creaked ajar, and Botolf entered with clean

bandages dangling from his hand. He wore his usual Hawaiian shirts and khaki pants. Carrot-colored sunsets flowed across the middle of his top with overgrown fuchsia hibiscus flowers strewn along the shore. Anyone meeting Botolf for the first time might mistake him for a rich, retired man who traveled on cruise ships in his spare time.

I stole a glance behind him into an empty hall; there was no scent of Sandulf in the house. Sandulf had to admit the mess was his creation. Perhaps he was still searching for Enre, or cleaning up after himself.

"Daciana?"

I glanced up.

"How are you feeling this morning?"

"Like shit." My voice engorged with pain. "Did they find Enre?" The twinges returned, my elbows gave way, and I fell back onto the fur.

"You need to rest and let yourself heal. Don't force it."

A scream clung to my throat, but my anger flared at the situation, not Botolf. Another round of stings hit, and my face scrunched up.

"Let me change your bandages."

Using all my strength, I turned onto my good side toward the window, relishing the sun's warmth. I bit back a shriek, wishing Botolf ripped the bandages off in one motion, rather than prolonging the sensation of tearing skin from the sticky bandages.

I spoke through gritted teeth. "Where's Sandulf?"

Botolf let out a long puff of air. "He hasn't returned to the house since the night you turned up."

"That was yesterday."

He slid the sweat-slicked hair off my cheek. "My sweet girl, you've been asleep for over twenty-four hours. Sandulf's been gone for a full day and night. It's Monday morning."

Dread filled me as I contemplated the dracwulf attacking Connell while I slept. What if he had given up on me already, moved on, and forgotten about our love? His words about me disappearing for nights at a time echoed in my throbbing head. The ache at my side reminded me I couldn't get out of bed, but I needed to know he was safe.

I tried to twist around, but Botolf pressed his fingers into my back. "Hold still."

Botolf stayed in the house because he followed the pack leader's order. Whether I had joined Enre on the hunt made no difference, Enre would have gone anyway. His stubbornness won most arguments, but it didn't excuse me from not stopping him.

In a victorious voice, Botolf said, "Done."

I rolled over as Botolf was wrapping the bloody bandages into a ball.

"How long does someone have to be missing before we send out a search party?"

His heavy brows lowered. "Don't blame yourself. This wasn't your fault."

I turned my gaze to the window, refusing to let him see my tears. "Yes it was. I shouldn't have encouraged Enre."

"Get more sleep. Hopefully you'll be walking by this time tomorrow." He patted my shoulder. "Your wound is healing faster than I expected."

Botolf departed and shut the door behind him.

The room sunk into silence, and I remained on my back beneath the blanket, praying for fast healing. My injury burned, and I fought against another surge of annoyance and shame. I slipped in and out of consciousness over the next few hours. Painful screams boomed in my head, but I was unable make out if they came from my fitful dreams or me.

uffled voices brought me out of deep sleep. I recognized the pack leader's scent along with several other wulfkin. With the blanket off me, I climbed to my feet and clutched my bandaged side. My fingers turned red.

Good news, the pain had died down. Bad news, I didn't pick up Enre's timber mark in the house.

Going through the pile of my old clothes Botolf hadn't thrown out yet, I dressed in gray hipster track pants that barely reached my calves and a faded black T-shirt with a rip in the shoulder, and then headed straight for the bathroom. I grimaced at my appearance. I looked like the Hulk bursting out of my clothes. My brown hair hung limp to my shoulders, tangled with bits of blood. Joy, I was a mutant about to confront Sandulf.

The need to vomit gushed forward. I bent over the toilet and let it out. My wolf jerked inside me, coiling on herself, stretching and pushing against my organs. Her whimpers sailed up my throat. The moon's call burned across my flesh crueler than before, and the desperate urge to rip free from my skin had to be the Lunar Eutine's lure. The nausea returned, and only bile rushed out that time. Inside of me, I already felt a change. Something primal and feral leeched to my insides, spreading like a toxic vine.

I relieved myself, washed my hands and face with the icy tap water. "Calm down," I told myself. "At least Radu has the book." I breathed one small sigh of relief, and headed into the main room.

The bright sunlight from the windows blinded me. I focused on the five heads turning toward me at once. Sandulf, Botolf, Radu, Matias, and Lutia sat on the fur rugs in the center of the room, hushing their whispers.

"How's your injury?" Radu spoke with a genuine caring tone.

I shrugged, unable to shape words. Between Lutia's grin and Sandulf's hard stare, my defenses rose. The alpha's khaki pants and shirt were clean and indicated he hadn't hunted for Enre that day.

"What's happened?"

The group exchanged glances. A twitch traveled over Botolf's face, betraying his calm mask. Had Enre's body been found? Glancing around the room, a folded newspaper nestled beneath the window, multiple plates stacked on a chair, and a mound of fresh wood gathered near the fireplace. No Enre.

I kept my voice low despite the heat bubbling inside me. "Talk to me."

Radu, Matias and Botolf bowed their heads forward. Lutia's lips broadened. Sandulf—on the other hand—stared at me with cold eyes, his nose wrinkled and lips peeling back. "You're obviously having a problem understanding my orders?" He stood up.

My instincts roared to get out of there, but I held my ground, refusing to let Sandulf push me aside. In a few days, I might never return to the pack house, and I couldn't keep running from him.

Sandulf stepped closer, and Botolf leaned out of his path. "I asked you to do one simple thing, and you let me down."

"I tried to stop the cops."

"No." His voice barked. "I said I would take care of the dracwulf. Now look what you've done." His gaze streamed over the other pack members who avoided his glare.

I attempted to fold my arms, but my injury refused to quiet down, and I almost lost my footing as I tensed through the pain. "But you didn't do anything about it."

His voice rumbled into a snarl like an approaching thunderstorm. "Enre's capture is *your* fault!"

A shiver snaked down my back. I'd crossed the line with

Sandulf, broken any faith he had in me, and he elbowed me aside in front of the entire pack.

The alpha moved with such swiftness that before I had a chance to react, he pinned me against the wall by my shoulders. "You keep pushing me," he growled.

My side stung. The words poured out of me, and I couldn't stop them. "You created a dracwulf, and you accuse *me?*" I roared, more like a lion than a wolf. "*You* should be out searching for Enre." The knot in my gut tensed. "*You* caused this mess. Enre and I were the only ones willing to do something about it."

"Who are you to challenge my authority?" Raw anger filled his voice.

I jerked away, my whole body trembling. "I'm the one who watched Enre being dragged away by the dracwulf. I followed the animal's trail until I blacked out. I'm the one who has to live with that image for the rest of my life." My breath quickened, and my wolf whined to come out. "He was my hunting partner. And we're all dead if the Varlac find out."

I searched the other wulfkin's faces for support. Radu shook his head and mouthed the word "stop." *Hell with it.*

Sandulf swallowed loud enough to draw my attention. "The Varlac is not your concern."

"Why not? Is that another secret you're keeping from us?"

His gaze hardened. "Your Lunar Eutine is almost here, and now that you're back home, we'll put this behind us. I'll find you a new mate, considering you got Enre killed."

"Don't you dare blame me!" I shouted, my voice climbing with each word. "What have you been doing for the past day? Have you found Enre or destroyed the dracwulf? You must know where the animal hides."

A howl burst from Sandulf's throat, his body quivered with rage, and I saw his struggle to control a transformation. "I can kill you for speaking to me that way."

"Go for it." I placed my hands on my hips despite the pain flaring through my limbs. I wasn't sure how much longer I could hold it, but damn if I would let him push me around when his actions created the problems.

Sandulf shook his head. With one movement, he slammed me into the wall with the back of his hand. "Is this what you want?"

I used the wall to hold myself up and refused to show weakness. My legs had a different agenda. They gave out beneath me, and I crumpled to the ground. "Did you tell everyone how you sent the dracwulf to kill humans I knew? Or about the encroaching pack?" Since we were sharing, I held nothing back.

He broke into laughter; it was forced and all for show. "I'd be careful of what you say if I were you, because sometimes what you care for the most can be taken away in a flash."

I lifted myself up, and strangled the angry words ready to fly free, suspecting he spoke of Connell. He knew about him —about us. An invisible hand trapped my heart, though Sandulf's implication that it may happen told me Connell was safe, for the time being.

Sandulf stalked toward the window and pretended something outside caught his interest. After a long pause, he said, "You've run out of options, Daciana. Accept your fate as a wulfkin, or die. No abandoning your pack. You seem very familiar with the rules, so I'm guessing you know no one can stop me from implementing that one."

Too many thoughts tore my mind to shreds. I still didn't know if Radu found a recipe or whether it would work, Connell was in danger, I blamed myself for Enre's capture, and my injury sapped me of whatever strength I had left. The desire to return to my room and crash was overwhelming, but I had crossed the line of no return.

Sandulf turned around. "The only reason I'm keeping you alive right now is because I need the police out of the woods.

Do that, and you'll have one more day in your precious human world to tie up any loose ends. Then you're mine. And don't try to run away, because I'll find you."

A heavy blanket of silence fell on the room.

Lutia's shrill voice finally broke it. "It's obvious she doesn't belong here; just finish her off, Sandulf." She somehow managed to climb to her feet in her mini denim skirt and tank top, and not flash anyone.

Sandulf's chest rumbled. "Let it go, Lutia."

She sauntered toward me with hands on hips, and heels click-clacking against the wooden floor. Her flaxen hair hung over her shoulders reaching her stomach, while the color of her eyes resembled storm clouds, always changing and unpredictable.

Lutia stood a bit taller than me. Her pulse sped, and I inhaled her scent. Every breath I took angered my wolf further.

"Daciana, take Sandulf's advice." Her strong Romanian accent, stretched my name to sound like "Dachshund." "Accept your future as a female wulfkin, and help expand the pack. That's your duty."

What concerned Lutia was Lutia, and I had no time for her hypocritical rant. I had disliked her from our first encounter. She appeared on our doorstep one morning, asking for protection from alleged hunters, and Sandulf, never one to turn away wulfkin in need of help, accepted her in our home. She ingrained herself into the pack. I never did find out where she came from before she joined us. Perhaps she left a rogue pack, after betraying them.

She wiggled her finger at me.

I could no longer contain myself and snatched her finger, twisting it back until her bone cracked. Her screeches pierced my ears. Swinging my bent arm, I threw my elbow into her face. Blood speckled my shirt and arms. At least, it stopped her howling noise.

"You bitch!" Lutia's voice trembled.

"Is that meant to be an insult?" I spun on my heels and bolted outside, needing air. Sandulf's voice drummed in my ears. "Let her go. She'll be back.

I hurried to my Jeep, retrieving the keys from the center console, and started the engine. I replayed what had just transpired, and I made up my mind: I would protect Connell, hunt the dracwulf, and find Enre on my own. Botolf, Radu, and Matias followed orders, so they couldn't be counted on. But I needed some alone time with Radu regarding the elixir. Sandulf and Lutia were a different matter. I refused to give into the alpha's threats.

I swerved with the bend of the dirt road, and the movement revived the stink at my side. The sensation that my injury split open, held together only by the bandages, flashed in my mind. I touched the wound, and pulled away fresh blood, dribbling down my fingers.

Romania's Animal Research Institute lay near. The clock flashed 5:45 P.M., and fortunately the place would be abandoned. Anyone who saw me dressed like the Hulk would ask questions, and I wasn't in the mood, especially from my boss.

Entering the building via the rear access with my keys, I quickened my walk, cringing with each step, and grabbed the first aid kit from the storeroom.

I tiptoed past an empty reception area, down the vacant corridor, into my office, decked out in wooden walls and flooring. Then I dove into the first aid kit. Clenching my jaw, I removed the sodden bandage and cleaned the excess blood with the clean edges. In haste, I wrapped a dressing around my waist and ignored the shooting pain down my leg. After encasing myself with three rolls, I stashed the kit under my desk and lowered myself into my chair, waiting for the pain to subside.

My life changed so much in the course of a few days. Connell would be panic-stricken by my disappearance, and I yearned to crawl into his arms. Sandulf might target him to teach me a lesson. Enre remained lost, and I had no idea how to tackle the dracwulf on my own. And I still had no elixir to take me away from Sandulf's barbarian leadership.

The door swung open, and I don't know who was more surprised, Vasile or me. My boss entered the room with two boxes in his arms, sneaking more crap into my office. At fifty-seven years of age, Vasile had no intention of retiring. Communism had made him hard. Thinning mud-brown hair floated on his scalp and bunched thick above his ears without a strand of gray. I often wondered if he dyed his hair to maintain a youthful appearance.

"I didn't hear you come in today."

Straightening myself, I smoothed down my hair. There was little I could do about the clothes I wore, or the blood on my top and arms, even if I did resemble a hobo off the street. I remained behind my desk. "Sorry."

His expression softened when he eyed the blood on my arm.

"I've had some personal problems." Partial truth sounded convincing, I hoped.

He piled the boxes on a stack already threatening to tumble over should anyone walk too close. Not the right time to complain, I reminded myself.

Shutting the door, he took a seat across from me. He wore the same blue suit from last week, and his white shirt revealed the smudge of accumulated sweat on the collar. No one was perfect.

He leaned forward, his arms over the desk. "What happened?"

Instead of telling him some great lie, I broke down and cried. It was embarrassing— that comes with weeping in public.

After wiping away the last tears with a tissue from my

drawer, I met Vasile's staid eyes. "I had an argument with my family." Saying it aloud lightened my shoulders.

"Did they hurt you?"

I shook my head. "This isn't my blood. I suppose you could say I got a bit angry."

His voice held a hint of humor. "Appears so."

On the inside, I laughed at Lutia nursing a bloody nose and broken finger. "I suppose."

"Families can get tripped up over trivial things. There is a bond and love between families so intense it can easily be tipped over the fence into hate's garden."

Vasile's poetic description made little sense. I nodded anyway.

"One thing you can be certain of is that family members will be the first to forgive and take you back. Sometimes it takes a bit of time." He reclined in his chair. "I myself have a brother whom I have not spoken to in thirty-three years, over a dim-witted fruit tree. I still hope that one day we will reunite."

Vasile's smile was magical and his delusional belief in humanity heartening. "I can tell you're a fighter. Stay strong."

A fresh sense of calm and inspiration splashed over me.

"I spoke with the police. I'm very disappointed to hear they question your expertise. You're one of my best animal specialists. Fill me in, Daciana."

"I attended a murder scene on Friday with a police inspector."

He nodded his head. "Yes, I heard."

"On Saturday I attended two new murder scenes, and the same animal was responsible for the killings. All three murders were of people I knew, but I have no idea why a rogue wolf attacked them." Honesty made my life easier.

He said nothing for a while, just scratched his chin and stared at me. "Fill out the field work, including your recommendation to the police, and bring it to my office today."

I looked at the clock on the wall. "It's past six o'clock. Can I give it to you first thing tomorrow morning?"

"No." Vasile's face twisted into a frown. "Dealing with the police is serious business."

I resisted yelling, as no amount of rationale would make him understand the police no longer followed Communist regulations. Romanian people fell into two categories: the new or the old generation. The older age group still feared the government and police, and it appeared Ceausescu still dictated their lives, even from his grave.

Without another word, Vasile walked out.

CHAPTER 12

I drove into the city with a sore hand. Vasile did not believe in modern technology and insisted all reports be handwritten. In truth, Vasile had taken a chance on me—an intern with no previous experience, but with my knowledge of mammals, he appointed me as the institute's behavioral specialist. To cover himself, he signed me up for a load of training that earned me a certificate and justified my right to hold the job. He took a risk on me, so I resisted outright questioning how he ran the institute or the decisions he made. So, I did things in a roundabout way.

In the document, my recommendation prohibited the police from hunting wolves in the Carpathian Mountains based on the endangerment of animals who might be killed in the process. If Vasile followed his usual routine of providing the authorities with whatever they wanted, then there was a danger of the dracwulf killing some of the police. That meant potential exposure to the pack if the animal was caught. I spent a bit of time scouring the aerial maps of the mountains, searching for any spots where the dracwulf might have set up her den. I planned to track those locations that very night.

But first, I had to check on Connell.

At the front door of my apartment, I paused, surrounded by the odors of curry cooking in a neighbor's kitchen mixed with an undercurrent of rotting garbage from the bins. No wulfkin scent. For some reason, I expected company.

A nippy coldness hugged the apartment, reminding me of an incident from years earlier in the pack house. Radu had placed a fresh rabbit, fur and all, straight onto the fire logs and in no time, a heavy smoke billowed through the pack house. We slept with the windows and doors wide open that night, and awoke to Botolf's fearful shouts from the main room. We found a brown bear, on hind legs, near him, snarling. We used raw meat from the kitchen to lure the animal out of the house, before it made a meal out of Botolf. Yeah, bears were deadly, but the incident was funny, and we never let Botolf forget how he squealed. Such memories would haunt me once I left the pack.

I strode inside and ignored the madness inside my head. If I ignored it long enough, it might leave me alone. The descending sun cast long shadows across the wooden floor. I headed straight to the fridge and took a raw T-bone steak, tearing a chunk off with my teeth. Two more chews and the first morsel slid down my throat, whole. I devoured the meat in record time, tossing the clean bone into the bin, and licked my lips.

The answering machine's red blinking light caught my eye, and the number nine flashed. Connell had left more frantic messages. That's when I realized I'd left my cell at home. *Crap.* I decided to visit Connell. I missed him, and he deserved an explanation of my whereabouts, even if I hadn't settled on an excuse yet.

Later, when the city slept, I'd visit Radu in his bunker, and then hunt the dracwulf. I'd learned enough from Enre to hunt on my own, and in moonwulf form I'd proven my strength was beyond most of the pack's ability. Two more nights before the Lunar Eutine and my life changed forever. For that reason I couldn't allow anything to stand in my way.

After a quick wash, I dressed in jeans and a black blouse with long sleeves, zipped up my black hiking boots and left the apartment.

The streetlights flicked on, and a breeze blew past me. I crossed my arms and avoided bumping into a group of young boys dominating the walkway and reeking of plum vodka. Fewer people roamed the streets along the lanes behind the main roads. The older districts were home to residents who lived there for generations. Potholes adorned the cobblestone paths while the concrete houses revealed cracks and rainwater discoloration trails, and dislodged chips of rubble had fallen onto the walkway.

Across the road I spotted a black rectangular sign with two taggers and the words *Barul Noapte*, which translated into "night bar", blazoned in red. Similar to other nearby buildings, dilapidation threatened the tavern. Black paint peeled off the wooden frames encasing the door and window, revealing a pale timber. Connell often mentioned the pub was a regular stopover after work, and I hoped to find him there; otherwise I'd continue on to his house.

I eased over the curb, waiting for a car to pass. Boot heels thumping, I hurried to the edge of the pub window and stole a glimpse inside. Candlelight lit the shadowy room. Bowls of peanuts decorated each table and a few patrons occupied the benches. I spotted golden hair and recognized Connell. He slouched alone at the bar. My stomach tingled.

I prepared to barge in when I noticed Connell standing up. He walked through a doorway with a toilet sign. That was my cue. I entered and the odors hit at once—smoke, alcohol, and perspiration. I bit my lip and hurried toward the bar as peanut shells crunched beneath my steps, and I struggled against the impulse to run out.

I hopped onto Connell's swivel stool and waited for his

return. I had no idea how he would react and hoped for the best. After all, I'd disappeared for the weekend after he witnessed Enre fight the dracwulf.

Fumbling with my hair, I slipped the strands off my face and tugged my puffy sleeves. I twirled in the chair and observed the other people in the pub. A couple of beefy men wearing blue overalls stared at their empty beer glasses in front of them. Four seedy boys lingered near the pool table, chuckling and pushing each other in a ritual to establish rank. No different from a wolf pack.

In the far left corner dwelled a lone figure with a black-hooded jacket. Slim, orange- stained fingers clasped the quarter-filled glass of ginger alcohol.

"Hey, miss." A low male's voice spoke from behind me, his words run together. "What'll ya 'ave?"

I spun in my seat and faced the bartender across the counter. He wore a tightly fitted black T-shirt with rolled sleeves, and his thick arms could wrestle a tiger. He was the epitome of brawn, perhaps no older than twenty-five or twenty-six.

"Sorry?"

He slowed his rushed words. "What would you like to drink?" The bear-shaped man leaned against the bar.

I inhaled his beer-infested breath and held his stare, unable to make a decision.

The boys at the pool table erupted into a concoction of hoots and screams. The bartender's gaze flicked over my shoulder. "Oi. Put the stick down."

For a full-sized man, he moved fast. One boy threw a punch and the other tackled him. The bartender grabbed a handful of hair and yanked them apart. One boy stumbled backward, and the bear-man's hand clutched the other boy's shirt, bringing him to his face.

"Get the bloody 'ell out of 'ere!"

With his three friends scrambling out of the pub, the

culprit wriggled free and ran after them.

Footsteps approached from behind. Connell's voice surprised me. "Decided to pop out from your hiding hole, hey?" For a moment, I had forgotten where I was, or why.

Rotating on my seat, my gaze swept upward over his white business shirt and locked onto to his mocha eyes. Golden stubble graced his face. I liked the rugged style, yet the dejected look in his expression and slumped posture added to my regret for letting him agonize over me.

Uncertain how to respond, I found my voice and sought a firm tone. "I'm dying of thirst here."

He said nothing at first. I guessed he contemplated whether to barrage me with questions or ease his way into the conversation.

He took a seat across from me. "Where have you been?"

I yearned to tell Connell everything. My heart fluttered at the idea of disclosing information no human should ever know. Enre and I hunted a dracwulf to conceal our existence in accordance with wulfkin rules. When hell broke loose, no wulfkin offered help, only humans. Funny, that.

"Something big came up."

His eyes rolled back, and he gave a slight shake of his head, the kind that told me he'd had enough. I couldn't take it anymore.

"I've been out cold for the past two nights. I'm sorry."

"What do you mean, out cold?" His brow pinched.

"I don't want to talk about it here. I really need a drink, please."

I sensed movement and cocked my head around. The bartender returned to his post, staring at us.

Connell turned to him. "Daci, this is Jai Hawkins from Australia. He's been backpacking through Eastern Europe but can't seem to leave Braşov. I've been stuck with him here for the past couple months."

Jai leaned forward and patted Connell's shoulder. "He's the only customer who hasn't been in a fistfight yet."

"Jai, this is Daci."

"Good to meet you," Jai addressed me with a joyous smile. "What's your drink?"

"Vodka, straight."

Connell was quick to add, "Place it on my tab."

Jai set the drink on the bar and disappeared into the restroom.

I swallowed the clear, crisp beverage, which heated my insides the instant it touched my throat. Connell's attention remained on me with a blank expression. I missed hearing his throaty laugh, the way it calmed and excited me at the same time.

"I thought I was going mad these past two days." He reached out to finger a lock of my hair off my cheek. "Are you in some kind of trouble?"

My heart thumped against my chest. "That's why I'm here."

His head tilted to the side. A sense of urgency passed between us, and I threw back the vodka, even if it did go straight to my head. I slid off the seat, and Connell was already leading me out.

Outside the pub, he tucked his arms into his pockets and we strolled toward his home, passing convenience stores and cafes, one after another. The quiet between us was uncomfortable and painful, when all I wanted was to jump into his arms and have him tell me everything will turn out okay. White townhouses with slate-colored roofs lined the footpath ahead, and the occasional tree or flowerbed adorned the front yards.

Connell said, "It's good to see you're okay.

"I'm sorry for everything."

He gave no response, just kept walking.

His house came into view in the distance, and in that split

second I panicked over what reasonable explanation I'd give about the dracwulf without sounding crazy. I needed to spin a small lie and make it convincing in case the truth ever spilled, even if the idea of lying to Connell irritated me to no end.

We rounded the path to his townhouse and entered inside. Connell strolled into the kitchen and flicked on the lights, revealing three chairs alongside a white-and-gray marbled bar.

I pressed my hip into the couch, remembering Enre from the other night, when he was still alive. Was he somewhere in the woods, maybe dead? I took a deep breath, locking away the raw emotions stabbing my chest. I glanced at the bookshelf concealing rum bottles and in the opposite corner was an overgrown potted plant with enormous palm- like leaves.

"I have juice, beer, spirits, or water. No vodka." Connell called from the kitchen. I joined him. "Water's fine."

Retrieving a clear bottle from the fridge, he reached up and collected two empty glasses from the cupboard, then settled onto a stool. Following his lead, I sat next to him and grabbed my full glass.

He studied his tumbler, running a finger down the perspiring glass. "What's going on with you and with us?" A long breath escaped from his mouth. "Your sudden disappearance this weekend, your friend's strange behavior—like he was more than a friend—and everything from that night seemed wrong, like I was missing something. I felt like an idiot."

My skin iced over, and my pulse thundered in my ears. His gorgeous face tightened, and his eyelids lowered as he said, "I feel like I'm just getting to know you. I don't like secrets, but I'm so in love with you that I'm struggling to walk away. And what scares me is that I might be heading right into a wall with my eyes wide open."

My voice softened. "Don't say that." I felt like the tug-o-war rope between Connell and wulfkin troubles, each needing my attention, and me refusing to give up on either of them.

He lifted his head. His hand cupped the side of my face and his thumb swept the tears from beneath my eye. I inhaled his warmness.

He said, "Please tell me the truth, no matter how bad you think it is. I can take it. But I can't take any more lies."

The faint tremble behind his words shattered my resolve to stay quiet. My entire life I followed orders, making everyone happy but me. Sandulf persuaded me to forget my mother with promises of a new life she would never accept, and I foolishly obeyed. I never knew my real father, but he obviously was a wulfkin from somewhere. I would give anything to turn things around and return to my real mom, to remove the grief she bore for losing a daughter. And now the alpha's action might see Connell ripped from my heart as well.

I blurted, "I come from a family of rogue animal hunters." While I didn't reveal the existence of wulfkin, I offered the next closest thing. "I'm sorry I haven't been honest with you, but it's been a family secret for generations."

Connell rubbed his mouth, and his forehead wrinkled.

"I've been hunting rogue wolves in the wild since I was a small girl. Enre is my tracking partner. Now when I say hunting, I mean capturing and re-locating the animal deeper into the woods. No harm brought to anyone."

I paused and caught my breath. "That's why he attacked the wild wolf we encountered in the city. From the time I attended the crime scenes with you, I've been trying to capture it." I fidgeted with my hair as I scrutinized Connell's face for a reaction. "I think this feral wolf might be a half-breed from escaped wild dogs or some other animal. It's a new wolf breed, and it attacked and killed those people in the city."

He stood and meandered to the sink, saying nothing for a long while. "Why haven't I heard of you or your line of work?"

"It's not something we want the public to find out. Our number one priority is the safety of wolves . . . and people, of course."

Connell scratched his head. "How do you hunt the wolves?"

"You saw Enre attack the beast the other night."

"By hand? That's absurd. Don't you use a weapon?"

"We don't want to hurt the animals. We've been trained to fight and capture wolves.

It's in our blood."

"Who trained you?"

"My family." I gulped the chilled water as tension pinched the back of my neck. Connell massaged his temples. "What do you mean by new wolf breed? The animal that attacked us was not a wolf. It was too large. And why is it only showing up now?"

I wondered the same thing and said, "For all you know, this creature could have been living in the Carpathian Mountains for a long time, and now decided to show its face." Connell spat out a laugh of disbelief.

"Put aside your skepticism. It's not uncommon for different species to mate." Images of Enre's body dragged through the woods flooded my mind. One moment I took a swig of water, and the next moment I said things I shouldn't have.

"The other night I traveled through the woods with Enre, and we had a run in with the wolf." My throat constricted, choking back a whimper. "It attacked us and dragged Enre away." I wiped my cheek. "I chased it, but couldn't keep up. God, I think it might have eaten him. That's why I was knocked out for a couple of nights."

The last thing I wanted was to reveal Enre's loss. Opening

my tear-filled eyes, I raised my chin and saw Connell sitting next to me again.

"Jesus Christ." His nostrils flared. "Why were you walking through the woods if you knew this thing was on the loose? Why would you do that?" He started pacing to the fridge and back, shaking his head. He faced me and a fierce expression contorted his face. "We need to report Enre's disappearance and start searching for him."

I felt broken and uncertain how to respond.

Connell continued his pacing. "I don't understand why you didn't come and see me. I could've helped." For a few moments he struggled to rein in his emotions.

"You would have stopped me if I told you."

He made a loud sigh and stared at me for a good minute, then wrapped his arms around my shoulders. "I'm sorry you went through that alone."

I melted into his chest and cried.

CHAPTER 13

The guilt of lying to Connell and the sorrow of losing Enre choked me into a crying mess. The dracwulf was unraveling my life, one thread at a time, all because Sandulf didn't finish her off. He would rather brush the pack aside than kill a creature that endangered everyone. Determined to finish the fiasco, I vowed to destroy her myself, not caring what rules I broke. The slight problem of the upcoming Lunar Eutine and finding the elixir constrained my time, but who didn't like a challenge?

Connell leaned closer, his hot breath on my neck, and his nearness confusing my thoughts. He took my hand and led me toward the couch in the darkened living room. I wiped my cheeks and sat down next to him.

He said nothing for a few minutes, then stated, "We should head to the station and report Enre's attack."

That was all the ammunition the chief needed to override the council and commence a full-scale wolf hunt. I shook my head, remembering Sandulf had given me one day to keep the woods clear of police. "Not now. I need some time to think."

He scratched his head. "There's a chance we might find him."

I swallowed the tension in my throat. "No. I don't want to report him missing yet." My gaze fell to my feet, and I refused to let guilt make me feel bad. There were too many other things to worry about and consider.

Connell slumped in the sofa like a stubborn child, and stretched out his long legs. "I don't understand why you want to wait. The quicker we start searching for him, the greater the chance of finding him alive. Daci, this is not the time to be stubborn."

I nearly spilled the truth, the burden caged in my chest. Would Connell believe me? *No. I shouldn't.* "Let it go, please. What my family does is illegal. I know this, but I can't have the police find out. I would lose my job and get my family into unbelievable trouble. I can only trust you."

"But I can't trust you." His face fell as he spoke, as did my stomach.

He started to stand, and I took his hand, drawing him back. "I didn't want to lie to you, but how could I tell you what I did? You'd never believe me and probably think I was mad or something."

"So the only reason you're telling me now is because you're stuck, and need my help. Otherwise, were you ever going to tell me?"

Most people might have looked away from his sharp tone, but I held his gaze and told the truth. "I don't know."

His strong expression softened. "I think that's the first time you've been honest with me."

"That hurts. I never lied about how much I love you or want to be with you, or anything about us."

"Then you should've trusted me." He sounded tired, not bitter, and ran a hand through his hair. He looked like someone exhausted after a long battle, too tired to care if he won or lost.

He stood up, pushing my hand away, and walked over to the cabinet, looking down at his hands.

"I can't lose you." My words quivered, and Connell returned alongside me.

"I don't want to lose you, either, but I also don't know how to move forward from here. Maybe I need time, or distance."

I leaned into him and placed a soft kiss on his lips. Rather than feeling hurt, I craved his touch and warmth. He trailed his fingers up my neck, cupping the side of my face and planted pecks on my nose and chin before finding my mouth again. I hungered for him and inhaled his breath as he pulled me into him. His roaming hands threaded underneath my shirt and guided me closer. I wasted no time climbing onto his lap. I stared into those chocolate eyes, which concealed no secrets, no uncertainty, just confidence of what he wanted: me. And that reassurance ignited my insatiable desire, leaving me breathless.

I lifted my arms and raised my shirt over my head to reveal a black sports bra. His face froze. "What happened?"

I looked down at my bandaged wound, and thanked the moon the bleeding had stopped, along with the pain. "A small injury."

"From the other night?"

I worked his shirt out of his pants. "It's just a scratch." I pressed up against him and seized his lower lip into my mouth.

His hands massaged my butt, and he greedily found my tongue.

I ripped the shirt off him in one motion, throwing it behind the sofa. My hands wandered over his firm pecs, snaking down his ribbed stomach, following the golden hair that vanished beneath his pants where his firm bulge waited to break out.

He whispered, "I promise to be gentle around your injury."

I relaxed into him, unable to get close enough. "Maybe I don't want you to be gentle." A smile curled on the side of his mouth with the promise of sex, and he gripped my hips harder, thrusting me against the hardness of his erection. I kissed him, and the heat drove me crazy. He unlatched my bra and tugged it off my shoulders. His head tipped and his tongue traced the edges of my breasts, flicking the stiff nipples in quick succession. His gaze met mine, and I knew he was teasing.

He gave them a light pinch with his fingers.

"Harder," I pleaded. My heart raced when he did. He blew a cool breath over my moist flesh, and an ache collected in the hot spot between my legs. I burned to feel him inside me.

Connell's hands fumbled with the zipper of my jeans. I pushed off him and he peeled both my jeans and underwear off at the same time. I stepped out of them as his fingers stroked upward the length of my legs, finding the fire between my thighs. And all my thoughts faded, replaced with a single one: for Connell to take me. A tingling pleasure rushed through me. His lips caressed my stomach, and my legs wavered.

Quick to unbuckle and drop his pants, he soon towered over me. I pressed against him, and his fiery erection nestled against my stomach.

"You still owe two hundred and forty kisses," I purred.

"You're going to get yourself into trouble with such talk." He sat back down. His hands were on my butt cheeks, kneading the hot flesh. "Especially since you owe me three hundred kisses, and I could call that debt any time."

Right there. In that moment, I wanted time to stand still forever. Connell was naked and lounged back, wearing only a sexy smile while his eyes and fingers devoured me. I let out a long whimper.

Leaning to his side, Connell pawed at his pants on the floor, snatched the wallet and with one hand yanked a rubber out. I knelt in front of him and placed a long, wet smooch on his tip. His head leaned back, and I loved watching him dissolve in ecstasy. I rolled the rubber on him in slow motion, enjoying the groans escaping from his throat.

Connell was sexy in every possible way, from his pouty lips, to the hard lines of his chest, right down to the way he slouched with a hard-on.

"Come closer," he said.

I straddled his thighs, locking my legs around his waist, rubbing against his heat. He crushed his lips onto mine, and I melted.

He licked my neck, and his hands cupped my breasts, fondling them. My earlier, troubling thoughts buckled under the pleasure of tingles enveloping my body. Grasping my hips, he positioned me over him and he slid deep inside me. I released a mewling sound. The perfect symphony of our moving hips escalated, and I seized his shoulders, riding him hard. I moaned with desire as the tightness between my thighs stiffened, and his firm plunges quickened.

My head flung back, my body trembled, and I didn't care who heard my screams. Those few elated seconds emptied my mind of everything.

We stared at each other, inches apart for a long time as I enjoyed the orgasmic feeling gushing through me. The kitchen light cast shadows across his face. He was gorgeous..

"I'll never get tired of that," I murmured.

Connell pushed off the couch, lifting me in his arms, my legs hugging his waist. He kissed my nose. "This isn't over."

He carried me into his bedroom. Laying me on the bed, he parted my legs, exposing my aching center. A sinful grin captured his lips. He crouched on the mattress in front of me. His mouth already trailed up my legs, grabbing small pieces of flesh between his teeth. He made sure to lick every part of me until he reached my mouth. He pressed his erection against my opening, teasing.

"Connell, please," my words were faint.

He rammed himself inside me, pumping fast and energetic, and with such voracity that his length kissed my back wall. His gaze lowered to meet my eyes, and I held onto his arms. I writhed beneath him, and without expectation I started to pulse with pleasure. Connell shuddered against me, and then he collapsed on the bed, gasping for breath.

I clenched my soaked thighs, elongating the titillating bliss. Connell's face always looked sincere after sex. My eyes slid shut, and I curled into his arms, forgetting everything.

CHAPTER 14

My eyes fluttered open to find morning had not quite stirred and night still draped the room. It took several seconds to register that I lay in bed with Connell asleep beside me. I stopped myself from crawling over to steal a kiss. He shifted a little and rolled onto his stomach. The tattoo of a long sword graced his right shoulder blade, a symbol representing his father: valor and justice, or so he had told me. His dad, who was also in the force, was killed by a robber he'd encountered in a neighbor's house. Connell hated speaking of the incident, so I left it alone.

I climbed out of bed and headed into the living room where I got dressed in a rush. Grabbing a paper and pen from near the phone, I left him a quick note.

Connell,

I have a few things to do, and I'll be back soon. Don't worry. I love you so much. Daci.

I spun on my heels and left the house. While the dracwulf remained lose, everyone I knew was in danger, especially Connell. I kicked into a jog, traveling in and out of pools of lights from the street lamps as the repetitive thud of my boots hit concrete. The sky still held stars and a plump moon, though the sun threatened to peek out at any second.

One day left before the Lunar Eutine. I hurried toward the forest.

A bitter chill encased my body, my toes froze and my stomach rumbled, though I continued trekking for most of the miserable early morning, ducking below branches and leaping over dead logs. I searched the areas I remembered from the aerial maps with no success, and emerged into an open space where the long grass reached my thighs. Bellows emanated from the woodlands, and I recognized the Caspian red deer mating call. A flock of cranes flying overhead complimented the orchestra.

When I picked up the faint scent of wet dog fur and urine, I iced over. My ears pricked, and I waited for a sound.

Silence.

I moved deeper into the woods, and between two trees I found a rough line scratched into the ground. The putrid urine stench had seeped into the earth, blending with the soil. Scattered paw prints in the earth confirmed a wolf, and placed the animal's size larger than a moonwulf.

The line dug in the ground was territorial and defensive. Wolf packs would cross such thresholds if they intended to claim another pack's land. The dracwulf's intelligence worried me; it mimicked our cousins, but on a grander scale. But one step closer to finding the thing that had turned my life upside down, my mood warmed.

I treaded over the line, scanning the bushes and darkness for any movement before tracking west. Occasionally, I sensed the dracwulf's trail. Pushing branches aside, I entered a dense portion of the woods where the trees grew close together. The breeze rustled the foliage, and I inhaled fresh blood.

As I strode deeper into the woods, the scent dwindled, replaced by the forest's crispness. No matter which direction

I headed, the scent distorted. I uncovered zilch—no other footprints, no tangled fur on shrubbery and worst yet, no dracwulf.

etracing my steps, I headed to where the giant pines grew sparse—to Radu's cell. He spent most nights there alone at Sandulf's command, who insisted the underground cell be manned each night in case of emergencies. Radu's passion for researching history over hunting awarded him that position. For years, he'd pleaded with Sandulf to let him attend the local university. I'd hinted to him that he should enroll as a virtual student without the leader's permission. He rejected the idea.

Pine needles at the base of a lush tree cloaked the trap door. I used my key, which I kept on me at all times, and descended inside, shutting the panel behind me. An orange glow from within the room threw shadows on the steps.

Before I reached the landing, Radu's melodic voice found me. "I hoped you'd visit."

Books were scattered all over the cobblestone floor. Some even managed to find their way into the locked prison booths. Radu sat on the ground, cross-legged, outside the cells, with two books folded open in his lap. His white long-sleeve T-shirt had the words *I Heart Braşov* printed across his chest.

"Nice top."

His silvery eyes glistened in the candlelight. "How are you holding up after yesterday?"

"Been better."

He paused, and I saw the struggle on his face. "Have you sensed the new landlord upstairs? I feel like she's been following me."

My gaze flicked to the staircase and back. "Yeah. Her scent is all over the woods, and Sandulf acts like it's normal."

He clapped the books shut and piled them at the foot of the table. "I haven't seen or heard her, but she's here. I sense her watching me when I arrive and leave my post."

My hands fisted into the pockets of my jeans as I imagined myself ripping the dracwulf apart and putting an end to her reign of terror. The idea of the animal sneaking up and attacking Radu boiled my blood. "So why the hell hasn't Sandulf stopped her? What did he say after I stormed out?"

Radu climbed to his feet and brushed down his gray pants. "He insists the dracwulf's no threat, and that you are using it as an excuse to not return to the pack." He gave me a questioning look, and I pretended not to notice. "He and Lutia are apparently trying to find the dracwulf's new lair tonight."

I hadn't sensed any wulfkin in the forest, so either they were hunting deeper in the mountains or not at all. The truth burned in my chest, and I doubted he pursued a creature that took Enre down with a weak wulfkin like Lutia by his side.

Poor Radu. He remained alone in the woods with a dangerous creature prowling the neighborhood just to appease Sandulf's rules. And that pissed me off.

Crouching, I grabbed several books until one caught my attention, *Wolves and Beyond* stamped in silver on a black jacket. "So, what'd you find in the book from Sandulf's stash?" My breath caught in my chest as I awaited his reply.

He stuck his hand into the front pocket of his jeans, pulling out a folded piece of paper marked with the distinct age spots of foxing. "It talked about the elixir all right, and in detail. This is what we've been looking for. But someone has torn out half the pages, so I could only get snippets of info."

"And?" I patted his arm.

He wiggled the page in front of my nose. I reached out for it, but he was too quick. "I have a recipe."

"No way." I covered my mouth, then broke into uncontrollable laughter, and jumped into Radu's arms, squealing. "What do we need?"

He paced to a prison booth as he unfolded the sheet, flattening it out against his thigh.

"The good news is there are only four ingredients, which are not that difficult to get hold of." His gaze fell to the crinkled sheet in his hands. "A pinch of salt. Crushed wolfsbane. Human blood. And the fresh petal of a wild petunia."

"Okay, so what's the bad news?"

"There are actually two bad things."

"Radu. Tell me."

"The wild petunia grows only on the night of a full moon, which means you can't take the elixir until your Lunar Eutine."

That sucked big time. I'd have to continue lying to Connell and keep Sandulf at a distance. "I guess I can wait. And as soon as the night hits, I'd have my petal."

I glanced over at him, and the way he was nodding his head told me it wasn't going to be that easy.

"Apparently for the elixir to work, a moonwulf must drink the mixture seconds before the moon on the Lunar Eutine turns full." He flipped the page over, staring at the spray of words. "The whole book was dedicated to the elixir, and it sounds pretty genuine, but every time I found details other than a hundred ways to obtain the ingredients, the page was ripped out. Do you think Sandulf did that, or he got the book that way?"

"Who cares? We got the recipe, and we'll work around the timing thing." I still couldn't believe Radu had found a recipe. Until that moment, the elixir never felt real, and for once I allowed myself to believe things might actually turn out okay. I did a hip- wiggling dance on the spot.

"I'll help you, but there are no guarantees this will work. I found no records of anyone ever taking this tonic, though they might be in the torn-out pages." He shrugged.

"The book was printed in 1564, and anything on side effects was missing. I have no idea even how this will affect you. What if it's dangerous and it kills you?"

The idea of the elixir not working was not an option for me. "I want to give it a go, regardless. I have to try."

He inhaled loudly. "I'll get the salt and wolfsbane, but you'll need to get me human blood," he said.

"Okay." I'd think of a way to do that.

"Oh, and there's one more thing that was made pretty clear in the book. Using the elixir is prohibited under Varlac law."

"Why would Sandulf have the book then?"

Radu stuffed the piece of paper in his pocket. "Why did he create a dracwulf?"

" Touché. Maybe he's still pining over Alina and he's filling his void with this beast.

After all, Alina was his first chosen alpha-female." I took a seat. "Speaking of the animal, did you find out any weaknesses on the dracwulf? Maybe an elixir that kills it?" I winked.

He spoke while continuing to clean up the mess. "No such luck. What's interesting is that they're not solitary creatures, and prefer companionship of their own kind, multiplying like rabbits if given the chance." He clasped another book into his embrace.

"On one brutal night almost three centuries ago, the wulfkin pack leaders from all over Europe united with the Varlac pack for the first time and held a venery. They swept in and eliminated all of the abominations. It was at this time that mating with wolves became prohibited with the intention to make the dracwulf extinct."

"A venery?" I raised a shoulder.

"You really should read more." The sides of Radu's mouth

lifted. "Venery is the sport of Varlac hunting wild animals, a leisure activity that is still practiced today by those born into privileged families."

Not a huge fan of hunting innocent animals for fun, I bit my tongue and nodded.

"A dracwulf will take over the forest it lives in, striving for dominance. It is exceedingly territorial and will kill anything in its path as it expands its area. A single dracwulf has been known to leave kills at the opposite sides of a forest on the same day to create an illusion there are many of them. It's a trickster animal."

My throat dried as I remembered the dead humans.

Radu leaned against the wall with books heaped in his arms, his gaze drifting upward. "The creature's irrational behavior is driven by the lust for flesh. They are born in dracwulf form and remain that way. Also, the moon has no sway over them."

"So what you're saying is they are an unstoppable eating machine?"

He nodded.

I carried some of the books to the half-empty bookshelf and forced them onto a ledge, sorting the disorder I created before Radu noticed. "How did the Varlac kill them?" Radu proceeded to arrange his books on the shelves, and then straightened the ones I added. "The texts don't give specifics. It just says they were slain."

"That's great."

Radu gripped the next book's spine so tight his knuckles turned white when he placed it onto the sill. His voice grew edgy, each word precise. "Sandulf has also taken Lutia as his mate. She is now our alpha female."

The news didn't surprise me, but it still stung for the simple reason that I didn't trust her. She would no doubt remember our last encounter when we crossed paths again.

Radu's eyelids lowered. "I can't believe you might leave us."

I slumped into the chair and thought about the pack's mess. "There's a longing in me that wants to explore my human side, find my mother and . . . " I omitted the part about Connell. "If I don't make a break for it now, after the Lunar Eutine, Sandulf will keep me like a prisoner." I met Radu's soft eyes. "I don't want to lose you and Botolf, but I can't live under his thumb my entire life." There was no easy way out. Whatever path came to me carried a price.

"You could still visit us if you became a human."

Like Sandulf would allow that, I thought but didn't say out loud. "How has Sandulf managed to save us from the Varlac?" I sat back into the chair.

Radu's mouth opened just as a scratching sound erupted from the entrance door.

I jumped to my feet. "We have company."

The noise escalated. I rushed up the stairs, taking two at a time, and secured the leather cable through a metal hoop mounted into the cement wall for extra security, while the dracwulf's scent poured over me.

I edged back to Radu and found him collecting the other books. "We need to get out of here."

Radu had never been a fighter, preferring the dreamy intellectual world. I refused to let another friend fall victim. "Is there another exit?" I asked Radu as I grabbed his wrist to stop his book gathering.

"The underground tunnels are not far. That's the closest exit, unless we head to the trekker's car park and follow the dirt road, but there's only one way out of this bunker." His eyes flicked to the door.

Stories from medieval times told of villagers using the tunnels to flee from the fortress into the forest at times of siege, but the tunnels were caving in and not ideal with a monster on your back.

The room echoed with the sound of wood splintering, and a piece of timber tumbled down the stairs. The animal bellowed and continued shredding the door.

Shit. Think, Daciana. I pointed to the closest cubicle. "Trap the dracwulf in the cell. Use me as bait."

A grim expression captured his face.

My words rushed. "No other way. Once it's followed me, use a chair or something to knock it out."

I knew that we stood no chance against the animal, considering even Enre and I failed, yet I couldn't live with Radu's death on my conscience as well.

I stared at the dracwulf's front leg rummaging through the gaping hole.

Radu slouched in the chair, his hands resting on his knees.

"Come on, it's now or never. Let's do it." What I didn't tell him was my intention to protect him from harm above my own safety.

He climbed to his feet and gave a simple nod, though the tightness around his eyes and lips showed his trepidation.

I concentrated and reached down within myself, praying for my inner wolf's return. A faint trace of her lingered, like rain on a breeze. My breath labored as I focused on drawing her out, but I made it worse, and she was withdrew, vanished into the abyss of my mind. Then an explosive popping sound cracked outside.

A gun. I met Radu's panicked look. The grating sounds at the door died.

"This is our chance," I said. "It will give you enough time to run back to the pack house. Don't stop whatever you do."

His lips parted, but no words formed.

"It'll be all right, just do as I say."

I dashed up the stairs. With the cord free, I raised the panel into the early morning light. All clear. Throwing the door wide open, I led Radu outside.

No gunman. There was movement in the corner of my eye—a large shadow zipped between the trees. I so needed my wolf right then.

The blackened dracwulf crashed past the trees about a dozen yards away, and my heart stopped. She released a guttural growl, and my gaze locked on her extra-long, sharp fangs.

"Go!" I yelled.

Radu dashed from my side. The dracwulf's gaze darted in his direction. I burst forward in a head-on charge knowing even in human form, my strength might help Radu escape.

I geared up to crash-tackle the beast somehow, but she slid away from me and made haste after Radu. Skating sideways, I leapt after her. The force from the impact drove me into the dracwulf's rump. I gripped fistfuls of fur and held on, bouncing on the rodeo- style ride.

Then the dracwulf stopped dead in her tracks, and I went flying over her side, landing nearby. I bound backward in one clean swoop. She looped around, sneering and slashing claws at the air between us. I recoiled, analyzing how to best avoid being sliced into pieces. I wasn't ready to die—not yet.

In a surge of adrenaline, I made a run for it away from Radu. Throwing a glance over my shoulder confirmed the dracwulf was in pursuit. I couldn't outrun her, but at least Radu's safety was assured. Now I just needed a plan.

The snarls at my back grew closer, and in my head, images of Enre's face propelled me faster. Swerving in between trees, I bought myself some time. The earth shuddered from the dracwulf's paws, and trees creaked each time she sideswiped them.

Two gunshots broke the suspense.

The dracwulf's thudding stopped, and I stole a glance just as the beast's shoulder smacked a tree.

I paused, pressing my back against a trunk, breathing heavily, adrenaline keeping my dread at bay. Behind the dracwulf, in the far distance, Connell stood with his legs apart, his gun pointed at us.

Unable to detect blood in the air, I guessed Connell had missed. He released another bullet but missed again as the dracwulf was on the move and whizzed right past me. Way too close.

The animal glared at me for an instant. Her muzzle creased, and her head trembled as she released a short howl. She dashed into the woods away from us both.

Connell remained frozen with the pistol aimed in the direction the animal vanished.

I ran toward him, all the while listening for the dracwulf's return. My voice came out more abrupt than I anticipated. "What are you doing here?"

"I came searching because I knew you planned to catch that thing on your own. I'm parked in the trekker's lot and as soon as I got out, I heard the growls. I came as fast as I could."

I inhaled his peppermint breath, and despite his stupidity, his actions revealed he still loved me. "Let's go before we become her dinner."

He dropped his hand and hurried toward his Audi. I tagged alongside him. No sign of the dracwulf, though I suspected not for long.

I jumped into his car and relaxed for a miniscule moment, collecting my thoughts. The digital clock on the dashboard displayed 6:55 A.M. There went Sandulf's claim that he would stop the dracwulf, not that I believed him anyway. And that made me furious, both at him and me for believing him. My mind wandered to Radu, and I hoped he arrived in one piece at the pack house.

Connell gritted his teeth and gripped the steering wheel with one hand. His eyebrows were raised on his forehead as he puzzled, "How can that animal exist?" He rubbed his mouth, and his words grew muffled. "I saw it before and now again, but still don't believe it."

Uncertain whether he spoke to himself or me, I kept quiet.

"I'm going to report this, and your statement will be needed." Pushing strands of golden hair behind his ears, he faced me. "Along with how you hunt animals. The thing out there—he pointed to the front windshield—needs to be caught today."

I twisted in my seat. "Me hunting the animal has nothing to do with the cops." "How you will explain why you were in the woods without lying?"

"They don't need to know I was here." Nervousness swelled inside me. I touched

Connell's arm, and he jerked away. His reaction hurt. "I don't have a license to hunt wolves. Please let me do it my way. I only need a day."

"This is beyond madness." His face fell dead serious. "Is this why the animal killed people you knew? It was following you because you kept hunting it?"

"No." A dread crept into my voice. Urgency to stop the dracwulf, and not destroy my relationship with Connell in the process, bit hard. "I know I'm asking a lot, and I need you to trust me a bit longer." Asking him to lie again scorched in my mind like pouring lava. "If I get rid of the wolf within twenty-four hours, will you leave me out of it?" Almost choking on my words, I couldn't believe what I promised.

"Dead bodies. A monster wolf. Telling me lies. Do you know what you're doing?" A look of exasperation crossed his face. "Let the police look after this. Why are you so adamant to catch it yourself?"

"This animal hunts early in the morning hours, so give me tonight. Then she's yours." I raised a shoulder and offered a smile, but my gestures were wasted. "I don't want anyone else to die, and I can stop it."

Connell faced the driver's window.

If I told him about wulfkin, he might turn the police onto the pack, maybe kill them, and I had no plan on revealing them anyway. Not for any reason.

"I must be mad." He refused to look at me. "I'll only consider this if I go with you." "No!"

He started the engine. "Then the deal's off."

I swallowed down nausea and turned my attention to the passenger window. A gust of wind blew dried pine into the air, tossing them about. "Okay, fine." That was a direct lie. I had no intention of sticking to it considering the dracwulf might be targeting Connell. It would buy me time, even if it took Connell ages to forgive me. "Please take me to the institute."

The bigger problem was saving him, and convincing Sandulf to kill his kin in just twenty-four hours before the police found out what Connell knew and started interrogating me.

CHAPTER 15

The tension inside Connell's Audi swelled like a blistering balloon ready to pop. Neither of us said a word for the duration of the drive. It was the longest argument we ever had, and I couldn't bear the excruciating void settling in my chest, or the sorrow blackening my thoughts. The agonizing ache that I might lose Connell twisted my insides.

He swerved into the institute's parking lot.

I wore my best pleading look. "It's okay if you're upset with me. I would be, too, but I'm not doing any of this to spite you. Please understand, the world I grew up in is a bit different from the one you know."

Connell looked away. "Go."

His attitude stung. I laid my hand on his thigh, and he didn't respond, instead he inspected the building in front of us. I climbed out and banged the door shut. He drove off.

I retrieved the cell from my pocket and punched Connell's number, staring at the digits, and then deleted them.

No. I needed to focus on capturing the dracwulf to protect Connell, finding Enre, and then turning myself into a human. There was little I could do about Connell's mood in the meantime.

The parking lot was clear of cars this early in the morning, and I stayed where I was until I could no longer hear his engine. Then I dashed toward the pack house. The woods passed by in a blur, along with a stunned fawn and tasty looking rabbits. I wished I could transform and run free. And that reminded me of my shy wolf, and I wondered if her absence was a sign of the upcoming Lunar Eutine.

I prayed Enre was still alive. After all, wulfkin could take a lot of damage and still heal. Regardless, the biggest problem was the dracwulf, and I'd have to stop her before she killed again, with or without Sandulf's support.

Gasping and exhausted, I emerged from the woods at the pack house. I burst inside to find Radu in the living room wiping his brow with a tea towel.

"Shouldn't you use a bath towel?" I bounced into his arms. "Thank goodness you're okay."

Radu panted. "I've never run so fast in my life."

"Maybe you should take up jogging?" I bumped him with my shoulder. "Where's everyone?"

He shrugged. "Probably at work."

I contemplated waiting for Sandulf to have a so-called civilized chat with him, but in the end decided showing my face at work, even if for a short while, ensured I could somehow stop the police from getting permission for hunting. "Got to head off, but I'll be back."

"Do what you need. I'll be here for you."

His reassurance boosted my confidence. I gave him a quick hug and bolted outside, starting back toward the institute. I sensed no dracwulf on the way and speculated the animal hid during the day to avoid detection.

While I only intended a quick visit to the office, I ended up spending a large chunk of day there, pouring over more aerial maps of the Carpathian Mountains, marking each dracwulf sighting, crime scene, and the direction Enre was taken. All the activity, except for the one attack in the farming district, took place on the side of the woods nearest the pack house, closest to the city. And I staked my life on her den being nearby those woods.

After making a brief, anonymous phone call to the police with sightings of a large wolf in the farming district, I headed into the woods, searching for any clues to her whereabouts. By late afternoon, my hopes dwindled as I found nothing new. I returned to the office, miserable, and placed a note on Vasile's desk excusing myself for the rest of the week, then jumped into a company pick-up truck. I'd grab a bag of clothes from home and dump them at the pack house to make it look to Sandulf I was serious about returning.

After an hour of incessant crawling and breaking, I abandoned the traffic-stricken main roads for side lanes and parallel-parked on my street. My gut croaked for food as I padded across the street. My priorities were: stuff my face, grab some clothes, and head straight to the pack house.

Rounding the hedgerow in front of my apartment, I collided into someone: Connell. My initial reaction was to fling myself into his arms. Resisting the urge killed me. His teeth chattered, and he blew hot air into his cupped hands. "I can't stop thinking

about what you said, and I'm ready to go out and track the wolf with you tonight. I'll help you stop it." He refused to smile, but I saw the slightest hint of one curling the sides of his mouth.

I just wish I hadn't told Connell about hunting wolves. In hindsight, disappearing from the city for a week might have done the trick. I retrieved the house keys from my pocket and stepped into the warmth of the building.

"You're a hunter, eh?" Connell's voice sounded nervous.

"It seems that way." My new policy: avoid saying too much.

In the foyer, brown-banded wallpaper curled at the edges of the cornices, and a heap of crumbled advertising leaflets collected beneath the mailboxes. I walked quickly toward the staircase with Connell on my heels.

"I researched wolf-hunting families today."

I stopped dead in the middle of the staircase and turned. I climbed a step to meet his height. "And?"

"There's no record of a family or businesses who hunt wolves with their bare hands, anywhere." Sarcasm marbled his voice.

"Like I said, it's something we keep private and in the family." I slouched on one leg, folding my arms.

"If in the process you hurt someone, then it borders on vigilantism. You're taking the law into your own hands." His eyes drilled into me. "I need to know everything about your family and what they do. I can help."

I climbed another step backward. "I want to stop the killings as much as you, so why are you interrogating me?"

He clasped my hand and raised it to his lips. "The last thing I want is to find your dead body in the woods. You mean everything to me. Please, Daci."

"Let's talk more at my place."

I climbed up the last few steps to an empty corridor and made my way to apartment 302 to find the door ajar. Convinced I had locked it, I searched for scents and picked up faint metallic blood. The fresh and delectable aroma teased my senses and awoke my wolf, which surprised me, since she'd been missing the past few days. Perhaps hunger was the trigger.

Connell placed a gentle hand on my arm and whispered, "Let's go back downstairs. I'll call for backup."

I shook my head. "Maybe I forgot to close it." Before he could draw me away, I pushed into the dimly lit apartment.

"Daci."

I surveyed the main room, finding nothing out of place.

In my hallway, the aroma of blood intensified, and severe cramps rippled through my torso like hundreds of scorpions pinching my insides. Nausea hit and my eyelids scrunched shut. I bent over, clutching my belly.

"What's wrong?"

My throat emitted a growl, and I knew what that meant. My wolf wanted out right then.

"Was that you?"

I bobbed my head and forced myself upright.

Connell already held his gun and stepped in front of me. "Don't be stubborn. Get out of here, and I'll check the apartment."

Ripe apples and meat flavored the air. I slipped past Connell, deeper into the hallway and felt my way into the darkened bedroom.

I switched on the light. On the carpet, next to my blood-splattered bed, sprawled a body. A slender woman, in her late thirties, was a tangle of ripped clothes, blood, and contorted limbs. Her glossy green, flat eyes were fixed on the ceiling. Her dark hair was matted into the carpet, and a bloodstain framed her fragile body. Across the room, a black stiletto without a single blemish lay on its side.

Connell broke into the room, shoving me aside. "Hell!"

The victim had recently died. Heat radiated from her like fingers reaching out to touch me. Whatever killed the woman fed on her in my room. Her gut was slit open, and someone had eaten her organs directly out of her stomach, yet left the rest of the body clean of scratches or bites.

No animal does that, unless it intended to leave the body as a warning. A faint trace of wulfkin teased my senses. I inhaled deep mouthfuls of the pungent air, without another hint of the muskiness. Instead, a strange scent wafted in the room, reminding me of chopped leaves.

Lutia came to mind along with our last scene in the pack house, when I had humiliated her in front of the pack.

Regardless, she wouldn't kill a human. It went against a direct Varlac rule. But then again, she might be adopting Sandulf's liberties when it came to pack law.

Connell approached the victim. Kneeling next to the body, he placed his hand on her cheek. "She's still warm.'

Heat rushed up my back, over my ears and head. The muscles in my shoulders stiffened, and the atmosphere changed from intense bitter scents to a nauseating, unbearable confinement. Recoiling, my back hit the wall in the corridor. I slid to a squatting position and cradled my bent knees, confused. I focused on the woman's legs and the blood stains speckling her thighs.

"Do you know her?" Connell's tone fell serious.

"Yes."

"Who is she? What's going on?"

"Neighbor from across the hall. But we never spent time in the woods." I dropped my head between my knees. It was hard to focus. Considering the front door of the building wasn't smashed up, I couldn't figure out how the dracwulf got inside, unless someone else was responsible.

"I can't cover you anymore, Daci. There's a dead person in your apartment now, and the police already suspect your involvement in the previous attacks." Connell, who was gazing into my bedroom, snapped his head around to look at me. "I'm calling this in."

My head lifted and tears swelled. "I don't know who did this or why, but it wasn't me."

"Is there a rival hunting family you haven't told me about?"

I shook my head.

Connell patted my arm and marched into the living room. He spoke on the phone, requesting backup.

A surge of anger rose within me. The only place I called my own—my sanctuary, my privacy—had been taken from me. I wanted to break into hysterical crying. My whole life

I'd lived and shared everything with the wulfkin pack, but the apartment was mine, something I owned.

Several hours went by as officers tracked through my home, and Connell did nothing to stop the other inspector from questioning me for most of that time. The young man with an Afro took notes about everything I did the past week, down to what I ate. With my mind still foggy with confusion, I barely remembered the lies I told Connell, let alone the new ones I needed to cover my tracks. By the end, I couldn't remember what excuses I gave.

The click of cameras and hushed voices speculating about the incident hurt my head. Hunched into a ball on the sofa, I observed the commotion unfold. Police, photographers, and lab geeks inspected every inch of my apartment. Eventually they carried the body out in a black bag.

I stared at the hole Enre had punched in my wall and pictured his body in such a bag. No, I would find him still alive. My tears rolled, and I brushed them away.

Connell stood next to me. "Look, Daci, you're going to need to leave your apartment, and since you're considered a suspect until they can carry out tests on the victim, they need to know where to contact you. You can stay at my place if you have nowhere to go." He guided hair off my face and sat down. "They will contact you about going down to the station for more interviews." He paused. "Were you at work all day?"

My heart froze. "I can't believe you think I did this."

He shook his head. "We need proof of your whereabouts. An alibi."

"I was at work from when you dropped me off this morning to when we met downstairs." I left out the small detour to the pack house.

He swallowed the obvious lump in his throat. "We will need to contact Vasile to confirm this."

I nodded.

Connell rose to his feet. I grabbed his arm, desperate for him to remain near me.

His hand clasped mine for a second. He retrieved the keys from his pocket. "I have to go to the station, but will join you at my place afterwards."

I slid the keys out of his hand, intending to visit the pack house first to find out how

Sandulf spent his day.

The pain in Connell's eyes worried me, and who could blame him? I wondered how he saw me right then: as a girl-friend who didn't trust him enough to share her secrets, or as a murderer?

His voice distracted my thoughts. "It's probably a good idea you leave." He glanced at his watch. "I'll take you to your car."

Not wanting to read too much into his suspicion, I gathered clothes and toiletries into a backpack, ignoring the bloodstains over everything in my bedroom, and exited the apartment with Connell. It was just before 11 P.M., and the air outside chilled my bones. The clouds were suspended midair, waiting for the perfect time to rain.

Connell caressed my lower back. "Are you okay?"

"I'll survive."

His gaze never left mine. "I have some paper work to complete, and I'll join you as soon as I can."

Connell squeezed my hand in his for a few silent seconds, and then jogged back into my apartment building.

I crawled into the car, throwing the backpack into the passenger's side and took off.

The busted heater ensured the ride through the forest was as comfortable as being a potential suspect in a murder case.

In no time, I arrived at the pack house. The engine ticked over, and I scolded myself for just staring at the unlit house from the car. *Be strong*, I repeated in my head, alighting from the vehicle.

At the front door, I paused for a few seconds, and then palmed it open into a dark room. Light wriggled out from the crack beneath the kitchen door.

I walked in. "Hello?"

My senses succumbed to the brewed coffee aroma, and I entered the kitchen. Sandulf lingered near the counter with a cup in his hand. He wore black track pants and a loose sweatshirt, resembling a broad-shouldered mountain man.

I waited for him to speak, anything to verify his mood. Radu would have informed him of the dracwulf attacking his underground cell, so surely he understood the priority in hunting the animal.

He cleared his throat. "Do you want coffee?" He retrieved another cup from the cabinet.

"Did you kill someone in my apartment?" My voice sounded more desperate than I intended.

Sandulf poured the coffee and offered me the mug.

I retrieved it with a quick motion.

He coughed. "You know you broke Lutia's finger and nose."

"Who cares? My neighbor was killed today."

Sandulf sipped from his cup, all the while his glare scrutinizing me.

"Did you have something to do with it? Was it the dracwulf?"

He said nothing.

I pushed on. "The dracwulf has to be stopped. You and me, we'll stop her tonight before the humans find her, and we can also track down Enre." I started to pace.

He inched forward, and asked, "Why can't you follow the rules? Everyone else in the pack listens to me."

Resolved to make him see logic, I continued. "You must know the location of the dracwulf's den." Heat engulfed my muscles, and I placed my mug onto the counter. His head cocked to the side. "Phfft. She's found a new home and I have no idea where she now hides."

"You created this thing. You have to stop her before we're found out."

His deep throaty laughter sent a shudder through me. "Are you challenging me?" He set his cup down.

The last thing I needed was to confront the alpha, but I didn't back away. Not this time. "No more pushing me aside. Tomorrow night is the Lunar Eutine, and until then I'll hunt down the dracwulf, with or without your help. I've done my best to delay the police hunting in the forest, but it's inevitable, especially now that they found a dead person in my place. I'll be investigated."

In a split second, he crossed the kitchen and wrapped his thick fingers around my arm and squeezed. With his free hand, he captured my chin, forcing me to face him.

Bile rose in my throat.

"The reek of human blood is all over you." His words raked my skin. "I sensed it the moment you entered my home."

"Was that your little surprise to get more cops on my tail? To force me to run back home to you? Is that why you're sending the dracwulf after me?"

Sandulf's nose creased.

I held his gaze. "Did you?"

"I'm trying to keep us together, not draw attention from humans. We can't be separated at a time like this. Our pack is in danger, and you're doing everything to make sure we get killed. Leave the dracwulf to me. Return home. That's all I want of you."

The disgust in his voice when he said "humans' irritated me more than the notion that he'd lost his mind.

"I'm taking care of the animal my way." His thumb caressed the length of my jaw.

"You need to remember your place." He gazed up for a moment. "You're feisty and strong, so I've decided to make you my mating partner for one purpose—growing and defending our pack."

I jerked from his grasp. "No." I recoiled. "That's never going to happen." The thought churned my stomach.

"Yes, it will. Tomorrow you will start a new phase of your life, and the dracwulf will be the last thing you will worry about." His breath, scented with coffee, danced in the air. "No need to worry about humans. Death happens all the time. It's normal."

My lungs filled with heated rage, and my hands trembled. "You're mad."

A wide, open-mouthed smile stretched his lips, and a horrible, dirty feeling washed through me. I wrapped my arms over my chest.

"I give you until tomorrow to return home and be by my side, or everyone you hold dear in the human world will pay." He strode out of the kitchen.

"Don't you dare threaten me."

As he pushed out the door, I spotted Lutia standing in the main room shrouded by darkness.

She sauntered into the kitchen, dressed in white cotton shorts and matching cropped tank top, her dead-straight blonde hair spilled to her waist. Her mouth broke into a smirk. "How does it feel to get what you've always wanted? Soon you'll be a full wulfkin."

"Don't you care that Sandulf's become a lunatic?"

"You don't know what you're talking about."

My muscles tightened. "Did you kill the woman in my apartment?"

She combed her fingers through her hair, and the slight shake of her hand gave her away.

Rooted in the kitchen, my legs refused to budge. "You're more stupid than I thought if you're carrying out Sandulf's idiotic errands. The Varlac won't care why you broke the rules when they come for you."

She stared at me with her deer-in-the-headlights gaze. A headache pulverized across the bridge of my nose and behind my eyes. "Just leave me alone, Lutia. Don't come into my life again, or I'll break more than your finger and nose next time."

"Don't be too quick to dish out threats. They might just backfire on you."

Ignoring her, I whizzed out the back door and hopped into the Jeep. I lost my apartment, and Connell no longer trusted me. Would he believe me if I told him the truth? I'd told so many lies I wasn't sure I knew the truth anymore.

The landscape swept by in a rush as I drove along the unforgiving track. Every so often, the descending moon glinted from behind clouds.

I was exhausted of everything, and refused to ponder about the things that swarmed my brain. The damage was done. I had to set things right before I started my new life with Connell.

I parked in the trekker's parking lot, jumped out and started hunting.

CHAPTER 16

Outside, the sun ascended, and the early morning winds raged. I kicked my foot into the car's accelerator and raced through Braşov, hoping to beat Connell home. For hours I had followed the dracwulf's heavy scent in circles with no result.

I laughed to myself. The Lunar Eutine ceremony was that night, and I was going into it uncertain if the elixir would work. My wolf roared awake inside me, a sure signal of the full moon's approach.

Finding Connell wasn't home meant one fewer thing for him to cross-examine me about. I staggered toward the bathroom and jumped into a scorching shower while I reflected on my last few shitty days. The dead body in my apartment screamed set-up. It was just another thing I had to address.

Emerging from the shower, I dragged on black jeans and a long-sleeve top. With a hot cup of coffee fresh from the percolator in my hands, I notice the clock on the microwave: 8:24 A.M. and still no sign of Connell.

I slouched on the kitchen stool and pondered how I'd collect a few drops of human blood for the elixir. The cutlery draw offered plenty of butter knives, and two huge carving blades. Not sure how Connell might react if I pulled either of them on him.

Uncertain what the day would bring, I decided to spend some time alongside Connell for a little while, and then depart with some lame-ass excuse about work to do more hunting. Most of all, I was tired of the bad luck I had when searching for the damn dracwulf, but I would find her today even if it meant ripping the woods apart with my bare hands. After the Lunar Eutine that night, if I turned human, I'd be as vulnerable as Connell against the creature.

The front door opened.

Connell strode into the kitchen, his red eyes half-closed and hair frizzy. A weak smile hung on his mouth as he placed the keys on the counter. Up close, I caught his perspiration and the stale police station smell. "I was worried you'd be gone when I returned."

"I'm here." I straightened my back. "Coffee?"

"Sounds perfect." He studied me. Detecting lies was something he probably knew a lot about, coming in contact with criminals on a regular basis. Most of my excuses to Connell were lies, and I hoped I did a good enough job to conceal them. "You're being a ninja today?"

Up on my feet, I threw him a pose with hands on my hips. "You like it?"

"You always look beautiful to me." The sadness in his voice tore my insides, and he dropped his gaze.

Slumped into the seat, I wanted to fall into his arms, take away the pain and remind him how perfect we were together. The past week I'd driven a huge wedge between us, but who was I kidding? The cracks were already there from months of hiding secrets and Connell's growing suspicions.

"I need a shower, or I'll fall asleep on my feet." He stumbled out of the room.

I placed my head in the crook of my arm as a headache pulsed in my temples. My back muscles pinched, and my wolf rose again, fiercer than during previous full moons, poking and thrusting against my insides, like I was nothing but a sack restraining her.

After fifteen or so minutes, Connell appeared in the doorframe wearing only blue jeans, and I couldn't take my gaze off his chest and six-pack. His hair tousled around his face in heavy masses reaching his jaw line, and he ran his hands through his golden hair, brushing it back.

He poured himself coffee. From across the bar, his chocolate eyes were intent on me. "Vasile verified your whereabouts yesterday, but the police will need to interview you again." He leaned his hip against the counter. "And I've held back the information about you hunting wolves, for now." He gave me a dark look. "You've got yourself into enough trouble."

I managed a half-smile. "Thanks."

"I've reported the attack in the alleyway and provided a detailed description of the wolf." He turned away. "And until they find who killed the woman in your apartment, you must remain in Brașov."

"When will they send out the wolf hunting party?"

"It's not that simple." He took another mouthful of coffee. "They only have my report as a witness." He shot me an expression drowned in resentment and sorrow, and then placed his cup into the sink. "We're setting up watchers on the perimeter of the woods later tonight, and any wolf sighted will be shot on the spot. No trekkers are permitted at this time."

My emotions tore between apologizing and confessing everything, yet all I managed to do was stare at his bare torso.

"Your institute has been issued passes to travel into the woods, and Vasile has yours. I can give you a lift there." He cleared his throat and took my cup to the sink. "You're awfully quiet."

Heat exploded across my skin, and I climbed to my feet. "My mind is a swirl of thoughts, but I can't pin any of it down. I'm devastated that my neighbor is dead, the police suspect me, and even worse, I feel you slipping away from me. So, what am I supposed to say?"

Instead of collecting me into his embrace and kissing me, Connell stood there like one of those God statues in museums that wore almost nothing, but were sculptured to perfection. I wanted to forget everything the day was about to bring and beg Connell to make love to me until I passed out. His hands dug into his pockets, pulling the jeans lower over his hipbone. My stomach tingled. He shifted his weight, and blond hair tumbled over his face.

"I don't know what's going to happen between us," he said. "I wish you would have trusted me to help you."

I choked up and started crying. For the past year, I pretended to be someone else, thinking nothing more of it until I fell for Connell, and as a result I was drowning in my own lies.

"I need some air." I hurried to the front door and didn't hear Connell follow me. Outside, the cloudless morning gripped me with its frozen breath, and I considered my options. With or without Connell, humanity was my destiny, not being Sandulf's slave.

Connell soon emerged from the house and joined me on the footpath, rugged looking in a fleecy top. "There's a park round the corner. A bit of fresh air might do us both good." His hands returned to his pockets, instead of wrapping around me. "So, are there many people like you around?"

My shoulders tensed. "People like me?"

"Wolf hunters."

"You could say it's a dying breed."

"How many wolves have you caught?"

Enre and I had tackled a lot of stray or dangerous wolves close to the city, and most of the time a growl and chase did the trick. We'd wrestled territorial bears, but never kept tally. "I don't remember."

He chuckled. "How many rogue wolves can there be in one forest?"

"You'd be surprised what a starved wolf or pack is capable of."

"So I'm guessing you're in the woods a lot, with your friend Enre? He did say he lived out in the farming district."

"You could say that." I stuck to my policy of not saying much.

We crossed the main road after a car sped past and followed a narrow path with white townhouses to our left and a towering terracotta-paved wall, spanning the length of the street, to our right. The whole time I stole glimpses of Connell.

The curved path brought us to an oversized iron gate spread wide open, complete with spiked bars. Beyond the entrance lay an open park the size of a football field. The path wove among trees stripped of leaves, and the breeze whistled past us. On the inner walls of the park, climbing vines clung to the bricks. At the right time of year, their flowers would bloom and grace the entire wall in an array of color. Now they hugged the bricks like shriveled veins on a carcass. A bench to the side caught my attention. My mind wandered to brushing off the leaves, taking a seat, and forcing Connell to kiss me.

"There are a few hunters left, and it's strictly a family business." I gave him a tidbit. From the corner of my eye, I spotted a smile crawling up his cheeks.

Ahead, the track forked in two opposite directions. Connell led me off the path onto the squishy soil. The wind zoomed past and carried a concoction of exhaust fumes, the tart aroma of wild berries, and wet dog fur.

I stopped, and an intense heat rolled over me as I scanned the perimeter. Even though the trees were scarce of leaves, the extensive space and multitude of trunks blocked much of the area. Then I caught sight of stormy eyes set in a porcelain-pale slim face and long blonde hair that flapped in the gust like a cape.

Lutia sauntered in our direction, exaggerating the swing of her hips. Clad in indigo pants, heels, and a translucent long sleeve shirt (revealing a black bra), she broke into a smirk.

She paused a few steps away. "Well, I can see why you don't want to leave this place." Her gaze slid to Connell and scanned him head to toe.

Connell straightened his posture.

"What did she tell you?" Lutia's voice was slick like a snake's hiss.

His brows bunched together. "I'm not too sure what you mean. Who are you?"

"Leave him alone," I said.

She curled a strand of hair on her finger. "Did she tell you she was already involved with another man? A man she got killed."

"That's a lie, and you know it." My fists clenched. Connell's soft voice said, "Enre?"

I turned to him. "It's a long story."

"Yes, Enre." Lutia's voice purred.

Connell raised a questioning brow. "What's going on?"

"She's lying. Enre and I used to date." Adrenaline punched through me at revealing a lie I had told him.

Lutia leaned her shoulder into a tree and watched.

"What do you want from me?" My gaze threw daggers toward her.

"What the hell is going on, Daci?" Connell's voice grew edgy. "Stop hiding things from me."

"She's hiding many things, aren't you?" Lutia reclined against the tree as if she was watching her favorite television show.

My reflexes snapped, and I grabbed a handful of her blouse, bringing her into me and muttering, "Remember my promise?"

Her expression fell serious, and her smirk vanished. "You can't hurt me. I'm the female alpha."

"Oh, I can and will."

She whispered, "Sandulf will kick you out of the pack once you turn." Her grin returned.

Connell squeezed my shoulder. "Let her go."

I brushed Connell's hand off and released Lutia, who said, "You little brat, you never listened to him and now you'll pay the consequence." The side of her lips curled into a snarl. "You're no longer the special one."

As tempted as I was to smash my fist into her perfect little nose, I simply said,

"Leave."

Her high-pitched laughter stabbed my ears. She stumbled backward, yanking down her crumpled shirt.

"Can't wait for the fun to begin tonight." Lutia strode back into the mass of tree trunks, disappearing from my sight like the wind. No matter what, Sandulf was determined to destroy my life.

"Tell me the truth this time." Connell's heavy voice crawled up my nape. "Who was that?"

There were so many untruths, I didn't know where to start. Connell believed I hunted wolves in my spare time with a crazed family I never spoke about.

He reached out for my hand, and I grasped it quick. There was no doubt regarding his devotion, even if it wavered, but could he accept the truth?

"Lutia is a family friend. And yes, Enre and I used to date."

Something flickered in his eyes, and he pulled his hand from mine. When he spoke, his words grew hard. "How long ago did you and Enre split?"

"More than a year ago."

"Why lie to me about Enre? What are you hiding?" The look of disgust etched his face.

"My family is complicated." I blinked away.

"Everything with you is complicated." His voice climbed.

I avoided his glare and surveyed my grimy boots—scratched and tainted with patches of dried mud. I didn't want to talk about me anymore.

"Strange things continue to happen to you. Like the dead body in your apartment, and who exactly was Enre, considering you said he was your family friend. Is that why you're embarrassed to tell me? Why does that girl hate you, and who is Sandulf? Isn't that your surname?"

"My family is hard to explain." I held his stare.

His cheeks turned a rosy hue, and his jaw tightened. "Until you sort yourself out, this thing with us," his hand flipped back and forth through the air between our chests, "is stopping right now."

I moved closer.

"Don't." The color had drained from his face, and he scrutinized a nearby tree, his eyes glistening. "I deserve to know the truth." Windblown hair slashed his face, and I yearned to run my fingers through the tangle.

"If I could tell you, I would."

He snapped at me. "Don't you understand? I lied to my boss for you. I've already been kicked off the case because I admitted we were in a relationship. I could lose my job."

A bitter gale blew through the park, and I let it rip me with its icy fingers. "I'm sorry. It isn't—"

He cut me off with a wave of his hand. "I don't want to hear any more of your lies." His shoulders sagged forward. "You've got me all wound up. I don't know what to believe anymore. Do you really love me, or is that a lie, too?"

The harshness of his words had my legs buckling beneath me. "Of course I love you." I grabbed his arm, squeezed and met his hard-edged gaze. We stayed like that a few moments, staring into each other's eyes.

"Tell me the whole truth, or I'm leaving right now."

What could I say? My tangled web of lies had me cornered, and at that point I suspected he wouldn't believe the truth. "Please, don't. Just give me some time."

He ripped his hand out of mine and strode away.

"Connell, no!" I froze. Tears saturated my cheeks, and I let myself weep, convinced I had lost any will to live. Was I worthy of him? My messed-up life kept me from ever knowing happiness, then I found Connell, and everything changed. Maybe he was better without me, without lies, without secrets.

I staggered to a bench and continued crying. I loved Connell more than anything, and the possibility that I lost him shattered my heart into a billion pieces. My thoughts distorted into nothing. I lay on my side, unable to fathom a life without him.

After a long while, I crawled to my feet and wiped my eyes. The sizzling heat spread to every part of my body, and I started the slow stagger toward the forest, my last salvation.

When I reached the edge of the Carpathian Mountains, I scoured the place for police— or watchers, as Connell had called them. Aside from the entrance gate, locked shut with metal chains, the area was clear.

I slipped inside and started to run, weaving between enormous trees and not caring that trunks scraped my arms or low-hanging branches thrashed me. I welcomed them.

CHAPTER 17

Onnell, the man I loved, was slipping from my grasp. My hair, slick with sweat, stuck to the sides of my face and neck, and the sickening burden of Enre's capture gurgled in my chest. His ocean blue eyes, behind strands of ink black hair pierced my thoughts with guilt. I was no closer to finding the dracwulf, regardless how many times I searched the damned woods. Within a week, I had managed to lose everything. A raw anger seeped into my veins. I wrapped my arms around my shoulders and shivered.

I had nothing left to lose. It was all taken from me. So I'd go down blazing, taking with me whoever stood in my way.

I returned to the area where the dracwulf marked her territory and heard a tiny whisper on the winds. Hunched near a thicket of bushes, I picked out Sandulf's scent, along with decayed flesh. I leaned forward and peered through the shrubs. The alpha kneeled over a dead gray wolf and patted the animal's body as his head shook.

I remembered the pack leader from my younger years, compassionate for the wolves and tenacious in his protection against intruders. Ever since Alina's passing, he hadn't been the same.

He climbed to his feet and walked away then paused by a tree, cocking his head toward the dead animal. A mournful expression consumed his expression. Without thinking, I stood and he snapped in my direction, a snarl hanging off his lips.

All kinds of questions raced inside my head. Had he stopped the dracwulf? Did he find Enre? How could he guarantee the Varlac would not hunt the pack down?

Sandulf's lips pressed into thin, white lines. An awkward silence fell between us, and unlike in our earlier years, Sandulf no longer felt like my father, but a stranger. He fooled me into trusting him, all the while hiding the real monster living inside him.

"Just tell me why you're risking the pack's lives for your selfishness?" I blurted unexpectedly.

He leaned against the tree, his posture casual, yet there was nothing calm about the fierceness in his stare. "Tonight everything will change for you."

My life had already changed, and I doubted things could ever be the same again. I dropped my gaze to the wolf. Insects circled and devoured the poor creature's neck. "What happened?"

"Someone shot her." Something in his voice softened.

"I'd say it was the police starting their wolf hunts. Another reason you should stop the dracwulf."

His nostrils flared, releasing a long, noisy breath. "There you go again, thinking you're in charge."

I fought the deadness wriggling up my body.

"I know you intend to leave the pack and remain amongst humans."

I shuffled a few steps back, and I almost tripped over a decaying log. That was the last thing I expected to hear from Sandulf, yet by the hardness of his tone, he was dead serious. Did he know about Connell, too?

"Change is coming. You can feel it under your skin, can't

you?" Pride sparked in his dark eyes. "You can't stop your transformation." A fiery color spotted his cheeks. "After tonight, you'll have no choice but to remain with your pack, unless of course, the police mistake you for a wild wolf."

Heaviness settled in my gut, and I struggled to speak.

"You lost the privilege to tell me what to do when you created the dracwulf and started killing humans. You're no longer the Sandulf I grew up with. I don't even know you anymore."

He gave me a look so fierce it could have ripped the skin off my back. "For your sake, let's hope after your change, you start to obey me."

Become my slave or else was left unsaid, but it was loud and clear in my head. I would rather die than submit.

Sandulf cut me off and started walking away.

I wanted to scream at him, beat some sense into his head, and make him see the that innocent people had been killed.

"Make the ceremony tonight a joyous occasion. Don't bring everyone down with your stories," he tossed over his shoulder before he leapt into a sprint and vanished into the woods.

With the dracwulf still lose, Enre lost, and the pack under a mad wulfkin's control, I refused to let him intimidate me.

The frigid mountain air reminded me how alone I really felt. I continued my search, numbing my thoughts with the hunt until high noon hit, and decided to retrieve my forest pass from work just in case.

Before long, I arrived at Connell's house and hoped he had left for work already.

Stepping up to the doorway, I gave a light tap and held my breath. After my second knock, the door flung open, and I gasped. Connell's messy hair revealed his flustered state. He wore creased, gray tracksuit pants and a T-shirt with the police emblem printed in cobalt. One hand pressed into his hip, the other gripped the door. "I didn't expect to see you back here."

Great. I scratched my head and mumbled. "I've come for my bag and Jeep. I'll get out of your way quickly."

His hand combed through his hair.

I slid passed him and into the house, tracking my bag to the living room.

Connell demanded, "How much do your family secrets need to cost you?"

My throat was parched. If only he knew the real answer. "That's not fair." I threw the backpack over my shoulder and toyed with the idea of telling him how fucked up my life really was, though I doubted I'd get much sympathy from him at this time.

"I guess not, but from my position, it seems fair I know the reason you keep lying."

The atmosphere in the room boiled, and my body trembled. I faced his rock-hard gaze. "You already know I can't tell you. Why make this so difficult?"

"What about us?" The anguish in his voice raked my skin. "I've already gone through one divorce because of lies, and now you."

My wolf's hackles rose. "I'm not like your ex-wife." I swallowed the dryness from my throat. I retrieved Connell's house key from the bag and threw my hand out. "Take it back." It killed me to do it, but anger won out. My patience was gone.

He stared at my open palm, considering it for a moment. "Keep it." The tightness in his expression grew painful to watch. "I should take you down to the station and have you confess everything you know."

Shoving my hands deep into my pockets, a quiver started to challenge my posture. "Connell, I just need another day or so to sort out my shit."

My pulse thudded and my chest stung. "Give me that, and

then I promise no more secrets. I'll tell you everything." I had the urge to fling myself into his arms, cry in his chest, and have him tell me everything would be okay. But I ccouldn't bring myself to let my guard down. Not yet. Not until I dealt with the pack and my ceremony, for I feared if I weakened now, I'd never gain the strength to make it to the end of the day.

I tore my gaze from his glassy eyes, and my gut clenched in anticipation of Connell stopping me, except when I strolled past him he remained still, making no attempt to do so. I wanted to return to his side and forget everything. Pretend the biggest night of my life was not looming over me like a tornado about to touch down. The troubling ache in my stomach screamed. Enre was lost, and I couldn't leave Radu or Botolf in a dysfunctional pack under Sandulf's rule. I was in a tight place with no way out.

I jumped into the Jeep and started the slow, monotonous drive to work. Sitting at a red light, I lowered the rear-view mirror and spotted leaves imbedded in my nest-like hair and started patting it down. What shocked me the most was the lightness of my gray eyes. By the time I reached work, my hair resembled that of a semi-sane person.

I said a quick hello to Alexandria, the receptionist. "There's an envelope in your office. It's from the police. A forest pass." I thanked her and headed down the corridor.

On my return, I contemplated paying the local hospital a visit with a desperate attempt to steal blood, then make my way to Radu's bunker to prepare the tonic. But the smell of wulfkin slapped me out of my thoughts.

I rounded the corner. In the main entrance area, my eyes set on two wulfkin. Matias's large frame bounced up from the visitor's couch when he spotted me. A blonde stood in front of the door. Her hair was pulled tight into a ponytail, drawing attention to her oval- shaped face and rose-painted lips.

My feet froze. "Lutia?"

She pushed open the door, all the while staring at me. A gale blew into the foyer, and rustled her white summer dress. "You coming?" Her smile widened more than usual.

Alexandria asked, "Is everything all right?"

Matias stepped closer. "Yeah, Daciana. Is everything all right?" His arms dangled by his side resembling a silverback gorilla. Black pants and shirt made him look the part of Lutia's personal guard.

My eyes trailed from Matias, to Lutia, to the receptionist. Work was not the place to create a scene. I dropped my backpack near the front desk and strode to the door.

"Yeah, I'm okay, Alex." I flashed a smile and stormed past Lutia on my way out. The door slammed shut behind us.

I snarled at Lutia. "What do you want?"

Her cackle sliced through the air. The desire to shut her mouth swelled with each hoot. "I don't want anything, my sweet Daciana. Sandulf has asked me to collect you."

I clenched my fists. "Forget it. I'm not going anywhere with you. What does he want now? I just saw him in the woods."

She flashed her teeth.

Matias gripped my wrist and squeezed.

"Enre would never want you to behave like this." I pulled the friend card, knowing the two shared a brotherly bond.

"Enre is gone because of you."

On the inside, I cringed at the truth in his words.

Lutia brought her face so close her sharp berry scent swarmed around me like summer flies. "Do you really want to make a scene where the receptionist is watching us through the window?" Her eyes casually glanced to the building.

"I'm not going anywhere. You can let go. I'll gladly go to Sandulf, no need for force."

"We're not stupid." Lutia met my eyes. Beneath her veneer

coyness, laid a treacherous wulfkin who would resort to any act if it meant getting her way. The malice in her eyes held no trace of guilt.

"You killed an innocent woman in my apartment." My limbs stiffened. "Don't think I'll forget that."

Her head flung back, laughing. "What if I said I had nothing to do with it, would you believe me?"

I inched closer to her, but Matias tugged me back by his side. "I know you were involved," I said. "I can smell your lie."

Lutia's fingernail twirled across my cheek, and I smacked her hand away. "Sandulf has a small proposition for you."

My muscles tightened further.

Lutia bustled toward Sandulf's black Land Cruiser in the parking lot at the side of the building. Matias scuttled alongside me, shoving me after her.

I jolted my arm loose from his grip, spun and landed behind the ape-like wulfkin, then kicked the back of his knee. He stumbled forward. Before the smack of his body against the concrete resonated, I'd already sprinted into the woods. There was no doubt Lutia would give chase, but a road didn't restrict me, and I cut through the forest in a direct line to where the pack house lay.

The landscape flashed by, and I cursed my carelessness. How long had Lutia been following me? What was Sandulf up to? I suspected the worse, except I just couldn't work out what that was. He had already managed take everything from me.

By the time I reached the pack home, my lungs burned. Voices mumbled in the backyard, and I dashed around the house, only to stop dead in my tracks.

Sandulf, Radu, and Botolf gaped at me.

But what caused the hairs on my neck to stand was the sight of Connell strapped in a chair with his mouth gagged.

CHAPTER 18

My stomach coiled in on itself at the sight of Connell—the only man I truly loved—tied to the chair. And I placed him in death's path.

Unable to meet his pleading eyes, I scanned the area. Sandulf stood in the yard across from Connell, his arms crossed, his body tense. Botolf and Radu lingered against the forest backdrop, both wearing heavy frowns.

The atmosphere around the pack had changed to something dark and bleak. The sight of Botolf wearing a plain white shirt confirmed it. It seemed inconsequential in light of the situation, but the only other time he wore non-Hawaiian shirts was when two bears slaughtered his sister years ago. His clothing choice brought back the poignant memories. I prayed they didn't stand in my way.

Behind me a car skidded, doors slammed, and footsteps neared. Lutia's movement caught my attention. She strutted toward Sandulf with her chin up and tossing her hair back.

"What took you so long?" Sandulf asked.

Her hand stroked his arm, and her lips slipped into a fake smile. "A slight mix-up." I wasn't sure who pissed me off more, Lutia or Sandulf. One thing for certain, Lutia just scored herself top spot on my hit list.

While I was busy deciding whether she deserved to be strung up by her Achilles' heel or hunted down like rabbit, Matias snatched my arm with such force it might have snapped if I were human. My foot caught on a branch on the lawn and I tumbled forward, landing on my knees not far from the pack leader's feet. I bit back the pain.

No one said a word. A current twirled in my hair, and the long grasses bent and rustled.

Sandulf simply stared at me, or perhaps tried to anticipate my next move. The creases on his brow revealed a wulfkin who struggled with his own thoughts.

I glanced at Connell. His recently polished leather shoes caught the light, and although I expected his feet to be tied, I didn't see a rope. My gaze inched up his body, past the charcoal tailored pants and half-buttoned business shirt. He'd never made it past his front door. His hands were wrapped around the back of the wooden chair, and a white piece of fabric covered the lower half of his face. It was his eyes, drowning in a mixture of terror and uncertainty, that killed me. He murmured something behind his gag, stirring my own rage.

Lutia's voice broke the silence. "Isn't he the handsome one?"

My wolf leapt awake, yearning to emerge and play. Transforming had crossed my mind, but Connell's presence suppressed my urge. I wondered if I was the only wulfkin left who fought to conceal her existence from humans. From the moment Sandulf announced his creation of a dracwulf, not one other member facilitated a hunt for the creature except Enre, and that cost him his life.

My attention returned to Sandulf. "Why is he here?"

His lips cracked into a slit. "A little insurance so you don't run away. When the dracwulf's nudges didn't work, I had to intervene." He shot a hard stare over at Connell and back to me. "She'd do anything for bit of nurturing and plenty of snacks. I guess she's not too different from most females."

"You set the dracwulf to kill those people? How could you? You've got me now; I'm not going anywhere. Let Connell go."

"If you behave and do as I say, then he'll be fine. I know about the relationship between you two. I've watched it bloom, and for what? An unhappy ending. I thought you knew better." He shook his head.

My suspicions were right, and the whole time Sandulf had been playing me, seeing how I'd react. "I've heard your promises before. He's a goddamn inspector, you'd know that if you watched me. Do you think kidnapping him will be overlooked?"

"You shouldn't have brought him into our life, then."

I regretted many things. I wished I never met Connell or fell in love with him or promised to move into his home if it meant he wouldn't get hurt. My chest rumbled. Regret was such a hopeless emotion. "Why did you do all this?"

"I told you before. Our pack is under threat by another, and I needed every member on board, including you. The dracwulf was a little surprise on the encroaching enemy. They'll never see it coming. She's still young and growing, but powerful. Their demise will be wonderful."

"You let humans die just so you could use the dracwulf as your weapon. You've completely lost it."

Lutia loomed closer to Connell with an extra swing in her hip and patted the top of his head. "Poor little Daciana. She might be losing it. It's too late for her now. You'll never see her again."

I snapped to face Lutia. "And is killing an innocent human in my apartment a part of your plan?"

For a moment, her face twitched. She squinted and grabbed a handful of Connell's blond hair, wrenching his head back. Her nails playfully dragged across his throat as she cackled.

My heart jackhammered against my ribs. A faint gash materialized on Connell's throat, and several red droplets rolled down his neck.

I jumped to my feet, yet Sandulf's iron fingers seized my arm. "Lutia, who have you killed?"

She scuttled closer to him. "But you . . . "

He backhanded her, wiping her mouth clean of words. "Never go against my orders again."

Lutia's lips parted and stayed open. She fiddled with her hair, avoiding everyone's stare.

Dispute among my adversaries. Perfect.

My body trembled. "What do you want? I already said I'll do anything you want. Leave him alone."

Connell stood no chance of surviving. Sandulf would finish him off, leaving me with one option—getting to him first. In that moment, I gave no thought to my future. If Connell wasn't safe, nothing mattered.

Lutia's snorted. "About time you smartened up."

Sandulf's shoulders slouched. "Remain with the pack during your ceremony. That's all you need to do."

"Fine. Done. Let him go." I gave little thought to the elixir, though I wondered if Sandulf knew. Regardless, Connell's well-being came first.

Lutia's cackle kicked off again like the annoying sound of a lawn mower. My pulse drummed in my ears, and I barely held back my wolf who stirred.

Sandulf inched closer to Connell. "This is why we have laws." His voice fell to a whisper.

I said, "And Enre? Don't you care he's lost?"

"Don't worry about him. You focus on yourself."

I bit my lip. "Why do you speak in riddles? Tell me where Enre is."

"Sandulf. Is Enre alive?" Unexpectedly, Radu asked from a distance.

Everyone's heads turned toward Radu, and Lutia marched toward him, with Sandulf trailing her. I didn't listen to their words. I took the chance and lunged at Connell, impatient to free him. His head bobbed in anticipation of his release.

I crouched and pulled at the twine.

Matias yelled, "She's freeing him."

I continue to pull at the knotted bind. Nausea rose as rapidly as my wolf attempted to claw out of my skin. My hands burned. I didn't stop.

Matias thundered my way. I swerved from his first blow and threw myself into a forward roll. My flesh prickled and stretched. He charged again, and I leapt to the side, avoiding his swinging arm.

My transformation had kicked off, and I couldn't stop it while fighting Matias. My talons pierced through my hands. Bones screeched.

Matias caught himself, spun about and grasped for my arm, but I spun and slashed his wrist. He recoiled, clutching his bloody wound.

Connell watched from the chair. I could see the look of horror in his eyes.

I was changing right in front of him, unsure if I could stop. Determined to save him, a half-howl, half-scream burst past my lips as I attempted to reverse the change. Dropping to my knees, the pain tore my muscles. Convulsions replaced the sting. Similar to squeezing clothes into an already full suitcase, I just managed to contain my inner wolf, which nipped at my insides, tearing flesh. It wouldn't last.

Sandulf clapped. "Don't fight your true nature."

Pulsating blood in my ears drowned out any other sound. Radu, who rubbed his cheek, and Botolf remained in the distance.

Suddenly, searing heat coated my body. My chest heaved, and I struggled for air.

Lutia bared her teeth at Connell and her pupils gleamed with excitement. She flung off her white dress in one quick motion. Apparently, she wasn't wearing underwear. "Do you like what you see?" Her voice smoky in a sultry tone, Lutia grabbed Connell's face, forcing him to nod.

She cackled. "What about now?" Her manifestation into wulfkin form accelerated. Bones stretched and flesh tore. Her body elongated. Lutia hunched over on all fours, and Connell's body thrashed, moaning, his eyes terror-stricken.

"Get away from him!" I hurled myself forward and grabbed Lutia by the arm, only to confront her wulfkin. The last bit of white fur sprouted over her body. She snapped in my direction, fangs exposed.

I released her paw.

Raised on her hind legs, she came for me.

My jaw tightened. I recoiled, wanting to place distance between Connell and us. Lutia advanced. She put all her weight behind a rushed snap of her jaws. I hopped back, but her swift blow threw me closer to Connell. She lunged.

I sprang to my feet and kicked my leg out. She crashed into the lawn face first.

Without hesitation, I flung all my weight onto her hairy back and plowed my fists into the back of her neck, one after another. Sandulf or Matias didn't jump in to help, so I guessed they enjoyed the show.

Lutia bucked the way a wild bull would in a rodeo. I lost my balance, flying directly into Connell. The chair broke beneath us, and the collision freed his hands. I clambered to my feet, drawing Connell by the shirt up alongside me.

He ripped away the fabric from his mouth. "Daci!"

My gaze swept the area. Matias approached from my right, clasping his blood-coated arm. On my left, Lutia rose to her feet. Botolf and Radu stayed out of reach. Sandulf stood in front. With Connell behind me, I nudged him farther back from the pack house, hearing none of his mumblings.

I said, "It doesn't have to be this way. Let him go, and I'll remain."

Sandulf's nose creased. "It's too late. He's already seen what we are."

"That's your fault." I held zero admiration for the alpha male. My affection for him

had long dissipated. My childhood seemed like another lifetime. The wulfkin in front of me was a mass murderer.

"You were a great hunter once. It's a shame," Sandulf said.

I swallowed a pocket of air infused with blood and wulfkin scents. When Sandulf started his transformation, a shiver seized my body.

"Connell, run. Get out of here, now!"

He covered his mouth and a dazed look covered his expression.

"Go." I shoved him. "Go!"

He coiled abruptly before bolting toward the dense forest without a glance back. Sandulf snarled, pointing his finger at Botolf and Radu. "After him."

Botolf and Radu both hesitated, and then pursued Connell. I prayed they disobeyed the

order.

Someone snatched my hand and whipped me backward. I landed on my rump. Lutia skulked close. Matias approached, and I counted on him resisting a transformation while his hand bled profusely at the risk of ripping the gash to a state beyond repair. Sandulf as a wulfkin was the real problem. He howled.

Three against one. *Oh joy.*

A grumble vibrated from my chest. Still on my bum, I crawled backward over the grass closer to the house, away from Lutia's grasp. I hit the wall and climbed to my feet.

No holding back. Odds were against me, so I might as well go down fighting. I let my true nature rip. In a hasty change, my skin burst, muscles swelled and bones grew too fast. Excruciating spasms threatened to topple me off my feet. I dug deep inside and let the mounting fury dull the pain. I stretched my spine and prepared to fight. I had nothing to lose.

Lutia attacked. Her razor-sharp teeth sliced skin and latched onto my leg. The pain shot up my body. My flesh split and blood poured free. I refused to whimper and instead whacked the side of my head into her snout. She released her hold and stumbled, blood gushing from her nose.

Matias rushed forward in his usual style—charging. I ducked, pouncing out of the way. He was quick.

Using pure muscle strength, I shoved my shoulder against his side, forcing him to trip into Lutia. They fell to the ground.

From my right, Sandulf advanced on all fours.

I rushed for Lutia who moved sluggishly and seized her shoulders with my talons. My fangs seized her neck. Her body tussled. I tasted the human she mauled in my bedroom. My eyes were on Sandulf, his creased snout, his trembling body. Lutia's legs kicked back in attempt to break loose from my grip. My jaw clamped harder and her body melted in my hold, slumping in my arms.

Sandulf attacked, and I thrust Lutia's limp body at him. He lost his footing and struggled to free himself from beneath Lutia's weight. I seized the opportunity and tore out of there.

On all fours, I ran from the pack house. My paws hit the earth. I was already deep in the woods by the time Sandulf's snarls reached me. His huffing breaths drew closer.

My heart pounded. In front of me, trees appeared to

move from my path as if I flew through the air, the wind slapping my face.

Certain it wasn't the case, I knew halting the transformation mid-way had caused more damage than I realized. Right then, I ran purely on adrenaline. Uncertain how much longer I could maintain the stamina, I continued my race.

I sniffed the air and leaped over a decayed log. Connell's scent led me right. I skated round an enormous trunk, tossing debris behind me. The mountain encouraged my sprint downhill. Sandulf thudded after me.

Almost upon Connell, I stole a look over my shoulder. Sandulf was rushing down behind us. The sound of his paws sliding across dried foliage resonated in my ears.

My entire body buzzed as my adrenaline decelerated. The world under my paws slanted and a blurry vision accompanied the dizziness, but I pushed on.

Something solid, with the strength of a truck, smashed into the side of my head. I crumpled onto the ground, losing all strength. The world was sideways, and my eyelids grew heavy.

My last vision was of an enormous black blur colliding into Connell.

CHAPTER 19

*A*long with consciousness, the ache in my skull also returned. Every movement drove a shudder through me, and the clunk of my heart caused the veins to pulse beneath my skin. Even breathing hurt, though the gentle pine fragrance caressing my lungs eased the pain. The wind's harmonica sounds accompanied by a swooshing of leaves played a rhythmic tune, and if it wasn't for the crunch of dried l eaves nearby, sleep might have claimed me once again.

I opened my eyes to a forest cloaked in night, and I lay on the earth below a round- bellied moon glowing in shades of copper and sanguine. The red moon hung low, and already the Earth's shadow slipped off the edges of its face, engulfing the globe in blackness.

The Lunar Eutine had started, and shortly the moon would plunge into the umbra, the time of my transformation.

My wolf roused, prodding me, eager for release, but I felt something else inside me—a rawness that chilled my bones.

Someone's breath chanted near, and I turned to find Botolf sitting cross-legged next to a pine, twice the width of him.

"How are you feeling?"

My throat croaked, and I held back a dry cough. "Where am I?"

"Deep in the Carpathian woods."

I stifled a growl and smelled other wulfkin on the breeze along with Connell's sweet perspiration.

Sandulf ensured we hid far enough from the city to avoid escape or anyone finding us.

Lunar Eutine ceremonies could be held anywhere, since the change would take place in my head, not the physical realm. Other wulfkin were needed for mere muscle power to hold down the thrashing animal; in this case, me.

So, there was no reason for Sandulf to haul us into the middle of the forest, unless he had other plans. And no reason whatsoever for Connell to be here except as a bargaining chip for Sandulf, to keep me under control, and for Sandulf to get what he wanted.

"Where's Connell?"

Botolf's chin nudged to the treeline in front of us. I cranked my head up and made out a black silhouette slouched against a trunk.

"Matias crash-tackled him hard." Botolf's voice sounded worn, and empty of spirit. Who could blame him?

A heavy sorrow lay in my chest, and I struggled to push myself upright, especially once I saw the shackle around my ankle with the chain wrapped around a tree. I blinked away the prickling panic smothering my skin. *Control.* I wouldn't lose it. Not yet.

"Your body's still healing." Botolf's soft words rang in my ears. "Sandulf knocked you out with a tree branch."

No surprise there. I rubbed the bump on my head, which stung. "Why the hell am I tied?" The dimness of the forest did nothing to conceal the dismay carved on Botolf's face, or the heaviness beneath his eyes. He shrugged.

"What happened after I fell?"

For a moment, he said nothing. "Radu and I wouldn't chase your police friend. We couldn't, and that enraged Sandulf." He inhaled a deep breath. "Once Sandulf hauled you back to the house, he beat Radu, who took each blow and scratch without a whimper. He's tied up in the house basement in worse condition than you."

I said nothing. Had Sandulf gone mad? As a pack leader, he was entitled to serve punishment on disloyal wulfkin, yet he never before dished out such cruel behavior. The news of Radu's punishment struck me hard, and dreadful images of him tortured and dying ricocheted through my thoughts until bile rose up my throat and threatened to spew out.

And then it hit me. I didn't have the elixir. No salt or wolfsbane. Even if I did, how could I get near Connell for human blood? Heaviness crushed my spirits, knowing I'd lost my chance at humanity, and at spending a lifetime with Connell. My destiny lay in Sandulf's hands, just as he wanted. A dark loathing coated my thoughts.

"I've seen a few Lunar Eutine transformations in my time," Botolf said. "I can guide you."

In truth, the ritual terrified me. Either way, I was about to lose everything, and couldn't change a thing. "I'd like that." *Anything to stop the drowning feeling.*

"*Eutine* comes from the ancient wulfkin language and translates to "true heart." It draws on the connection you have with your wolf, and when the moon is completely shrouded in black, a new you will be delivered. Don't be afraid of it. It's a wondrous gift, and the ceremony is different for everyone. In mine, I was a pup again, huddled in fur blanket. Radu found himself trekking through unknown mountains, and Enre hunted a dark shadow, but every vision ends the same way: you wake up a wulfkin." Botolf's cheeks lifted. "Don't fight the allure, welcome it."

He inched closer and whispered, "The Lunar Eutine is not your problem. Saving your human friend might be, especially since—" He pulled his hand out of his pocket and revealed a bottle with a small amount of red liquid sloshing about, and just as quick he stuffed it away. "Look at what surrounds us."

I covered my mouth as I gazed upon the field of miniature white flowers everywhere. The wild petunia.

"Radu told me everything. We both had a vial as a backup plan. Lucky for you, I took turns guiding Connell out here, and I had to cut him for blood. I felt terrible for it."

The fire in my chest rekindled. Maybe my dream was possible. Botolf returned to sitting cross-legged, his head bowed.

"I'm sorry you had to find out that way," I said.

"Don't be. You need to do what's right for you. We'll always love you."

I nodded. We were in the woods for the sole purpose of the alpha finishing Connell. I knew that, and if I woke up as a human, he'd finish me off, too. I needed a plan and fast. Botolf and I kept silent for a long while, and I racked my mind for possible escapes involving Connell. Sure, I could take on Lutia and Sandulf. It had been done before. But there were no guarantees, especially when Matias was thrown into the mix.

Nearby, something snorted and rustled. A wild boar with spiky tusks approached, its snout deep in foliage, making all kinds of grunting sounds. It nudged something that clanked. The animal raised its nose and sniffed us, then squealed and scrambled away.

I crawled close enough to see my keys to Radu's bunker in the grass, but no matter how far I stretched my arm, I couldn't grab them. Someone had patted me down. I met Botolf's stare. "Whatever happens, know that I love the pack. Well, maybe not all of them."

"I know." He clutched his chest and that simple gesture broke my heart. I wanted to take him and Radu with me, so they'd never fear Sandulf again. The guilt of leaving them alone with an irate alpha, and Enre still lost, sickened me. I glanced up at the eclipse, which had now swallowed half of the moon.

Lutia's voice broke the peace. "How adorable, sharing your feelings. So human."

Sandulf, Lutia with a bandaged neck, and Matias, sauntered in our direction. The wulfkin's scents swirled on the wind, and memories of my life under Sandulf's rule surfaced —a time when the pack house provided a haven for wulfkin, protection, and the collective nurturing we craved. He destroyed it for his own self-interest, and I wondered again how far Alina's death had broken him.

Sandulf hadn't attempted to kill me yet, and that small, unnerving detail gave me hope that a part of the old him remained somewhere inside.

"I sense you're troubled." Sandulf's voice grew dry and hoarse.

Matias paced back and forth like a caged animal alongside the alpha.

I pushed myself to my feet.

Anger flared across Sandulf's face, twisting his features. Just as quick, it dissipated back to a calm mien. "We're family. So either do what I say, or I'll show you no mercy." Did he realize his comment was one huge contradiction? "I'm here, aren't I?" I offered.

Darkness slithered behind his gaze, like a surging tsunami, relentlessly pushing forward, engulfing everything in its path. His wolf roused inside him, eager to erupt and eliminate the defiant opponent: me.

"Tonight's Lunar Eutine is partial to a matriarch, coming along once every three hundred years or so."

"And?"

"You're a fool, Daciana." Lutia interrupted.

Sandulf stepped forward. "Any female moonwulf changing on this night who is stupid enough to take a certain elixir is asking for trouble." His gaze swept to the keys in the grass.

My throat closed up, and I couldn't take another breath. *Dear God, he did know about Radu helping me find the elixir.*

"If you go poking around in someone's items, they'll know. And Radu will be lucky to survive the punishment coming his way. He'll never betray me again." He inspected his hand and fingernails. "Then there's you. What to do with you."

"You've got what you want. I've lost everything. Do what you want." I glanced at the white flowers around me, guessing Sandulf didn't know about Botolf's secret.

Matias's back arched. His muscles twitched beneath his skin. Sandulf placed a hand on his shoulder. "Not yet."

"Let's get one thing straight, Sandulf. You got what you wanted in the end. You won, okay. Let the human go, and I'll be your willing mate." I struggled to keep my voice calm and my wolf under control.

"I'll hold onto my insurance, and take you as a mate anyway."

Lutia should never play poker, because the fury of Sandulf's words reddened her cheeks and thinned her lips. "I'll take the human and finish him off myself," She said, her eyes fixed on me.

I clenched my fists and imagined daggers streaking toward her, and for the second time, I wished another wulfkin dead. Wiped from existence. And I'd feel no grief, only joy.

Botolf cried out, "Sandulf, stop this! You've broken the law by allowing a dracwulf to be born, letting humans die, and now bringing one to our ceremony." He crossed his arms over his chest. "The Varlac will kill us. Don't you care? What's happened to you?"

Matias roared like a bear toward Botolf. Lutia giggled.

Sandulf's eyelids closed in slow motion, all the while his

head bobbing back and forth. "The Varlac are no threat. My contact has assured me of this, and perhaps you should control your tongue."

"And you gamble the pack's lives on this contact?" I asked.

"Would I risk the pack when I'm trying to protect them?" Sandulf's voice was shaky, his nostrils flared, and his bunched hands trembled.

He made no sense. Maybe that was part of the problem. Perhaps he had been losing his mind for years, leading the pack astray, but why hadn't I seen it before? Maybe I didn't want to.

"Let the human go. Release Daciana. Let's be a pack again, not enemies." Botolf's nervousness scraped the length of my arms, feasting on my own nerves.

"Phfft.'

Matias dropped on all fours, his body a spasm of convulsions. He was going to change any moment if he didn't control his rage.

Swallowing hard, I tussled to restrain my own wolf as each limb ached to transform. My body twitched, and my legs gave out. I hit the ground hard..

A movement at the corner of my vision revealed Connell attempting to stand, despite being secured to the tree. His words muffled into the gag around his mouth.

Lutia spun toward him. "Daciana—or should I say Daci— is tied up right now." She moseyed closer to Connell, while Matias crawled toward Botolf, and the whole time Connell's eyes stared at me.

My lips opened in a silent snarl, and I dove forward on all fours toward Lutia, but was caught on my chain. "Do not touch him!" I voiced each word loud and precise.

"You love this man?" Sandulf scratched his chin.

"Yes." I staggered to my feet.

"And he loves you?"

I flashed Connell a quick look. Behind his mask of fear, affection reassured his love for me, and I nodded.

"Good. Once you turn, convince him to never speak of us again. If the police start sniffing near the pack home, I will hunt him down. Will that arrangement make you happy?"

The sudden change in Sandulf's demeanor and the compassion in his words caught me off guard, and I stared at him for a long while. My insides burned, but he was giving me what I desired, Connell's freedom.

So why didn't I believe him?

A slice of moon dangled in the sky, and my legs wobbled beneath me. The unsettling sensation resurfaced and raced through my veins.

Sandulf marched toward Connell and spoke with his back to me. "By your silence, I take it you agree. Then you won't mind if I use him a bit first."

Tightness gripped my skin and my balance rocked. "L . . . Leave him alone." Connell's legs kicked at Sandulf.

"I won't hurt him much." The alpha snatched Connell's arm, causing the chains decorating his wrist to clang. Sandulf transformed his arm into the furry kind and slashed my beloved's forearm. "Lutia," he said. "The cup."

She scuttled to a tree and seconds later, appeared with a mug. She pressed it into Connell's flesh, collecting the sweet nectar that already laced my nostrils.

A long, throaty growl hugged my words, and I refused to succumb to the heaviness of my limbs. "What are you doing?"

"Fresh blood helps wulfkin through the Lunar Eutine. It's not smooth sailing for us, you know." His words and body shook as he raised the mug to his mouth.

The other wulfkin also writhed and fought to control their bodies. Matias lay on his back, a faint wail floating from his mouth. Botolf's body jerked, yet he held my stare.

Lutia's slurping sounds engorged my own hunger. The desperate urge to tear free and rip her apart was excruciating. The blood belonged to me. Long breaths blew past my lips. Despite Connell's gaze sealed on me, I salivated, tugging against the chain.

It became too much, and I collapsed onto my side. I yearned to rip Sandulf and Lutia apart. They had tasted my Connell.

Botolf's voice floated on the breeze. "Daciana, the Lunar Eutine is here."

I glanced over as he threw the vial at me. I snatched it out of the air.

His words spilled into a howl, and soon Matias joined in on the wolf's song. I pushed myself to my knees and pulled the cork off.

"Don't," Sandulf cried and ran full tilt toward me.

I ripped a handful of petunias and grass, stuffing it into my mouth and swallowing it down with the tonic.

Sandulf's foot collided into the side of my head, throwing the bottle into a tree. I flew backward and hit the ground.

The sky was changing, shrouded by blackness and descended around me. Sandulf's half-growls, half-murmuring words fell into the background.

I'd never wanted anyone as much as I desired Connell—his love, his affection, his blood, which was sweeter than I thought. No more crying, no more regrets, and no more guilt.

I opened myself up, releasing the wolf, welcoming the tearing of my flesh. Pain flowed free, and it concentrated around my hip. Rawness spread through me, unnerving and familiar at the same time. It called to me, hauling me inward like previous transformations, except that this time, something other than my wolf waited inside of me.

CHAPTER 20

It was too late to hide. The Lunar Eutine grasped me in her hold. One moment I streamed deeper into my mind with blackness veiling my vision, and the next thing, I stood naked on a dirt track in the middle of the woods, studying the endless passage weaving into the distance on either side of me. The tops of the pine trees swayed in the winds and the branches creaked like forgotten ships anchored in the sea and ravaged by storms.

I remembered Botolf's words, and knew I was inside my head. A hallucination maybe, a vision, or something more spiritual.

The last fragments of light faded from the heavens, and the breeze died away. A heavy stillness swathed the woodland. Then a cloying stench of wet dog fur hit me.

"Hello?"

The beat of paws against the earth echoed all around me. Trees crashed to the ground. A glowing, vermillion silhouette moved back and forth amid the trunks next to me, encroaching ever so close.

I readied for whatever lurked to pounce out.

Instead, a lone wolf with fur brighter than the blood

190

moon emerged and sat in front of me. Its pupils were frosty white, concealing what lay beneath. Sanguine lights sparked from beneath the animal, spreading and illuminating every inch of the ribbon trail that entwined through the forest farther than my sight allowed.

The red wolf's head tilted as if it considered me and trotted closer, nudging my hip in the exact spot where Enre had left a scar. For that split second when we made contact, everything made sense. A new future lay ahead of me, it was shrouded in black, but it was mine. A serene calmness fell over everything, and not a single thing worried me.

Out of nowhere, a swarm of itchiness spread over my body. Invisible fangs sank into my skin, and the insect-like bites slithered across my arms and legs. I scratched and ripped my flesh. Screams bellowed past my lips, and I clawed myself, unable to reach the burning inferno. I fell to my knees. "Make it stop!"

The wind rushed past, and the red wolf vanished in a blur from my sight, along with the path, replaced by more trees. My gaze dropped to a red fur pelt around my feet and I wrapped myself in the blanket.

Inside my head, the blur cleared. The red wolf represented the blood moon, my spiritual guide, and with her pelt around me, I'd embraced my new life. My future was neither as a wulfkin or human.

"Child, rest a while as I have unfinished business," a female voice sang in my head. Somehow I knew it was the red wolf speaking to me.

"I will take over your body and mind for a short while," she continued. "And you will have no control, but no harm will come to you. Don't resist me, child. Your new path needs to be wiped clean, and I cannot allow his death on your hands."

A wolf's howl cried behind me, and I spun to find myself thrown into darkness. Something new lived inside me now;

the red wolf. I embraced the warmth spreading through me like my life depended on it, and I faded into the background of my mind, where everything was calm.

Awailing sounded, and I snapped open my eyes. The Carpathian woodland gleamed beneath the sickle-shaped moon radiating copper from the heavens. A new time. A new world. It had been a long while since I last walked the earth.

Climbing onto my feet, I stretched my wulfkin form. A shattered fetter lay on the ground nearby. I resisted Daciana's desperate memories pushing forward. I was eager to rid my head of useless emotions. Instead, I savored the purity and power humming through my veins.

Wulfkin scents encircled me, along with a human's sweet tang. Perfect. I needed something to eat.

A shrill voice rang in my ears. "You're too stupid for your own good, Daciana."

I coiled around to see a thin, white-haired female grinning foolishly. Her tart scent, a poisonous berry on my tongue, left pinpricks on my throat. One swift movement of my paw, and she crumpled to the ground, gripping her bloody cheek.

Behind me, an aging wulfkin emitted a fire's heat and filled my lungs with fresh kindling. He carried a strong heart. Alongside him stood a fighter baring teeth, yet he trembled. I inhaled his concoction of earthy fungus and tree sap, a pure soul who'd lost his way.

Someone else approached from behind me. It swam in an odor of decayed animals and briny lichen. I faced the black-eyed man whose betrayal foamed in my mouth like methane gas rising through water. He was beyond saving. His heart had turned the color of burned wood, drowned in sorrow long ago. The alpha.

He studied me as he pulled off one boot. "You went against my order, in a direct violation of pack law." The other boot fell to the ground. "I shall deliver your death swiftly and show you I am still a compassionate alpha." In one abrupt movement, he peeled off his shirt. "But it's my fault." With his pants removed, he gripped his hips. "I should have finished you before the ceremony for going behind my back with the elixir." He smacked his hand into the side of his head. "The moment I knew someone took my books, I should have stopped you."

The young, warrior wulfkin left his post by the tree and loomed closer to the alpha, his body tense and ripe for combat. The older one's voice called out, "Sandulf, please don't do this. Let her be."

The alpha's lips pressed tight into a smirk. "Too late." He shed his human form and slipped into a pelt the color of sludge and delivered a trembling howl that proclaimed to the group his reign over them.

I swept my gaze toward the encroaching alpha. My head lowered, and I leapt for him, snatching his neck between my claws and constricted. Too many lives had paid for his treachery. The warrior recoiled.

The alpha's rock-hard fist connected with the bridge of my nose, but I clenched my muscles and held him, peering into his cavernous soul. I sneered. Heat tumbled off him, stuffed with ferocity, rage and regret. There, deep in the depths, the real wulfkin lingered. He was too far gone now, his mind snapped, and I pitied what he had become. But he'd suffered enough. I'd seen his true heart and that left me with one option. I called to the spirit world in my head and demanded his swift end.

He kicked and squirmed. I released him. Toppling backward, he lost his footing and fell. A growl choked in his chest, and he pounced from a crouched position, latching onto my shoulder, ripping into me.

I stumbled against a tree truck, the alpha clawing into me. His slurping and sucking noises sickened me. I endured the agony and id nothing. His torso slid against mine, coated in blood. Nausea tested my balance and patience. Yet I waited.

He started to flinch. He jerked and shoved me into the arms of another tree.

His paw dragged across his muzzle, wiping the blood that I knew scorched him. He gurgled, foaming at the sides of his mouth and clutched his chest. Dropping to his knees, he slid back into human form, his body slackening. His breath grew raspy, and his torso slumped forward. "What have you done?" An unrecognizable voice hissed. He gripped the shrubs nearby to steady himself.

The blonde rushed to his side. "No, Sandulf, get up." Arched over the alpha, she pried his chin up, then shrieked and recoiled.

Around the alpha's mouth, the flesh peeled from the bone, exposing a skeleton jawline. Threadlike capillaries caged his back teeth. His pupils rolled back, and he screeched a sound engorged with a torment no living creature should ever endure.

The young female looked at me with fierce eyes. "Stop it, you're killing him!" She knelt near, but was too afraid to touch him, and sobbed in her hands.

Red blotches dotted the alpha's torso, widening and dissolving the skin. The girl wailed louder. He collapsed face first into the earth from which he came, his body limp and unmoving.

Despite the gasps and moans from others, I felt no sympathy, no grief, nothing. In my mind, a perfect image of the alpha materialized. He stood in the path between the parted forest, and a bright smile curled on his lips. I glimpsed a silver wolf trot out from the woodland, and happy tears trickled down the alpha's cheeks. The silver wolf spoke to him and while I couldn't hear the words, I sensed a tremendous flame radiate from them, and understood—a reunited love.

The warrior's voice dragged me into reality. "Oh, Daciana." His cheeks were ashen, his hands trembled, and he held his arms against his chest. "What have you become?"

A sweet scent teased me, and my snout jerked up. In the distance, the old wulfkin squatted next to the human man, fumbling with something. The human shot to his feet and stared my way with huge eyes, gasping for air, then sprinted into the wooded forest.

I went dashing after him. The voices and shouts fell behind me. Inside my head, Daciana pushed forward, her scream deafening. She begged me to stop. I couldn't. I craved meat, and my meal just bounded away. Someone crash-tackled into my side, and we collapsed. Jumping to my feet, I shoved the warrior off me, and bolted after the human.

Stomping footfalls chased me.

The faster I pursued my prey, the stronger his succulent aroma teased me. Deep inside me, Daciana pleaded for me to stop, that it was wrong. But how could it be? Humans were meat.

A blanket of mist unfurled on the mountain, masking the man but not his scent. The trees swiped at me and the debris pinched my legs, snagging on my fur. I salivated and skidded to the right where the aroma strengthened. The ground beneath my feet sloped downward, and I stepped into a clearing.

I spied the human in the distance, huddled near a tree, his hands fiddling with his leg. His quivering arms rose, and he clasped a black object, pointed at me. In the man's aura, valor lingered, and I halted. My entire body buzzed with adrenaline.

Daciana was saying he, a human, would help the wulfkin.

That couldn't be, but he was part of her future. A heavy feeling in my stomach confirmed what I sensed. No, I refused to believe it.

An explosion erupted in my ears.

I sensed nothing. The world under my feet slanted. Suddenly I was on my knees, then on my side. The man dashed from my sight.

Had I imagined it? A thick weight on my chest made breathing difficult. I shut my eyes and let myself slide back into my world.

CHAPTER 21

The caress of fingers along my cheek awakened me, and Botolf's timber scent teased my nostrils. He looked down at me. For a moment a honeyed glow encased him, then it faded. Darkness circled his eyes and sorrow consumed them.

"Good to see you're awake." His voice was chirpy. I liked that.

I lay in my bedroom in the pack house and breathed in the cool air, tasting the crispness of dawn on my tongue like sharp stings. Light seeped in around the drawn curtains, and I tried to recall the ceremony. Memories of the vermillion wolf calmed me at first, and then everything else came flooding back.

"God, I...the red wolf tried to eat Connell. She controlled me."

Botolf wiped my forehead with a moist towel. "But you didn't."

"Because he shot me. But it wasn't me doing it. Where is Connell?" I blurted out all at once.

"I let him go, even though he might come back to kill us.

He's your friend, and I did what I thought you'd want. I tracked him to the city. He's safe."

Botolf's face paled. "Every small noise makes me jump. I keep thinking he's coming for us. He knows what we are."

The idea whirled in my head. Would Connell come back with guns blazing and the whole police force behind him? After I betrayed him, there was a slim possibility of such a return, and I prayed it didn't happen. Worse yet, I might have lost him forever. Never to feel his touch, his soft lips on mine or the loving words he whispered in my ears. Sadness weighed heavy inside my chest. If I were braver, I might have told him about the wulfkin, about me, and convinced him none of it matter because of the love we shared. But with a bunch of lies thrown in, why would he take me back? Something gripped my throat, and refused to let go.

I remembered seeing everyone the previous night as if through someone else's eyes. I had lost control. Connell was nothing but meat to me. I killed the pack leader and felt satisfaction. How the hell did my blood burn him up like that?

"Sandulf." The name dripped off my lips. He'd returned to Alina's arms. Happiness had radiated from them as they united, and yet their reunion did little to squash my guilt. Where was the grief and sorrow death promised? I felt none of it. Instead, I lay broken with jumbled emotions. And after all that hassle with the elixir, I still turned into a wulfkin.

Botolf looked away. Sandulf had been his family for more years than I'd been alive, and I took him away. I opened my mouth and three hushed words rolled out, "I'm so sorry."

He wiped his tears. "It's done now."

My gut stung. I was a full-blown wulfkin, except something was wrong with me. I felt what lay in others' hearts. Not to mention my blood burned Sandulf from the inside out. I was a freak. Uncertain how much of my recollections I could trust, I prayed the incident was a singular event, yet I doubted it. Knowing my luck, I'd probably start zapping people dead with my gaze next. "I'm not right, am I?"

"Being a wulfkin is different from a moonwulf. You have more power and control. That's all you're feeling."

"No, it's not all I am feeling. You saw it last night. What I did to Sandulf. Don't tell me that's normal."

He said nothing for a little while. "You smelled like pure wolf with no hint of the Daciana I knew. You behaved as if you didn't know us, and your blood—it was acid." A pained expression conveyed his repulsion.

That hurt. "It wasn't me. I watched the events unveil and couldn't stop myself." I lifted my chin higher. "Did the red wolf visit you in your ceremony?"

His gaze drifted to the ceiling. "No. A path lay between the forest and the city, and I crawled out of a warm fur blanket, then walked into the woods." He dry-washed his hands. "The red wolf symbolizes the matriarchal soul of the moon. Maybe she wanted it this way."

I pushed myself to a sitting position, noticing I wore pants with tears up the legs and a faded sweatshirt. I was the she-Hulk again. If anyone knew about the matriarchal moon, Radu would, and then I remembered Sandulf had punished him.

"How's Radu?"

"He's in the other room, badly injured, but alive."

Too much devastation lingered in the wake of the ceremony. I reached over to the shoulder Sandulf had ripped into, only to discover there was no lesion, no injury, nothing but smooth skin beneath the fabric. The other side was the same. "But he bit me. The blood—"

"It seems you heal quicker than any of us now." Botolf glanced out the window, his expression blank. "I've never heard of anyone healing like this, though. Maybe you've been gifted?"

Uncertain what part of my deranged life needing fixing

first, I clutched the fur blanket to steady myself, imagining myself in Connell's arms.

Botolf's warm touch helped. "Let your body ground itself before you get up."

Footsteps sounded outside the door. A beam of light defined Lutia's hunched posture as she entered the room, and her tart berry scent wafted into the room around me.

The sight of her affected me in a way I hadn't anticipated. Bandages hid her cheek and neck. All life had drained from her pallid face while her expression held no trace of its usual savagery. Sweat coated her flat hair, and blood splattered her track pants. I should have been angry, should have wanted to rip her throat out, but I didn't. Not when the misplaced look in her face revealed regret. I killed the man she loved, or so we were led to believe, and such a loss was enough heartache for anyone to tolerate.

She knelt near me, her head bowed.

"What are you doing? Get up."

"Daciana," Botolf said. "She is showing you respect. You are our alpha now."

A sudden coldness knocked into me. Everything I touched messed up, and now a wulfkin pack reported to me. How long before I screwed them up even worse than they already were?

"What?" I managed.

Lutia's gaze found mine. "Well, you did kill Sandulf."

Her brazen comment didn't shock me, even if I was the new alpha. And just thinking the word to myself had me breaking out in goose bumps. The trauma of everything I'd lost was raw. I never asked for alpha status. Sandulf shouldn't have died, and the chance that Connell might take me back was close to minus zero.

Would he still love me? I wasn't sure I could keep going without him. I wanted to return to a time before the dracwulf entered our lives. A time when Sandulf was a caring father, and when I cherished life more than anything. The pack's lives were changed forever, and I doubted my ascent to leadership would put things right again. And just thinking of the dracwulf pushed my pulse to racing speed. First thing on my agenda was to kill the beast and then find Enre.

Lutia curled a blonde strand around her finger. "I'm guessing with you in charge, I'm no longer in line for alpha partner?" Her tongue licked her lips. "Unless you want me to be?"

I raised an eyebrow. She had to be kidding. Right?

"Okay, just asking." She tossed her hair over her shoulder. "Was it worth it? Is being a leader everything you thought it would be?"

Despite her docile façade, the fire still roared within her.

Botolf interrupted. "Lutia, remember who you're speaking to."

The smile wiped off her lips. "His death is on you."

"If you're here to insult me, this conversation is over. If you have something to say, say it," I told her.

Lutia straightened, and at once I sensed her heat rise.

Botolf cleared his throat. "Lutia, watch yourself."

She huffed. "Everything I did was an order."

"That doesn't alleviate you of your mistakes."

"Don't you understand? He used me to get to you."

Her words came as no surprise. "So? You always have a choice."

"No reason to hide it any longer." A twisting smile curled on her lips. "Go deep into the woods." The coldness of her voice chilled the room. "Go east until you reach the rock caves. Don't waste time."

"Is that where the dracwulf hides?" Why the beast chose the rock caves baffled me. Exposure to the weather and vulnerability to other predators made the location a deadly one. No wolf in her right mind would hide there. Though in hindsight, I cursed myself for not checking the location earlier.

She started to stride away, swinging her hips. I leapt forward, shoving my hand into her back so hard she smacked into the door, which clapped shut. "This is your one and only warning. Disobey me again, and I'll rip your head off." I couldn't help myself and banged her head into the door for good measure, just in case she didn't get the message. "Now. Is the dracwulf in the cave?"

"Yes." Her voice muffled.

Her whimpers did nothing to make me feel pity.

I pulled back.

"Just because you're now a super wulfkin, don't think you can do anything you want to me," she spat.

I spun her to face me. "What super wulfkin?"

"That's what you've become. When a female wulfkin takes the elixir on a matriarchal moon, there's a slight chance she'll evolve into a super wulfkin, or whatever the term Sandulf used. You have different abilities, and lucky for you, once the Varlac find out, they'll be wanting to meet you, since your kind is in high demand." The side of her mouth curled up. She tucked her head into her chest and scampered out of the room.

Sandulf had torn out the pages from the elixir book, ensuring no one knew the truth. Perhaps he feared if someone found out, they might chose to become the super wulfkin on purpose and challenge his alpha status. I shrugged. Just my luck for the matriarchal moon to fall on my turn.

Botolf's expression told me he had no idea about the so-called "super wulfkin." Whatever it was, if the Varlac took interest in me, I didn't want it. Maybe she made it up and lied. I'd find out. I grabbed my old joggers from the pile of used clothes and stepped into them.

"I want to see Radu."

Botolf nodded and climbed to his feet. He gingerly touched my shoulder. "I'm not upset with you. Sandulf carved his own path. I'm saddened by the disarray he left behind." His emotions seeped through his defeated posture. He cared for our wulfkin pack much more than Sandulf ever had. Botolf should have been alpha.

I hugged him.

We then made our way into the other bedroom. Within seconds, my vision adjusted to the darkness. The musty air mingled with Radu's wolf. Botolf flipped on the lights. Radu lay on a pile of fur blankets drawn to his chest. Cuts coated his arms, upper chest and neck, and I wondered whether Sandulf used a whip. He whimpered in his unconscious state, and that single sound seized my heart and squeezed it.

"Oh, Radu." His helpless and injured body tore me apart. Since childhood we had done everything together, and now I regretted getting him involved with finding the elixir. I'd ask him about the super wulfkin part later.

I moved to his side and stroked the hair behind his ear. He twitched, and his wild, silvery eyes snapped open.

Botolf was at my side. "It's all right, you're safe," he reassured Radu.

I backed away until I hit the wall, asking, "How could Sandulf do this?" Radu twitched, and I prayed for a fast recovery.

Botolf ushered me from the room and closed the door.

Once in the hallway, I shook my head. Silence permeated the house. How had I allowed such chaos to rule our pack? Lutia's words had reminded me of the dracwulf still on the loose, and I needed something to kick and punch. Plus, the pack remained prey to humans and the Varlac with that animal on the loose, regardless of what guarantee Sandulf promised us. And with him gone, any guarantees he had were now in question.

"I'll be back as soon as I can."

Botolf frowned but said, "Do what you need to do."

I dashed outside and followed Lutia's instructions, veering east. With no idea whether or not I was walking into a trap, I pushed forward with purpose.

The morning's crisp breeze promised a cold day. Forest animals scurried out of my path. Even the sun appeared to shine extra brightly in the cloudless sky. Entering a denser part of the woods, I slowed to a walk. Tree branches creaked, leaves crunched beneath my sneakers, and all the while the dracwulf's faint scent trickled past me.

Worry crept forward, and I contemplated the off chance that the beast had captured Connell. Though Botolf did say he left the woods. No sign of police at the pack house meant either Connell never made it home or he was freaking out all alone. I wished for the latter, no matter how mean that sounded. Once the dracwulf was dealt with, my focus was getting Connell back, no matter what it took. Otherwise, the emptiness settling inside me might kill me.

Distant murmurs caught me off guard. I halted. The wind shrilled, carrying a soft groaning noise. I hurried forward and soon emerged into a clearing. Farther on my left, the mountain range dropped into a wall of jagged boulders, overlooking woods rarely visited by humans.

Large animals never occupied the area due to the utter sheerness of the stone formation. Massive boulders protruded from the ground and bunched along the mountain's side with dozens of small caverns between the rocks. The lack of trees meant exposure to the elements as well as predators.

I hopped onto a jagged boulder, then another, making my way to a narrow sill. Once there, the path allowed only one easy way to get across without falling to my death. With my stomach pressed hard against the stone, I slid sideways. My fingers gripped the tiny ridges in the cliff for stability, despite the gale sawing at my clothes, and each step was calculated to avoid placing weight on loose or crumbled pebbles.

Over my shoulder, I observed the steep fall and the endless forest in the catchment. Treetops spanned out to the horizon. An eagle glided across the scenery. Braşov huddled on the other side of the mountain, unaware of what stalked its woods.

I neared the end of the narrow passage and I leapt onto the flat, wind-worn ledge jutting out of the mountain like a colossal bench. The frosty gale pinched my skin when a familiar smell hit me with such ferocity it left a coppery taste in my mouth, and in the same moment, the freezing winds tugged the smell from my grasp.

A wide curve of the rock formation brought me to a winding, ragged passageway. The wind occasionally stirred the metallic fragrance into the air, and I chased the trail to an upward tapered breach in the rock face. The wind's ferocity twisted around me, and I held onto the rough edges, peering inside. My shadow blocked the best part of the light, but blood overwhelmed my senses—and the familiarity returned. My legs weakened.

"Enre?"

Had the beast gorged on him out here? Lutia was so dead if that was the case. I bunched my hands, inhaled a lungful of icy air and burst into the cave.

Brown stone coated the inside, but diminished to total darkness deeper into the cavern.

I stepped aside and allowed light to spill forward. A current of wind shrieked past me, and I caught sight of someone lying at the back of the cavern. The floor ascended in front of me and the roof dropped. A body was elevated at the back. My breath caught in my throat.

He lay motionless on the stone platform, daylight spraying his body. His blue jeans hung on him, and a white T-shirt sandwiched between his back and the sandstone.

Despite his frail body, he was intact. The lesion at his neck had turned black, and someone had tended to his injury—Sandulf no doubt.

I rushed forward, forced onto all fours where the roof tapered downward. Lowering my ear to his nose, I listened for any signs of life and heard a frail, shallow breath, wheezing. *God, he was still alive.* I touched his pale cold cheek.

"It's me, Daciana. I'm here now," I told him. His face blurred behind my tears, and a tremble seized me. Why hadn't the dracwulf killed him?

Sandulf had kept Enre alive, tended to his wounds, fed him. But why leave him out here with a creature on the loose? Lutia knew everything and did nothing.

"Enre." I shook his shoulder lightly. "Can you hear me?" My tears dripped on him, and I stroked his forehead. "I found you, that's all that matters."

Emotions bubbled in my chest. They stung. Rage, sympathy, and loathing fought to gain control. I wrapped my arms around his legs, and inched them off the raised platform. I slipped my hands beneath his shoulders, looping them under his armpits, and shuffled his torso halfway down the ascending rock form.

A foul taste slicked over my tongue, awakening me to my surroundings, and I froze. Someone else had entered the cave. I recognized the newcomer at once and a sensation of death swarmed around me, like nothing I sensed before.

I jumped to my feet, or at least tried. My head banged into the ceiling, and I crashed onto my rump. A pulsating ache pounded across my vision, blurring the menace before me.

CHAPTER 22

A guttural rumble droned in my ears. Banging my head into the ceiling was not one of my brighter moments, but the small issue of my skull killing me didn't compare to the humungous problem, which loomed closer— the livid dracwulf. I shuffled away, and kept Enre at my back. Running away was out of the question. I wouldn't leave him. No way.

The dracwulf's enormous size blocked most of the light, and I recoiled. How the beast managed to squeeze into the narrow fissure still amazed me, yet there she was. Her broad chest heaved, frothing saliva seeped from her fangs, and her fierce roar bellowed across the cave. The hair on the back of her neck puffed and if the space permitted, the dracwulf might have even risen on hind legs.

She slinked closer, and my anger flared. Sandulf had known about her killing spree and did nothing to stop innocent people from dying or save Enre from his imprisonment. The dracwulf ate five humans in an uncontrollable frenzy, yet Enre remained untouched. I considered the possibility she sensed his wolf side, but her sudden conscience made no sense.

Standing in the cave with a monster left me with two choices—fight or die. Still unclear what changes my super wulfkin form might bring to the party, I curled my hands and started to lift myself up, even if every part of me screamed *run*.

The notion that my blood might kill the dracwulf crossed my mind, along with the risk of allowing her to chomp into me. Then another idea spun in my mind.

"He's mine, back off!" I shouted.

The dracwulf sprang forward, her talons extended and lips curled, exposing pointy teeth. I tripped backward over Enre's body. The beast gave a high-strung whimper and withdrew her arsenal midflight, landing so close her hot, pungent breath gushed over my face. She sniffed Enre's body like a caring mother and licked his cheek.

Her sneer grew with menace. Her squinted eyes fixed on me.

The notion of Lutia setting me up, hoping the animal finished me off in the cave, seemed credible.

The dracwulf shoved her snout into my chest with such force I smacked into the wall behind me. She continued to smell Enre's body, checking for injuries perhaps. Her close proximity nixed my escape plans.

Then it hit me, and I couldn't believe I'd been such a fool. The dracwulf had chosen Enre as her mate, and it hadn't occurred to me until now. *Idiot*. Why else would she protect him and shove me away? Kind of sweet if it didn't involve a blood-frenzied animal. The downside meant the beast would kill anything in her way to keep him.

My mind fled to Sandulf's casual take on Enre's capture. I cursed myself for not picking up the clue earlier. Perhaps Sandulf wanted Enre out of the pack, which left him in charge of only the wulfkin who would not dare challenge him, no matter how many rules he broke.

Jaws snapped in my direction, yet never close enough to

bite. If Enre were conscious, he might even radiate in pride, knowing two females were fighting over him.

Change of plans. "I don't think you're his type." I landed a hard blow to the bridge of her nose. She reared back and shook herself. In that split second, I rocked forward, and took hold of Enre's head. The hairy monster exploded in a growl, her mouth gaped open and her wicked fangs exposed.

To transform might leave me vulnerable for a few seconds, so I slipped my hands further beneath Enre's shoulders, to his armpits. The dracwulf lunged for me, and I jerked away, heaving Enre's body upright in one movement between us. His weight fell against me, and we stumbled into the wall. I locked my arms around his chest.

The next time the dracwulf went for me, I threw my forearm out in defense. Her teeth grazed my skin, tearing flesh and drawing blood. Quick to pull my arm back, I waited for a reaction. She tasted my blood after all, and it had killed Sandulf the other night.

The beast surged closer, now lashing higher, and with Enre's head slumped forward, she nicked my ear. *Shit, nothing.* Why had it burned Sandulf, then?

Short of breath, I edged toward the exit, sliding my back against the cold stone wall. Just my luck to pick the longer route but at least it was progress. I resisted the urge to wipe the warm trickle running down my neck from my ear and ducked behind Enre, while I staggered closer to the light, despite my trembling legs.

The animal screeched and paced, each time swatting me with her claws.

I whispered into Enre's ears, "Hold on, we're almost there."

The dracwulf nipped my arms. She thrashed herself about the cave, bumping the walls, charging at us, and then stopping at the last second. Her nostrils flared, heavy with whines.

Exhaustion started to claim my strength as I stumbled across another bumpy surface. But when sunlight warmed the back of my shoulder, I straightened up and found a new surge of adrenaline. Armed with a deep breath, I braced Enre tight and forced us backward through the gap. My arms scraped the rough edges, and I squealed in pain.

The dracwulf half-howled, half-barked in acceptance of a challenge I didn't mean to instigate. *Crap.*

Outside, the sun gleamed, and the wind thrashed my body. A line of blood snaked down my shoulder. Enre's weight tested my balance, yet I dragged him along the platform and hurried to put distance between the dracwulf and us, knowing I couldn't hold him for much longer.

The growls turned to whimpers. Her head was wedged out of the cave's mouth as she pushed herself through. If the dracwulf had not slaughtered innocent people, I might have felt compassion for her. Pressed against the rock, I inched farther away, the sun beating down on us. Unsure how we would cross the open path between the rocks and forest, my worries turned to the beast who exploded onto the ledge, causing rock fragments to cascade over the cliff.

Hunched low to the ground, she crawled toward us like a spider. Her ears pricked, fur bristled and incisors on display.

I reeled backward, exhaustion winning the battle against me. The coldness of the blustery weather didn't help. Under no circumstance would she allow me to take him. With Enre tight in my grasp, I kept moving.

She threw herself forward, and I shoved Enre and myself backward. Her razor teeth caught flesh and snagged on my sweatshirt at my side. She yanked with such force that Enre slipped from my arms, and I landed hard on my hip. The beast dragged me closer to the edge with her forward motion.

The fabric ripped from her mouth, but her talons stabbed into my calves as her hindquarters dropped over the cliff, dragging the rest of her down, trapping me in her plummet. I flailed about, screeching as the dracwulf hauled me over the stone surface toward my death. I grabbed for anything on the rock platform and came up short. My body rushed over the rock's edge, pulled by the mass of the dracwulf.

My talons burst free and scored the ground until they latched onto a ledge in the stone. I had stopped our descent, though we now both dangled off the side. She struggled and shook us both.

"Stop freakin' moving." Excruciating pain laced my legs and crept upward.

She didn't. Her claws dug deeper into me. I screamed, my voice echoing in the catchment. Her talons tore down my calves and gripped my joggers. The sensation jerked up my body. My shoes were slipping off and the dracwulf lost her hold and she dropped. Her wail was ear-shattering.

I hung from the ledge, and numbness started to crawl through my arms. Breaths rushed. I drew on my last rush of adrenaline and hauled myself up. Huddled on the sill, I glanced downward and willed my hands to take human form.

A swarm of trees encased the catchment. I calmed my breath. No birds flew around us, only the gale sang on the breeze. My gaze dropped lower. The dracwulf lay on a single ridge with no easy passage into the forest. She was still alive and already climbed to her feet. From the fall itself, she should be dead. Damn, I wanted her dead and every last bit of Sandulf's betrayal removed from the pack.

But now a small opportunity of time opened up for me to escape, and I rolled onto all fours, crawling toward Enre.

The animal already started bellowing.

I lifted Enre's fragile body, and a tingle buzzed up my arms and legs. His skin was tepid to the touch. My heart froze when his eyes slid open a crack, revealing the blueness of his pupils, which had washed away and no longer held the deepness they once radiated.

"Enre, it's me, Daciana. Can you hear me?"

No response. He just stared at me, like a lost child too scared to voice his words. A cold wind wiped the heat clammed to my skin. If someone had told me a week ago that I would lose Connell, kill Sandulf, rescue Enre, and become alpha, I would call them mad. Everything I desired had been ripped from me, and I questioned my own sanity now. Winning back Connell and saving Enre were my sole motivations, and I refused to give thought to my purpose if those things were taken away.

I pushed into a sloppy and slanted walk. My mangled legs stung each time I pressed weight on them, and a trail of blood followed behind us.

Sliding sideways along the rock form, I kept a vigilant eye out for the dracwulf. Once we reached the sharp boulders, I slowed my pace and stumbled downward in slow motion. At the gap between the rock and forest, I had no choice but to jump. Taking a few steps back, I tensed and ran, leaping at the last moment. My feet hit soil, and Enre's body bounced in my arms. Dropping to my knees, I whimpered. As soon as the pain in my legs subsided, I was back up and rushing into the woods.

I kept my focus on reaching the pack house before the dracwulf escaped from the precipice. Every part of my body trembled, but I refused to stop.

CHAPTER 23

*P*ast the rocks, I hastened into the forest, blundering past low-hanging branches and over dead logs. I had no energy to do anything more than walk straight. The mid-morning sunlight slanted through the canopy of trees, and its warmth wrapped me in a sense of false security. Unable to move faster, I kept checking over my shoulder and listening for noises, anything to indicate the dracwulf was closing in on us. I had taken her mate, and like me, she would never surrender. Her attack was inevitable once she managed to climb out of the gorge, especially with the easy-to-follow blood trail.

Enre's weight in my arms, which grew heavier the farther I trudged, bothered me less than the tears that refused to stop each time I thought about no longer having Connell. I'd lost him. A few times, my legs wobbled beneath me, and I leaned into a tree for a rest, never letting Enre out of my grasp.

At last, we reached the pack house, and I inhaled the scent of fried sausage on the wind. I rushed inside, greeted by silence. My foot kicked backward and slammed the door shut.

"I need some help!"

The kitchen door flung open, and an exhausted Botolf appeared. His hair was ruffled, patches of redness smeared his white shirt, and his expression turned aghast at the sight of Enre.

"You have another patient, doc." My voice choked on tears.

He stood still for a moment, placed a shaky hand to his forehead and mumbled,

"Dear God, you found him."

The air thickened and my breath accelerated. Botolf collected Enre into his arms and hurried toward the bedroom. A wave of heat shook me. I used the wall to steady myself and let out the uncontrollable sob I had held inside. I let everything out, so I'd be ready for the next round of onslaughts.

I wiped my cheeks, preparing to join Botolf, when Lutia stepped out from the hallway. I paused, waiting for her smart-ass mouth to kick into overdrive. Instead, she stood there, her posture tight, crumpled forward, and her gaze darted to mine.

She fidgeted with the collar on her black trench coat-style dress. "I'm glad you found him alive." Her words rang soft and polite. "I know we haven't been getting along lately—"

"Actually, we've never gotten along."

"You're right, and I should've tried harder." The side of her mouth pinched together.

"But I'm hoping we can change that and forget the past."

I inched closer. "I'm not in the mood for your jokes."

"I gave you Enre." She backed away. "I deserve some recognition."

My first reaction was to jump her, certain it would give me satisfaction. My muscles tensed as the words grated past my throat. "You left Enre in a cave with a dracwulf, you killed a human in my apartment hoping to frame me, and kidnapped an inspector, revealing us to him."

She shifted her weight from one foot to another. "Nah. Sandulf, gave me the orders."

"You didn't have to follow them."

"He would have hurt me."

My fist pressed to my lips, and I inhaled deep. "I don't believe anything you say." Her mouth dropped open.

Botolf entered the room and halted.

The sour taste on my tongue relighted. How I yearned to break her and make her beg for mercy, but then, would that make me any better than Sandulf? He used force and threats to control the pack. I intended to change things under my leadership, which meant doing things differently. "I'll give you a task to perform. If I'm satisfied, you'll gain yourself the lowest rank in the pack, equal to moonwulf. If not, you're out."

Her chin dipped into her chest. "What do I have to do?"

"Every little thing Botolf asks of you. He will be your mentor." I turned to Botolf. "If that is okay with you?"

He nodded. "Of course."

"Settled. Botolf will inform me of any instance where you don't follow his instructions, and there will be no second chances."

"For how long?"

"Count yourself lucky. Now get out of my way."

She remained frozen on her feet with her fingers splayed out in a fan against her chest, then turned and dragged herself into the hallway.

I should have thrown her out of the pack instead of giving her another chance. I must

have hit my head hard in the cave.

"You did the right thing. I'm proud of you." Botolf squeezed my shoulder. "Did you know your ear's bleeding?"

"It's nothing." I wiped my injury and discovered a nice chunk of flesh missing from my earlobe.

"Stop being stubborn, let me at least bandage the wound and clean the scratches on your arms."

I agreed and followed him into the bedroom. Enre lay on the fur blankets on his back, and anyone else might have guessed he was asleep by the color in his cheeks. I cringed at the deep pain shooting in my ear as Botolf cleaned the torn flesh.

In no time, Botolf patched me up, and I washed the dried blood off my arm. Before long, I stood in the kitchen, leaning against the countertop and stuffing a third sausage into my mouth. The sway of trees beyond the window numbed my thoughts, and I welcomed the silence.

Botolf entered.

"How's he doing?"

"I can't believe he's survived the injuries. Someone tended to his wound, and what he needs now is rest. We'll have to wait until he's stronger to know if he will heal completely."

"A need for survival can sometimes aid healing." Had I just tried to cover up for Sandulf?

"Survival can't wash clean a mortal wound," he said with a strained voice.

"We both know Sandulf kept Enre out there in the cave." Botolf shook his head, and my gaze fell to the floor as I warned, "The dracwulf will soon be here and not too happy, either. She wants Enre back."

His body stiffened. "Why didn't Sandulf finish her off?"

"He was scared of losing the last real family he had after Alina's death, though I don't know why he just didn't have pups with Lutia." I stuffed another sausage into my mouth, and gulped the morsel in one go. "Not that it excuses his behavior."

I proceeded to tell him about Enre's capture, Sandulf's threats to me, the larger pack coming for our territory, the attacks on the humans, and the police wolf hunts. I didn't leave anything out, except my love for Connell. I stared at my hands, remembering the last time he held me in his arms, tight and devoted. He promised to love me forever, but would he now? The sting in my chest returned. I wished I hadn't turned into a wulfkin, I wished I could have spent my life alongside Connell, smothered in his affection. Sadness spread inside me, and I had no idea how to even begin letting go of the constant hurt.

I started to walk away. "We need to bolt down the house. I'll do the outside." "Maybe Sandulf was confused."

I stopped. "What could possibly confuse him? That he mated with a wild wolf and allowed the animal to kill humans while he protected the bloodthirsty beast? Or that he condemned our pack to the Varlac and exposed us to a human? What part could have possibly confused him?"

"Let's be rational in our thinking, Daciana. Things don't just happen." Botolf gripped his chin. "A series of events would have made him behave the way he had."

Sandulf knew a menace dangled over the pack and did nothing. "It doesn't matter, he's gone. He was ready to join Alina a long time ago, and we didn't see it." Drawing closer to Botolf, I gripped his forearm. "There's no time to evaluate every scenario. Sandulf is guilty. The dracwulf is on her way here, and we're not prepared."

"I admit, I saw it coming and hoped I misinterpreted his actions. I've sat back and let too much pass me by in the years gone," he confessed.

His struggle to accept Sandulf's betrayal was difficult to watch. "We need to focus on the problem at hand."

He stared through me, at nothing in particular, and I didn't expect him to respond.

"I'm not as strong as I once was, and it's only us and Lutia. Matias hasn't returned to the house since your ceremony. He's agitated by what happened and took off into the woods.

Radu has no strength to fight. Lutia probably does, but she pretends she doesn't."

"I don't trust her. Maybe get her to lock up the windows inside the house." I pushed the sleeves up on my shirt. "Move Radu into my room near Enre. It's easier to protect them if they're together." I wondered if the basement offered a better hiding spot. But its entry and exit was a flimsy wooden panel, and left us cornered, so I kept to the original plan.

Snatching the last sausage, I pushed past the back door. How I would take out the dracwulf on my own, I still needed to work out. I toyed with the idea of using Lutia as bait or a distraction, and laughed to myself as I pictured her horrified reaction if I suggested such a thing.

The outside air held scents of pine needles, soil, and greenery, but no dracwulf.

At the kitchen window, I unlatched the metal clasps on each of the thick wooden boards on either side of the glass. Sandulf made the house defensible against potential attacks by other wulfkin packs. Every opening of the dwelling sported a covering, and once in place, only two doors permitted entry or escape. The security planks were not impenetrable, but they bought time. Never before had the shutters been drawn and yet there I was, locking down the place. The irritating notion that I didn't stand a chance against the dracwulf tested my nerves. Bites and scratches were all I managed during past encounters against the animal, but I reminded myself I was a powerful wulfkin now. After all, I had killed a wulfkin with my blood. If only I knew how to turn that ability back on.

I wrenched shut the heavy slats one at a time. Due to their weight and force, I shoved my palms against the timbers to bring them together. The harsh movement stung my ear. I grasped the iron-studs on the short chain and clasped the panels shut. Once closed, the fasteners were removable by industrial clippers. Yeah, a bit of overkill, but needed when dealing with beasts with unnatural strength.

The crunch of dry leaves from the woods roused my attention, and my senses sharpened. I crept closer to the sound. The direction of the wind masked the scent of the culprit and my wolf readied to emerge. I stepped into the undergrowth, scanned the trees, plants and foliage.

For a second, everything fell silent. My chest heaved. When a gray rabbit hopped out of the huddled shrubs, I cursed under my breath and relaxed. Tempted to catch the bunny for a snack to serve it up for frightening me, I returned to the next window and continued securing the house until my feet nudged the basement door.

After securing three sides of the house, my arms ached. I paused and let the tingling sensation fade. At the front of the property, I latched the last two windows. Stepping away from the house, I admired my handy work. It resembled an evacuated property, boarded up by the government to stop squatters moving inside.

The soft drone of a car engine distracted my musing.

In the distance, a flicker of metallic red flashed between the trees. A car curved off the track and an Audi pulled into our driveway. The tires crunched to a halt on the gravel. Connell climbed out and shut the door with a thud, and my heart melted. He scanned the surrounding area before striding in my direction, his blond hair tumbling around his face. The wrinkled state of his hooded sea green sweater and black jeans said it all.

He was freaked.

My feet stuck to the ground, unable to move, let alone say anything.

A wave of heated rage accompanied his harried, wild expression, though he managed a neutral smile, as if we might be passing each other on the street.

"Connell." No other words formed because all I yearned

to say was *take me back*. He folded his arms across his chest, stopping a few steps in front of me. "Nice to see you, too."

My voice quivered, and I couldn't stop the babble. "I'm sorry for everything."

He exhaled noisily. "I didn't know what to expect, but I had to come back here." He

cleared his throat. "My mind's been going through the events. Over and over. In theory, yes, maybe werewolves exist, but my logical mind refuses to accept it, even if I did see it." He looked around him as if expecting someone to jump out from the woods. "I couldn't tell anyone at the station without being ridiculed and forced onto medical leave. That leaves me in a very uncomfortable situation. Do I get the police involved to stop this man-eating beast at the risk of looking like a fool, or continue to lie to them, at the cost of my career?"

I swallowed hard and decided to divulge everything to him, refusing to feed him any more lies. He was already privy to our ceremony and transformations, so why pretend otherwise? But a lengthy conversation was out of the question right then, as the dracwulf could turn up at any moment, hungry to reclaim Enre. I didn't need Connell to face any more danger because of me.

He said, "Why couldn't you be upfront and honest like a normal person?"

"It killed me to not tell you the truth."

"Oh wait, you're not normal, are you? You attended those murder scenes and knew what was responsible for the killings. You lied to my face."

His words stung, and while his anger and uncertainty spoke, insults made any wulfkin defensive. "Would you have believed me? Of course not. That's why we're trying to catch the animal ourselves."

He clutched his chest. "Trying. So it's still on the loose. Your methods aren't working. That much is obvious." His hand reached to his lower back and retrieved a handgun. "I should have done this the first time I saw the animal, instead of listening to you."

A sudden coldness hit me. "Planning to shoot me again?"

"I didn't shoot—" His words trailed off. "That was you? But . . . how? My head hurts." His hand dropped and the gun dangled from his fingers, pointing to the ground. He staggered toward the woods and slumped to his knees, murmuring something about a dream. Boundaries between sanity and madness were easily crossed, and I worried for him.

I walked to where he crouched. "I wasn't myself that night," I said, in a calm voice, and placed a hand on his shoulder.

He flinched.

I knelt next to him. "I can only imagine how difficult this is for you. It's tearing me apart to have you push me away. The fact of the matter is wulfkin—or werewolves as you call them—do exist. For your own good sense, you need to accept this or it will eat away your mind."

"Goddamn it, Daci!" He snapped to face me. "You think I'm crazy because I can't accept you're a bloody werewolf." Hysterical laughter rolled past Connell's lips, though his expression held no hilarity. "They don't exist." He tucked his head into his bent knees. "I must be going mad."

Aside from chirping birds, a quiet enveloped us. Berating myself for being a colossal fool and not trusting Connell earlier, I stretched my legs out and tried to devise an excuse for him to leave without pushing him farther away. I had lied to him, like his ex-wife, and now my jar of secrets lay smashed open. There was nothing for me to do until he decided to forgive me.

"This is not an easy thing to admit to myself. I've been working on the force for years and there's always been a rational explanation for every single incident. This, here," he looked sideways at me, "is not rational."

"I know you're confused, and I owe you a complete explanation of everything. And then it's up to you whether you choose to accept the truth, or let it drive you insane. No more lies from me. But you need to leave this place. Now."

He frowned. "Why do I always fall for the liars?"

Holding myself tight, I ignored the lump in my throat swelling. "I can't say sorry enough times to show you how terrible I feel, and I'll let you decide once you've heard my side. But I can't do this right now. Please Connell, you have to leave." I stood up.

His brow creased. "No, tell me now. I can't cope with not believing my own memories."

I paced across the yard. My hand rubbed a sore ache settling in my forehead. My initial instinct was to physically force Connell into his car, thought that might scare him into never coming back to me.

"That creature you saw in the city is on her way here, and she's not coming over for a cup of tea, if you get my drift." I squatted next to him to appear less intimidating. "She's on her way, and really pissed. That's why you need to go."

Lines formed at the sides of Connell's eyes as he squinted against the sun's glare. "If you're hunting this wolf, why is it coming to you?"

"Because I have her mate."

"God, I'm so confused. Why is this animal so bent on attacking people, and you're not?" His glance darted to the woods.

"The animal that attacked us in the city is different. She has no human side, and is pure wolf, but ten times more territorial and vicious."

Connell climbed to his feet, and I clutched his arm. "You need to leave now." My fingers squeezed. "I'd die if anything happened to you."

His mouth opened and closed several times before his words spilled. "I'm not going anywhere. I'll help you stop it."

I took his hand in mine. "You'd be safer at your place. I'll come and see you afterward. Please." The drumming of my pulse thudded in my ears.

He drew his hand out of mine. "I wasn't safe when I was abducted. How do you think I found you? I didn't even know you lived out here."

Oh joy, he's never going to forgive me or take me back, but rather than self-pity, anger flared awake. Furious words rushed toward my lips, but a great roar bellowed from the surrounding forest, and I froze. Hairs on the back of my neck spiked as if hell itself licked the length of my spine.

Connell lifted the pistol to his chest. He stumbled closer to the house in quick, jerky steps, all the while scouring the perimeter.

My stomach clenched. "Fuck. She's here."

Connell stepped in front of me, pushing me behind him. His touch quivered with the thrashing of his heartbeat. "Go inside the house, Daci." He drew a fast breath and scanned the forest, clutching his pistol tight.

I paid no attention.

On the wind, the sound of branches cracking and the beat of paws pounding the earth accelerated. A loud cacophony of birds squawked as they burst free from the crown of trees nearby, and there in the distance the dracwulf emerged, plunging through the woodland, her strength crushing shrubbery and undergrowth like a military tank ramming opponents.

"Shoot her," I cried.

Gunfire exploded, and I cringed from the *bang*. The bullet tore half the dracwulf's ear off, though she continued her rampage without a flinch.

"It's moving too fast," Connell's voice quivered.

When a second bullet fired and caught her on the shoulder, she skidded to a halt across the driveway and roared. Her head bowed forward, and her lips curled over pointy incisors.

I contemplated my chances of transforming to take her on my own, but knew Connell would intervene and probably get himself killed. I dropped the idea.

Taking a few quick steps toward the house, I dragged Connell alongside me. "We'll need more than a few bullets to stop her."

We spun about, dashed past the front door, and slammed it shut behind us. I hurried to lock the second, metal door. At the same time that the deadbolts clicked into place, a thunderous blow smashed against the wall. The whole place shook, hinges creaked and wood splintered.

Connell started to pace. "This is really bad."

I switched on the lights and watched him slide loose hair strands behind his ears. A low, droning growl echoed from outside.

"Why the hell does it smell like a barnyard in here?" Connell inspected the empty space.

Botolf tore into the room with rushed breaths. "Bloody Sandulf and his dracwulf." He spotted Connell, whose perspiration tickled my nose. "Probably not a good idea for him to be here right now."

"Too late."

"I'm standing right here. You can talk to me," Connell said to Botolf.

I eyeballed him. "This is Botolf, the eldest of our pack. He released you the other night in the woods."

For a few moments, he said nothing. "I remember you cutting me and collecting my blood in a vial or something. Glad I could provide you with a snack."

"It's not what you think. He did it for me," I said.

Connell scratched his head and then offered his hand to the older wulfkin. "I'm Connell, Daci's friend."

Friend? Had he just called me a friend? My mind froze, unable to process anything. Tapping my fingers to my lips, I stared at Connell who gave a slight shrug.

I turned to Botolf. "Well . . . seeing you've met my friend, why don't you take him to the bedroom, so everyone is in one place." I narrowed my eyes at Connell. "I'm going to do a quick check for the dracwulf, since she's fallen too quiet for my liking."

"Daci—"

I lifted my palm at Connell and stopped his words. He looked as uneasy as I felt. Maybe I should pat his arm and thank him for making the decision to break-up an easy one for us, or kiss and beg him to tell me he wants me back. I didn't know what to do. Was he still my boyfriend? I strode into the kitchen like nothing bothered me, when I yearned to run away crying.

Slumped beside the countertop, I contemplated the possibility that Connell might have just broken up with me, officially. Was I really surprised? I kneaded my chest, easing my breath. Why call me a friend? Why not partner, girlfriend or lover? And the way he shrugged, that small gesture, jabbed my heart a million times. The cold awareness started to cut into my stomach like razor blades, shredding deeper. I leaned forward and hugged my gut. Every part of me shivered and constricted.

A long exhale escaped my lips. It was the wrong time for me lose my cool, or let my personal issues distract me. I had a dracwulf to eliminate.

I lifted my chin and re-entered the rest of the house, listening for the beast's whereabouts, leaving the bedroom for last, but all I could hear was my pulse hammering inside my head. There were no sounds outside, so I joined the others, greeted by a wave of fear, electricity, and a heavy stillness in the room.

Connell leaned into the far corner, and I refused to meet his gaze. Radu slumped in an old armchair that once belonged in his underground post. His forehead gleamed with sweat and every so often, his breath rasped. Lutia sat against the wall, her legs stretched out and arms behind her head. She studied me, yet fell short of any crafty remarks.

I touched Botolf's shoulder. "How's Enre holding up?"

"Still asleep."

Enre's fragile body, lying on the fur blankets, reminded me of how I found him in the cave, clinging onto life. A coral complexion bathed his cheeks, and I suspected his stubbornness kept him alive.

"What's happening out there?" Botolf asked.

"Zilch. Not a thing. She's possibly checking the house for the best point of entry. That's what I would do." In truth, the silence terrified me because she could break inside at any moment, and I was still short a plan.

Botolf cleared his throat. "What are we going to do?"

Lutia's loud cackle broke the silence. "She's not going to hurt anyone if we give her Enre."

"Are you mad?" I said.

Connell pushed himself from the corner. "Why is she here? It's obvious she doesn't care about the rest of you. Even I can see it, and I've been here two seconds."

"Idiot human. Shut your mouth." Lutia's face twisted into a feral expression. "Lutia." A rumble echoed my voice.

Connell marched toward her with determination and swung the gun into her face. "Don't think I forgot you trying to eat me."

She waved a hand in dismissal and forced a strained smile. "I wanted to scare you, not taste you, though I bet you're sweet." She shot a glance my way and winked.

Connell's eyes rolled, his nostrils flared. "You don't fool me. I vote on throwing her to the wolf thing while we get away." The sarcasm in his voice was lost because he wasn't kidding around.

For a long moment, I considered his proposal for no reason other than to torment Lutia.

She gripped her knees. "You're not going to listen to him?" Her eyes met mine.

I ran a hand through my hair. "It's tempting."

She squinted, her lips thinned, and her words quivered. "You wouldn't."

I touched Connell's arm. "Put down the gun. We're all here for the same reason. Keep focused on the enemy who's outside." To my surprise, I managed to keep my voice composed.

He withdrew and tramped over to the far wall, holding Lutia in his sight. "I don't trust her."

"Good, that makes two of us."

"I have a shotgun in my trunk. Maybe it will buy us time," Connell said.

I nodded and stretched out an open palm. "Give me your keys."

He shook his head. "I'm coming."

"No, you're staying in here until I return." Unintentionally, a snarl hung off my last word, and despite his racing heartbeat, he didn't flinch.

He retrieved the keys from his jean pocket and threw them at me. I caught them in one hand and stepped backward, refusing to give any thought to his rigid posture or parted lips.

"Lutia, you'll keep guard over Enre and Radu. Botolf, you're with me." Connell would keep an eye on Lutia, and I counted on him using the gun if needed.

I headed into the hallway. "Let's go."

Once in the main room, Botolf said, "Maybe we should wait for the dracwulf to tire herself out."

"She won't give us that chance, you know that." Even as I spoke, I sensed the animal outside. "I'm going to distract her and give you enough time to grab the gun and dash back inside." I dangled the keys for him to take.

He clutched them, turning his knuckles white. "What's your plan?" "When I yell, just do your part, don't worry about me."

"But, you won't—"

"Leave it to me. You focus on keeping safe."

Instead of resisting me, his shoulders straightened and he stood ready to fight. After a quick hug, I hurried into the kitchen and unlocked the padlocks with unsteady hands.

The backyard was deserted. Stillness clung to everything. Not even the tree branches swayed. The breeze froze with bated breath, and I released a loud whistle, carving the peace.

The dracwulf hollered and materialized at the corner of the house, growling and slobbering on herself.

"Botolf, go!" I slammed the door shut and sprinted into the thick underbrush, toward the forest.

A sudden wind wailed between the oversized trees, carrying the smell of dung and wet wolf fur. The thudding of paws behind me quickened. She was damn fast. Just a bit of time was all I needed. I hurried, ripping the underbrush getting caught on my jeans.

Her grunts grew closer. Louder.

My foot snagged on a tree root. I tumbled forward and rolled onto my back, jutting my arm upward.

Enormous jaws latched on my forearm, and the pain belted through me. She shook her head, shaking me with her. A hot, putrid breath gushed from her nose and over my face. Her saliva seeped onto my chin, while tiny eyes with intelligence behind them studied me. I admitted my plan to remain in human form was flawed. Strength always won over agility.

Desperately, I smashed my brow into her nose and regretted the decision as soon as the dancing lights distorted my vision. She jerked, releasing me with a growl. I dragged myself backward, but not for long. She leapt over the top of me. In reflex I threw my damaged arm to cover my face. Her teeth tore a chunk of my flesh. Nausea flashed through me, and I released the ululating cry burning my throat.

She freed a triumphant howl.

A banging sound resonated in the air, and the dracwulf stiffened. Her head jolted up, and she thrust herself off me, heading toward the house, growling.

An itchy inferno spread through my insides. I embraced my unrestrained fury, rushing a full transformation while I climbed to my feet and scampered after her, knowing too well it might hamper my injured arm from fully healing.

I bolted to the front yard to find Botolf splayed on the hood of Connell's Audi, and the dracwulf standing over him. The shotgun lay strewn near the front wheel. I stopped dead in my tracks.

The dracwulf twisted her head my way, and I swear she wore a grin.

Botolf winced.

I held the beast's attention, giving Botolf enough time to slip away. He slid beneath the beast's arm and crawled underneath the Audi.

Quick to respond, she started to ram her side into the car. Each collision lifted the vehicle farther off the ground, and in no time it would expose Botolf.

I leapt forward, throwing my entire weight into the dracwulf. She fell onto the front hood, smashing the windshield.

I landed on my rump and jumped to my feet.

"My car!" Connell's voice shrieked and shot two bullets into the animal's hind legs, just missing me, followed by the click of an empty ammo chamber.

Blood darkened her fur, marking the Audi. She slipped off the vehicle and onto the ground. Her long, viscous tongue drooped between sharp fangs.

My gaze shifted to Connell whose rapid breathing called

to my hunger, and my pulse sped. Not good. His eyes bulged as he watched me. A dazed guise captured his expression. His grip strangled the gun in his hands. He deserved major brownie points for not running away.

The dracwulf, already on all fours, retreated behind the car.

Jumping to the front of the vehicle, I yanked Botolf from beneath it.

"I thought that was the end of me." He grabbed my paw and struggled to his feet. Then I spotted Connell crouching near his Audi, collecting the shotgun.

"Get out of there!" Botolf shrieked.

The dracwulf reappeared from behind the vehicle, targeting Connell who was too busy fiddling with the weapon to notice the oncoming menace.

I launched myself toward him.

He was quick and hurled the butt of the shotgun toward the beast's snout. She dodged it and bit into his thigh, tearing through material and flesh.

Connell yelped; a horrific sound. The gun fell from his grasp.

The dracwulf snatched it into her jaws, chomping it into several pieces.

Connell fell backward against me.

The dracwulf sneered, blood spilling from her wobbly legs.

I stepped in front of Connell and pushed him toward the house.

My sliced arm blazed in pain, but my thoughts centered on retribution. A cool breeze swished the hairs along my neck. I threw myself forward. The dracwulf slipped out of reach, stepping sideways. Catching myself, I mimicked her low posture. We both crept counter clockwise, holding each other's glares. I attacked, and she swiped her large paw, slashing my cheek. Stooped lower, I lurched forward again, that time biting her front leg, crunching bone.

I retreated slightly and circled the wounded animal.

A peek over my shoulder saw Connell and Botolf safe near the front door. While wounded, I might defeat the beast. Maybe. But at the cost of permanent damage to myself. In a final decisive act, I spun about and sprinted into the backyard. The dracwulf took the bait and gave chase.

Skidding into a sudden turn, I plunged through the wooden doors to the house basement. The wood split under my weight, and I tumbled down the stairs, thudding to the cement floor. Perhaps that wasn't the best tactic. There wasn't any time for a rational plan.

Up on my feet, I hurried a transformation back into human form.

The dracwulf plummeted into the darkened basement behind me, tumbling onto her side.

I snatched the padlock keys and dove inside the farthest pen, slamming it, knowing the locks clicked shut once the doors closed.

Standing at the back of the prison, I coaxed the dracwulf to follow in the adjacent cubicle, by dangling my arm through the bars, hoping she fell for my trick.

Desperation drove the dracwulf to plunge into the empty cell. I rushed forward and kicked my leg out between the metal rods, banging the door to her cell. She was locked inside.

I shuffled away from her cell.

Her body smashed into the bars, and the enclosure shook. Ramming the dividers, she howled.

I unlocked my padlock and got out.

The prison would hold the dracwulf for the time being, at least until I got Connell to safety.

Back in the house, he was propped alongside the wall

with both hands clutching his wounded thigh, and tension gripping his face.

"What were you thinking? I told you to remain inside," I said.

His mouth opened, but when his gaze found me, his brows lifted. A mix of shock and pleasure comprised his expression. Fair enough, considering I stood in the middle of the room naked.

Connell's skin paled; blood coated his hands and pooled around him.

Botolf entered, holding a towel. "Where is she?"

"In the cell downstairs." My voice raced with adrenaline.

"I'm going back to finish her off. I just need a knife to make it quick."

Botolf's body stiffened. "I can't stop his bleeding. It's too deep. He needs to get to a hospital before he loses any more blood."

I looked over at Connell, who was as pale as a sheet of paper, and then turned to Botolf. "This is why you need to get a driver's license."

I cringed on the inside and held back the rage flooding my chest. And there was no way I'd trust Lutia with Connell. They'd probably end up killing each other.

Connell's smoldering eyes were still on me. How could I say no to saving his life? The man I loved.

"Shit," I said. "I'll take him. But you need to keep watch over the dracwulf since the cell won't hold her for long. Take Lutia with you. I'll be back as soon as I can."

I hurried to my bedroom. Quick to slip on ripped jeans and a hooded top, I snatched black sneakers from the pile of old clothes and joined Connell again. The first thing I noticed was that the wound on my arm had already closed up and healed. I knelt near Connell and proceeded to tie my shoelaces. "Let's head off then."

I wrapped my arm around him and helped him to his feet.

"Rest your weight on me." With Botolf holding his other side, we carried him to his battered Audi.

Once outside, Botolf cleared away the shattered glass from the front seats. I leaned forward, holding Connell's weight, but his hand pushed me away, and he inched into the car on his own.

I was in for one fun car ride.

I ploughed the Audi along the dirt track toward the city with only the repetitive sound of a grunting motor and crunching gravel reverberating through my skull. Connell remained slumped in the passenger seat and groaned each time the car hit a bump. The non-existent windshield poured a gush of air over us.

Ironically, inside my head a relationship between him and me was possible. Why not? My secrets flew free, and if he loved me for what I was, no problem. Except for the small hitch of him accepting the existence of wulfkin and then wanting to date one. On top of everything, I had placed him in harm's way, and he knew it. There was no undoing that mess.

Branches slashed in through the battered window, and I jerked out of instinct, swerving off the track.

Connell moaned.

Rather than make the situation worse with a smart-ass comment, I focused on a smooth ride.

At the edge of the woods, a policeman waited. Connell forced himself to sit upright, covered his leg with his hand, and turned to me. "Keep going, don't slow down."

I guided the car over the curb, leading us out of the forest and onto a city road, while Connell flashed his badge to the guard. He slumped back into his seat after that.

Past the line of concrete apartments, tall buildings jutted out in a halo curve where the hub of the city sat like a gray wasteland.

We stopped at the traffic lights, and I patted down my wild hair.

"Dumpsters don't come any closer than the trash you're driving."

I cringed at the young male's voice from the car alongside us. Unfortunately, on that particular street, young boys raced each other in jazzed-up cars, and they came complete with wisecracks. I turned to face the guy who traveled alone, snapped my fangs out and snarled.

He jolted in his seat, yelped and floored his vehicle through the red light. *Oops.* Lucky for both of us, no other cars traveled on the road.

"Real classy, Daci." Connell grumbled beneath his breath. "You could have killed him."

"You're never happy, are you?"

He released a rushed breath. "Not since I found out you are one big lie. I might as well be in this car with a stranger, because I don't know a single truth about you."

I raised an eyebrow. "Not completely true. You know I'm a wulfkin, my pack lives in the Carpathian woods, and I've trapped the dracwulf in my basement. So, you know more about me than anyone else outside the pack."

His head shook. "That's not what I mean."

I strangled the steering wheel. "Then what? I told you before, I couldn't tell you what I was, and even if I had, would you have believed me? Look at how you reacted when you did find out." I waved my hand in front of me. "All freaked out."

"Don't you dare."

"What?" I stole a peek across my shoulder and met his scowl. Some blood from his thigh had spilled onto the leather seat, teasing my nostrils.

"Don't turn this on me."

The light switched to green, and I kicked my foot into the accelerator, thankful the chilly wind ripped the scent from my grasp. "I get it, you're angry at me. I lied and kept information from you, but—"

"You don't get it."

I caught sight of his flushed cheeks.

"You exposed me to something I didn't understand, and . . . ." He paused, staring at his bloody hands like he was deep in thought. "When will it happen to me?"

"What are you talking about?" The notion that his mind snapped beyond repair crossed my thoughts. Not to mention hysteria.

He stared at me, incredulous. "When will I turn into a werewolf?"

I burst into laughter at the absurdity and considered it a blessing to find anything funny at that point. "Don't believe everything you see on TV."

"But the animal bit me."

"Yes, it did." I swerved the car off the road. "I'm a wulfkin, which is a different kind of wolf, not a fictional werewolf."

His head cocked to the side.

I inhaled a shaky breath. "Wulfkin are not changed by bites. We are born that way.

We're not controlled by the full moon, and silver doesn't affect us. We rule our wolf side and transform at will, and our senses are better than most animals. I can smell your shampoo fragrance, what you ate this morning, and hear the racing of your pulse each time you're around me."

His lips parted and the hardness in his gaze melted. He

worried about transforming into a creature like me. So, how could he love what he feared? My stomach plummeted along with any hope I had of rekindling our relationship.

Connell shifted. His jaw clenched as he pressed his palms into his thigh. "There was always something different about you." He lifted one shoulder. "But I never thought more of it. Like your enormous appetite yet you remain slim, your knowledge of animals for someone so young, and the unexplained nights I couldn't track you down."

"I had no choice." I reached over and slid a fallen blond strand off his cheek. "But I never intended to hurt you. I want to be with you."

He watched me. His mocha eyes glittered in the sun. Maybe he considered my words and pondered how to respond, or maybe the pain he felt from his injury froze him in a tomb of agony.

I thrust the gear into drive and started to take off when his warm, sticky hand found my leg. "Daci, I won't lie to you. I can't stop loving you, even if I tried. But you've hurt me, really bad. And I don't know if I can continue this with you." He fell silent for a few moments. "Maybe I need more time. I don't know."

My throat dried and the last spark in me dwindled. I refused to look at him and instead mumbled a word, which sounded like *okay*. The road ahead of me stretched into a never- ending conduit, and every part of me crumbled on the inside. Connell was splitting up with me. I chewed on my lip and bit hard each time a tear threatened to spill free. The wind became my friend, wiping my waterworks clear, and a sick miasma swirled in my stomach.

He withdrew his arm, and already I missed his touch, his warmth fading with each passing second.

"Please Daci, don't make this harder than it is."

A million excuses floated in my head about why he

should reconsider and take me back, but only three words drizzled out.

"I love you."

Tears ran down my cheek, and I swiped them clean. "I risked everything to be with you."

"You didn't have to kill that Sandulf guy for me." The strain lines returned to his mouth. "And what about the animal in your basement? What happens now?"

"First, that's what a pack does. When the alpha endangers those under his leadership, he has two options, and Sandulf had no plans of walking away from us. Plus, he was going to have you killed." I brushed hair out of my face. "Second, I won't release the animal in my basement. She was never meant to live, so you don't need to worry about her."

"You make it sound like I should be happy you killed this alpha." He tore his gaze from me and studied the apartments blurring past.

My heart struck my ribcage. "No, it's not what I mean, but forget it, you wouldn't understand anyway." His accusations were more than I could handle in one day, and a void slowly crept through me.

We approached the center of the city where the traffic picked up, but our conversation flatlined.

Connell twitched in his seat and scratched his forehead. "The urine tests from the crime scenes have revealed some strange results."

I stared at him and the bloody streak across his brow.

"The police detected what they're calling mutated wolf DNA." He cocked an eyebrow. "They're keeping the case open until they find the animal, and search parties are being dispatched into the woods today or tomorrow."

"And the wolf hunts?"

"The Council has voted against them, which means no kills, only search parties. No one will be allowed to enter the mountains except those with permits."

Relief weaved through me. With the dracwulf captured and the pack under my orders, the cops were welcome to wander the forest until their shoes wore out.

"The police will also poke around your house in the woods. They have five dead bodies to explain to families, and the public and won't give up easily."

"As they should. It's their job." A smile forced itself across my lips

Connell frowned. "Don't you understand? You won't be able to run around in your wolf form."

"I know what you mean. Once I deal with the wolf in my basement, we'll have nothing to hide. We will be park rangers doing our job. As long as you keep our secret." "If you're asking that question, you really don't know me."

He turned his attention to the buildings rushing past us. "You'll be called into the station soon regarding the victim in your apartment. Though it seem they don't have anything to pin you to it as Vasile validated your alibi of being at work all day."

After another bout of the silent treatment, I swerved into the hospital parking lot, switched off the ignition and climbed out. By the time I reached the passenger door, Connell was already limping toward the front doors of the Sfântul Constantin hospital; guarded by a number of smokers.

Ambulance sirens cried in the distance, and I slipped beneath his arm, taking some of his weight. He didn't protest.

"Daci, I tried to keep you out of police involvement, but with the other detective in charge of the murder case in your apartment yent, I have no say." He expelled a pained hiss. Squeezing his eyes tight, Connell stopped for a few seconds, and then staggered on.

"Don't worry about that. Let's get you help," I told him.

My head whirled with questions, like was I still suspected

of murdering the woman found at my place, had the police found wolf DNA there, and what other abnormalities did they uncover at the crime scenes? I asked none of those things, and instead held Connell tight against me.

Once we were in the foyer, antiseptic and lemon bleach smells stung my nose. We hobbled through the corridors toward reception and in no time gained the nurses' attention.

I explained that a wild dog attacked him and counted on them giving him rabies' shot, just in case. Connell's whines intensified. He sat in a wheelchair, they whisked him away, and I was right there by his side, our fingers intertwined.

We passed patients attached to drips shuffling down the pale-green linoleum. A heart monitor went crazy and beeped. Doctors and nurses barged past us to get to that patient.

Connell's pulse rose, and his hold squeezed. Sweat beads caked his brow.

"It'll be okay," I said. "You've lost a lot of blood."

We entered the emergency ward, and the nurse wheeled Connell to a vacant bed. His hand slipped free, and my arm dropped by my side. A young man sped from across the room, accompanied by two more nurses, and moved to Connell's side. "He'll need stitches for sure, and cleaning. Prep him," the young doctor said and dashed to whomever needed him next.

I slipped farther back from the commotion and stared at the blood on my hands, ignoring the whimpers and cries in nearby cubicles. Connell lay on the bed, nurses fussing over his leg, yet he kept his eyes straight ahead. On me. The silence between us exchanged more than words—it acknowledged recent events and reaffirmed our shared feelings. Right then, my thoughts faded, and all that mattered was the love he expressed. The possibility that he might take me back was all I needed.

I mouthed the words, *I'm sorry*, and turned to leave,

unable to sit around with a loose thread hanging over the pack: the dracwulf.

CHAPTER 26

In the past week, I'd made one hell of a mess of my life and dragged down those around me. My heart still belonged to Connell and always would. And the thought of losing him was too much. I wouldn't think about it.

I swerved all over the track through the woodland, mainly because I wasn't paying attention. I drew in a deep, hiccupped breath. An exasperated scream gushed past my lips, and it felt good to release something. Anything to let out the pain trapped inside.

The afternoon sunshine concealed the true, darkened mood of the day, and when I arrived at the pack house, the dracwulf's hollering pierced the ominous silence.

Parking on the grass to avoid the smashed glass all over the driveway, I studied the boarded-up windows in disbelief. Memories of violence that should never have occurred rolled across my mind. Still my adrenaline persisted each time I recalled the Lunar Eutine. A part of me grieved for Sandulf, while the rest of me teetered between relief and rage. He never explained why he chose the dracwulf over us. I understood I wasn't his child by blood, yet he'd never treated me as anything but, until the last few years. His rejection cut me up, though I'd never tell anyone.

I got out of the car and bumped into Botolf in the doorway. "Why aren't you with the dracwulf?"

"Just popped up to check in on the boys." He stroked my arm. "Everything go well at the hospital?"

I refused to talk about Connell and changed the topic. "Has Matias returned?"

He shook his head. "Matias never knew where he stood in the pack, and he blamed you for Enre's capture."

No shockers there. We went inside, and the dracwulf's cries ricocheted through the house. My nerves prickled with each angry bellow.

Radu slept on the couch, while Enre remained stretched out on the fur blanket, wearing only blue jeans. A rosy streak graced his cheeks.

To my surprise, Enre's eyelids opened. I rushed to his side, clutching his hand, and swallowed the dryness in my throat. "Welcome back."

Enre licked his dry lips.

Botolf was at my side. "He's already taken a liter of water and not said a word."

"It's a good sign, isn't it?" My gaze never left Enre's. I caressed the side of his face, thankful we hadn't lost him to Sandulf's stupidity.

"I don't know. He may heal rapidly, but if he's unable to cope with his trauma, he may never be the same again." Botolf placed his hand on mine, and the warmth of this touch was like a blanket on a frosty night.

I wondered whether Enre registered what we said. Probably not. I moved to the doorway, pressed my brow into the frame, and blinked hard to avoid the waterworks. It still baffled me how Sandulf sacrificed Enre to please the dracwulf.

"Daciana, you should rest. I'll keep guard over the dracwulf."

Sleep was the last thing on my mind. I left the bedroom and staggered through the darkened house to the kitchen, listening to the persistent shrieks of the animal in the basement. I debated on the one thing left to do—how to finish what Sandulf had started. I retrieved the longest knife off the magnetic strip on the wall. Feeling the comfortable wooden handle, I tightened my grip. The animal didn't deserve to suffer. It wasn't her fault she was brought into this world. She was doing what came naturally. So, I would end her life quickly.

Botolf joined me. "You're doing what Sandulf couldn't."

"I can never make up for what I've taken from you." I turned around. "But I promise I'll do whatever I can to make things better."

"It's not your fault." His voice quivered. "You'll be a stronger alpha than Sandulf ever was. We all have flaws, but he let his consume him." Botolf's words broke off; obvious he struggled to control his emotions.

"We'll get through it together." I wrapped an arm over his shoulders, and for a short while, silence enveloped us.

He pulled away and wiped clean his flushed cheeks, though the pain in his eyes was clear.

The rage streaming through me intensified. Sandulf managed to leave behind a distraught family, frayed and disoriented. Not caring for the mess he made. "We can make the pack what it should have been." I raised my chin. "Things will get better from here." I started to believe myself.

His gaze lifted to the ceiling. "Do you hear that?"

"No. What?"

Botolf bound to the back door, and I tracked him. "She's free."

He was right, the dracwulf no longer howled. I unlocked

the door and rushed outside where the vivid sunlight shimmered and stung my eyes.

The need for stealth had passed. No more running or hiding. The dracwulf skulked into the clearing from beyond the overgrown shrubs and trees engulfing the back yard. Even from a distance, I recognized her bared teeth as a warning.

For the length of a heartbeat, I believed the dracwulf broke free of the prison bars, and defeated Lutia—brawn was not her forte after all. But when Lutia emerged from around the side of the house, I realized the awful truth. She had freed the dracwulf. Stupid me. Why had I trusted her?

I regretted many things, but nothing compared to the guilt of not stopping her earlier. Damn my conscience. So much for giving her a second chance. That won't be happening again.

"What have you done?" Botolf's voice demanded of her

Lutia stepped backward, away from the house, her gaze targeting me. "You don't deserve alpha status. What have you done for this pack? Exposed us to a human. Went against Sandulf's orders, yet you live. And then you killed him for no reason. For that, the pack should rip you to shreds. Instead, they bow at your feet."

"And I guess killing a human is justified?"

She snarled and flashed her teeth. "Just like Matias, I'm leaving this pack. It's falling apart. And your soft spot for humans will get everyone else killed—Botolf, Radu, and Enre. All because of you." She turned and strolled away.

I licked my lips, and gripped tight the blade in my hand. The rules allowed the alpha to kill any wulfkin who abandons the pack. Anger burned away rational thoughts. I moved after her, but noticed movement in the evergreens to my side, and stopped.

The dracwulf raised her square head, ears flattened against her skull. Her solid, fiery eyes locked onto me. She rose from the undergrowth, like the dead climbing out of a graves. Black matted dreadlocks of fur bounced against her body and revealed her earlier injury still

"Daciana," Botolf said. "Forget her. Focus on the dracwulf."

The animal rocked forward, and an unvoiced snarl rumbled within her chest. She moved toward us, her body hunched low in the dancing evergreens, narrowing the distance between us.

My pulse grew too wild, too loud. I focused on the beast and stretched my spine. In a split second, I flung the knife at Lutia, aiming for her back, then threw open the floodgates to my wolf. Lutia's screeches fell into the background. Within seconds, I embraced the torturous pain of my skin splitting and shook myself free in the cool breeze.

Galloping through the foliage with purpose, I roared. No sooner had I taken a great leap forward than the dracwulf slammed into me and sent me flying backward. Pain hit me as I struck the outdoor table. The wood splintered beneath my weight. The dracwulf was right there, next to me, ripping into my leg. Her assault knocked the air out of my lungs, and I gasped for my next breath. Bright lights dotted my vision.

Botolf, now in wulfkin form, charged the dracwulf, colliding into her side. It gave me the distraction I needed. A whimper streamed from the animal, and she staggered side-ways. I ducked and rolled forward, jumping on top of her. She thrashed, half- howling, half-whining. I sank my fangs into her neck and tore into the flesh. Blood dampened the dracwulf's pelt and transformed the greenery at her paws into a sanguine puddle, and I slipped off her.

She snapped around, unaffected by the massive blood loss. It was obvious that, like me, she ran on pure adrenaline. Her lip curled and deadness consumed her expression.

I rushed her. The dracwulf mimicked my actions. Thrust into a clash of bodies, we smashed together, and then I bounced backward. A severe dizziness weaved through my skull, not to mention the double vision. The dracwulf clawed my torso, and I reeled, sacrificing my arms.

I growled, waving my tail in the air, which made the dracwulf snap her jaws at me. Her head shook with rage.

Botolf crept up behind her.

Saliva dribbled from her mouth. Our eyes locked. I crouched low, ignoring the pain in my leg. She copied me, and a fiendish yowl rumbled out of her.

Botolf attacked and snatched her tail as I leapt forward. But it didn't stop her. While my jaws clamped on the side of her neck, the dracwulf's teeth latched onto my shoulder, her incisors impaling deep. My spine arched, and my legs wobbled. I slackened in her grasp, my grip released, and I started to slip into human form.

Blood filled my mouth. *No. That's not how it would end.*

Botolf threw himself into the beast. I dropped from the dracwulf's mouth and slumped on the ground.

Motionless.

Get up, I told myself.

The dracwulf tore bits of flesh from my back, and I gritted my teeth with each bite, but couldn't move. My body refused to budge. Botolf's new roar ceased her attack, and she leapt out of my vision after him. The thudding of their paws against the ground vibrated in the earth, and grew more distant.

I dug deep within myself, concentrated and drew on every last bit of strength I owned. A sudden spark jerked down my body, and I shuddered again and again. On the next breath, a blend of flavors smeared my tongue. An earthy kindling scent wrapped me in warmth, and in my mind I spoke to Botolf—*keep running, get away from her.*

Then the sweetness of tree sap engulfed my senses, and images of Sandulf torturing Radu sent a twitching sensation through my limbs. Everything fell aside when the rawness of wet soil and fur spread in me. I needed my pack, but Radu remained comatose.

Enre stirred in my thoughts. I said his name, called him. No response.

My inhalations grew brassy. In the distance, the dracwulf was now trotting my way. There was no sign of Botolf. Barely able to push myself upright, I willed myself to stand and fight. I wasn't going down easy. I edged toward the house, but the beast was almost upon me.

Then something black emerged from within the house. It dashed past me in a blur and knocked me off my feet. I froze on the spot, not even a breath escaped my lungs as I expected the beast to tear into me. Nothing happened. Instead, an eruption of barks and yelps erupted. Wood splintered and cracked.

Pushing off the ground, I caught myself and watched a wulfkin fight the dracwulf. Part of the house had been smashed in, leaving a gaping hole in the laundry room.

My first thought flew to Botolf, but he was staggering into the yard from the woods in human form. And it hit me. The wulfkin with the thick black pelt with silver splashed over the tuffs on his ears, his chin, and underbelly was Enre. I stumbled forward.

The pair tangled in a brawl. I no longer saw where one began and the other ended.

When Enre's body tumbled across the yard, blood caking his torso and snout, I threw myself at the dracwulf who had eyes only on him. Something came over me, a new sense of purpose and a newfound strength. I bit her flesh, and wounds dotted the animal's body. Her yelps and whines did little to stop me.

With the dracwulf dangling from my mouth, I shook her like a toy, just as she had done to me. I cast her onto the remains of the fallen wall and gave no pause as I leapt onto her collapsed body. I spat out a chunk of black pelt on the rubble and barked a threat to the defensive beast. She never whimpered in response. Her breath grew raspy and distant. I stabbed my dagger-sharp teeth into the animal's jugular, leaned over and let her life bleed away.

Her pulse faded, slowed, then stopped.

I stood, leaving behind a crumbled tangle of flesh and fur. The dracwulf lay dead. A flicker of electricity hummed along my nape, and a sudden coldness hit me. The ground caught my fall. Botolf appeared at my side, helping me toward the back door where an injured and naked Enre slumped.

He raised his head and his eyes captured a satisfied gleam. A wide smile graced his lips, and his gaze met mine. "Missed me?"

CHAPTER 27

I leaned against the house and wiped my brow.

Radu threw another piece of drywall into the wheelbarrow and stared at the gaping hole in our pack house. "How are we going to fix this?"

Botolf emerged from the damaged laundry room, carrying a tray with mugs and pastries. "You worry about the mess, leave the fixing to me." He stepped over the rubble and into the morning sun. I helped myself to a cup and croissant.

"Yeah, you two enjoy yourself while I work hard." Radu winked at me. "We wouldn't want a bear to accidentally stumble into the house and terrify us." His gaze locked onto Botolf who pretended not to hear a thing and placed the tray on the ground. He stuffed a pastry into his mouth while gazing out into the horizon of trees.

I broke into laughter, croissant crumbs flying everywhere, and cherished the ease of things in the pack. There was a time I didn't think I'd ever smile again, let alone laugh. But it was over. The end of the world for the pack had vanished. My life returned to some kind of new normalcy, given my new duties as pack leader and the unknown situation with Connell, though I have never given up on getting him back. I figure a bit of time might make his heart grow fonder, not to mention letting him get used to the idea of me as a wulfkin. My love for him hasn't dwindled and I can't stop thinking about him.

A week has passed since I killed the dracwulf, whose body we buried so deep in the mountains I doubt we could find it again if we tried. The police continued to scour the Carpathian forest, aided by the park rangers—the pack. I survived the Lunar Eutine and transformed into a full-blown super wulfkin. So, anything was possible.

Even though I didn't quite understand my new abilities yet, time was on my side for once. And I plan to research my powers and understand what they all meant.

Botolf glanced my way. "I know Sandulf would be happy for us."

He was right. The heaviness no longer burdened our shoulders. We gave Sandulf the burial he deserved in the wilderness and paid our farewells to the wulfkin we remembered from happier days. I don't feel guilty about his death. I killed him to save the pack. In a macabre kind of way, it was probably the best thing that could have happened. Plus, Sandulf returned to Alina's arms. I knew that.

But a few other problems remained unresolved, like Matias's and Lutia's whereabouts. After the fight with the dracwulf, Lutia had vanished, and her blood trail dried up deeper in the forest. We all agreed Lutia posed a danger, and if seen again, we wanted her dead. I suspected our pack was not the first she had betrayed. Matias's whereabouts, on the other hand, caused us concern, more for his safety than anything else. Every few nights, a couple of us took turns to search for him without any luck.

I finished off the last bit of flaky pastry with tea. The biggest surprise came in the form of Enre. He was alive.

Connell had taken up residence in my mind, more each day as I waited for him to visit me. I'd never been strong when it came to him, and I doubted that would change. In hindsight, I realized my mistake. My purpose was never about getting what I wanted or what made me happy. No, it was about protecting the pack, even if it was at the sacrifice of Connell's love. Despite this realization, it still hurts and I can't shake off how much I long for him every day. Every hour. Every second.

What I never thought possible, especially after our arguments, was that I could trust him to guard our secret. And I regret not telling him earlier about the wulfkin's existence. He would never have betrayed me, and instead of darting around trying to fix everything on my own, scared out of my wits, Connell could have helped. Major lesson learned.

Someone touched my arm.

Enre stood next to me. "I've been talking to you. You didn't hear a word, did you?"

He shoveled a whole tart into his mouth, causing his cheeks to puff out like a chipmunk storing food, except the bridge of his nose pinched and his eyes narrowed, taking away from the cute rodent look.

"What were you saying?"

He flung his arms into the air and muttered while swallowing his food. "I said my parents are coming to town."

I suddenly had the urge sit down. Regardless of whether they were Enre's parents or not, I suspected they weren't coming just to see him. If there was one thing I learned from Sandulf, it was to never trust the Varlac. "Why? They've never come before. Do they know about the dracwulf?"

"What do they really want?" Botolf approached us.

Enre gave a half-hearted shrug. "You're both too paranoid. They probably want to see their son. Plus, it's customary for new alphas to be assessed by a Varlac. So, my dad took the job."

"How did they find out so quickly I'd become an alpha?"

He shrugged again. "Does it matter? We have to fix up the

place before they arrive, and . . . " Enre distanced himself. "I need a good explanation as to why I'm not the alpha."

Really? Just when I thought my life was settling down, it kicked back up. One good thing was that I'd be able to request help from the Varlac against the encroaching pack. If Sandulf feared them, it would make sense for me to get a handle of the real danger. "What exactly does this assessment involve anyway?"

"No idea." Enre returned to my side. "I'm sure it's nothing major." He wrapped his arm around my shoulders, and his warmth spread through me. "You worry too much." His fingers caressed my neck. He leaned into me and whispered, "And don't think I've forgotten. You promised me a date." His breath tickled my ear, and I tried to frown, but instead gave a crooked smile.

I nudged Enre's arm off me. "I think we've got more pressing issues here."

He turned to Radu. "Come on then, let's get this place ready."

I was suffocating in my thoughts.

Botolf, who watched me, asked, "Are you okay? You look a bit flushed."

"Yeah, I just need some time to think. I'll be back." As the alpha, I had nowhere to run, and I couldn't help but wonder if the Varlac somehow found out about the dracwulf.

No, it couldn't be. It was my paranoia on overdrive.

Botolf nodded, and I strolled toward the treeline with no destination in mind.

I decided to listen to Enre and follow his laid-back attitude. What's the worst that could happen? I gulped and pretended I didn't just ask myself that. Pushing into a run, I sprinted forward, interweaving between trunks and relishing the freedom, the sharpness of the wind and how much I loved being a wulfkin. There, I just contradicted myself. But those things happen.

Stopping near a huge tree to catch my breath, I sensed someone near. Twigs snapped and footsteps crushed pine needles. I peered round the trunk, and in the far distance I spotted several cops, tracking through the forest. But someone else stood right behind me, and I took my time turning around.

"How's the leg?" I asked.

"Pain killers do the trick." Connell rubbed his thigh. "I never thanked you for taking me to the hospital. So, thanks."

I shrugged. "Of course. I couldn't let you bleed to death. What sort of girlfriend would I be?"

We stared at each other for a long while, and Connell's stoic expression gave nothing away. On the bright side, he hadn't dismissed me when I called myself his girlfriend. But what did that mean? We were on or off?

I hadn't heard from him since the day I took him to the hospital, and I wasn't sure what to say next without sounding like a lovesick teenager. Though, in truth, I wanted to throw myself at him.

He studied his feet. Was he upset or missing me? Did he desperately want to pull me against his chest and devour my lips? Or was that just me?

"Did you get rid of the wolf?"

"Yep. You'll find nothing here except a peaceful wilderness. But I know you have to go through the motions."

I yearned to give in to the ridiculous standoff and dash into his arms. He might tell me how much he loved me.

"Daci." He swallowed hard. "I can't believe I'm about to say this."

My breaths strangled in my throat. My legs quivered. Oh my God. He was planning to break it off for good to my face. To tell me what a horrible person I had been, and that he never wanted to see me again. Tears collected in the corners of my eyes, and I shut them, preferring not to see his gorgeous face when he said the words.

Silence.

I thought of the pack, the Varlac, my heritage, and what I'd become—all the elements responsible for shaping me into an alpha. I belonged to the wulfkin. They were my family, my protection, and where my loyalty lay. And maybe soon I'd have the strength to forget about Connell if he didn't want me. Though I doubted it.

Dead leaves crunched beneath Connell's steps. I slipped open my eyes. He stood in front of me. His hands glided around my waist, and his face was inches from mine, grinning mischievously "You know you owe me three hundred kisses. I couldn't go anywhere until I collected."

"Even as a wulfkin?"

He raised my hand to his warm lips. "You could be a swamp monster, and I'd still want you."

I threw my arms around his neck, pressing my mouth against his. He lifted me off my feet, spun me, and we tumbled to the ground. We kissed some more, and I don't know how much time passed. But what I did know was that my life was bound to change and for the better this time.

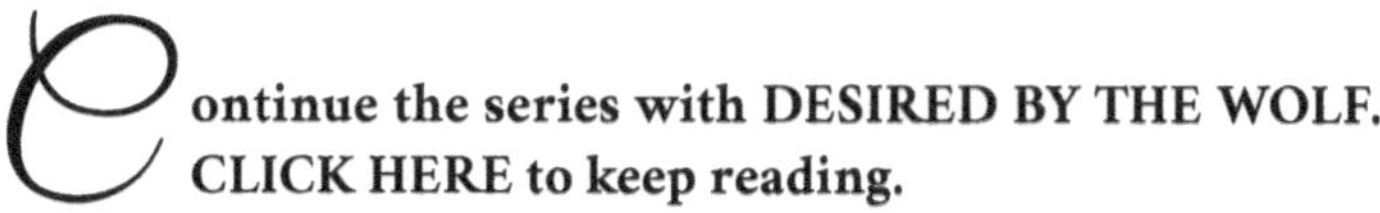

ontinue the series with DESIRED BY THE WOLF. CLICK HERE to keep reading.

TO SEDUCE A FAE

LUTHER IS THE MOST BEAUTIFUL OF MY CAPTORS.

STILL I HATE HIM MORE THAN THE OTHERS.

AND I HATE MYSELF FOR CRAVING THE PRINCE OF THE DARK FAE.

FATED MATE ROMANCE

START THE WINTER'S THORN SERIES

BOOKS BY MILA YOUNG

Thanks for reading Shadow Shifters.

Reviews are super important to authors as it helps other reader make better decisions on books they will read. So if you have a moment, please do leave a review here, HERE.

Find more Mila Young books.

Gods and Monsters
Apollo Is Mine
Poseidon Is Mine
Ares Is Mine
Hades Is Mine

Wicked Heat Series
Wicked Heat #1
Wicked Heat #2
Wicked Heat #3

Elemental Series
Taking Breath #1
Taking Breath #2

Fallen World Series Co-write with C.R. Jane
Bound
Broken
Betrayed

Broken Souls Series Co-write with C.R. Jane

<u>School of Broken Souls</u>
<u>School of Broken Hearts</u>
<u>School of Broken Dreams</u>

Haven Realm Series
Hunted (Little Red Riding Hood Retelling)
Cursed (Beauty and the Beast Retelling)
Entangled (Rapunzel Retelling)
Princess of Frost (Snow Queen Retelling)

Beautiful Beasts Academy

Manicures and Mayhem
Diamonds and Demons
Hexes and Hounds
Secrets and Shadows
Passions and Protectors
Ancients and Anarchy

SPIRIT SERIES
Spirit of Christmas

Best-selling author, Mila Young tackles everything with the zeal and bravado of the fairytale heroes she grew up reading about. She slays monsters, real and imaginary, like there's no tomorrow. By day she rocks a keyboard as a marketing extraordinaire. At night she battles with her might pen-sword, creating fairytale retellings, and sexy ever after tales. In her spare time, she loves pretending she's a mighty warrior, walks on the beach with her dogs, cuddling up with her cats, and devouring every fantasy tale she can get her pinkies on.

Ready to read more and more from Mila Young? Subscribe today here.

Join Mila's **Wicked Readers group** for exclusive content, latest news, and giveaway. Click here.

For more information...
milayoungauthor@gmail.com